# Bro



Born … ucated at Kin …

He … d as a ma … here he kept an inn for thr … in the West Indies, managing a ho … h Columbia, where he now works in the Britis … rest Service.

His first book – *Mirror Image* – appeared in 1972 and was followed by seven more, in addition to many contributions to a wide range of SF magazines. His novel *Charisma* is also published in Pan.

Married with three children, Michael Coney now lives on Vancouver Island.

Previously published by
Michael Coney in Pan

Charisma

Michael Coney

# Brontomek!

**Pan Books** London and Sydney

First published 1976 by Victor Gollancz Ltd
This edition published 1977 by Pan Books Ltd,
Cavaye Place, London SW10 9PG

ISBN 0 330 25334 4
Printed and bound in Great Britain by
Richard Clay (The Chaucer Press) Ltd, Bungay, Suffolk

# prologue

The beach was a long crescent of pale sand, bright in the sun so that I had to replace my sunglasses. A large number of people stood there – all of them, without exception, looking out to sea. The water was shallow, low waves rippling in lazily from a long way out. Beyond the line of breakers I saw movements, black fins cutting to and fro.

There was a girl standing near; a tall tanned girl who looked at home here, who was probably able to explain. I watched her for a moment, summoning up courage. She was pretty in an outdoorsy way, her hair bleached by the sun, a rim of white showing above the top of her bikini where she had pulled the flimsy material down as far as she dared. My feet made no noise on the sand so I cleared my throat as I approached, but still she didn't look my way.

'What's going on?' I asked. 'Is someone in trouble out there?'

She didn't reply. She stood still as though listening. I could read nothing from the expression on her face.

I turned and looked back at the town. Houses stared back at me with empty windows; a handful of people picked their way through the parked hovercars to join the growing numbers on the beach. Further down, where an outcrop of sandstone shelved down to the water's edge, a man stood with raised hands. He was saying something: I couldn't make out the words but I recognized the hectoring tones employed by outdoor religious speakers and patent medicine quacks.

I'd never felt so alone ...

I'd tried to get out of the town a couple of hours previously. I'd driven back along the road towards Premier City, and after a while had come across a block.

A uniformed soldier had stuck his head through the open window of my rented hovercar and said, 'Get the hell back the way you came.'

I asked, 'What's going on? I couldn't get any sense out of anyone in Oldhaven.'

'If you don't know, I sure as hell don't.'

A knot of soldiers lounged against their vehicle nearby, grinning. The interior of the car was getting hot. Sweat started somewhere behind my ears and trickled down under my shirt.

I wanted to drive away fast, but I wanted to talk, too. I didn't want to go back to Oldhaven, where the zombies were.

'Look, why can't you let me through? I came this way only a few hours back. There was no block then.'

Another soldier ambled up, chewing. He leaned on the car roof, drooped his head through the window and said, with peppermint, 'Nobody comes out of Oldhaven any more – that's our orders. If you came along the road from Premier City you must have seen the refugee camps. Christ. They've got no food, no johns, and not much water. Stay in Oldhaven until this blows over, will you?' His voice was not exactly unkindly.

'How long will that be?'

'Your guess is as good as mine.'

'For Christ's sake, I only arrived on this goddamned planet today. What kind of a place is this?'

'You have your Immunol?'

I fingered my bottle of small white pills. 'They issued me with them in Premier City.'

'Well, you'll be all right, then. And if you didn't see any fighting in Oldhaven, that means everything's all right. Maybe the whole thing's over. I don't know. Be a good guy, get back, huh? Otherwise I'll just have to burn you a little,' he said sadly, fingering the button on his laser.

I took a pill and started the engine.

'They should have told you in Premier City,' he said regretfully. 'But maybe you didn't ask. You just landed at the spaceport, rented a car and drove out, huh? Too bad. Too bad nobody thought to tell you about the problem we're having on Arcadia right now. I tell you this,' he said, 'I reckon they're ashamed to admit, back in Premier City. They're ashamed to admit there's something happening they can't handle. And so you're out of luck. Like I said – get going, man.'

Smiling, he flicked the button on his gun. There was just the slightest hum as a sliver of hot invisible light zipped past my nose and out of the far window.

So I drove back to Oldhaven.

I rechecked the address on the Interspac Telex which I'd carried all the way from Earth and found I'd been right the first time. So once again I drove to 1678 Second Avenue, parked the car and rang the bell, then hammered on the door. I made enough noise to rouse the entire street from its siesta, but there was no response. Beckenbauer was not at home. My one contact on this planet was unobtainable.

Then I heard a noise from behind, a concerted shambling as of many feet. I wheeled around, heart pounding. In the stillness, the sound had shocked me. A line of beasts straggled down the street, heading for the beach. They were akin to the terrestrial cow: angular with protruding bones, wise clowns' faces rather goatlike. They lurched from side to side as they walked with swaying udders. The leader paused as she caught sight of me and the followers piled up behind, butting each other gently in the rump. There was a moment's confusion as they watched me uncertainly.

I felt nervous and outnumbered. I recognized the brutes as Arcattle from pictures I'd seen, but I was not sure of their temperament. They looked harmless enough – but I had the weirdest notion they'd taken over the town. After all, they seemed to be in charge: there was no human around to shoo them back to their stalls.

Then, still watching me, they began to sidle furtively past. They were just as scared as I was, after all.

I climbed back into the car and headed for the beach again: there seemed nowhere else to go. I saw no other animals in the empty streets, and no people.

By now the crowd on the beach had assumed immense proportions. Most people stood at the water's edge although numbers were now sitting on the sand, watching the sea through the legs of those in front. I saw a little girl nearby: she was about nine years old and appeared more alert than most. She was shaping the sand into neat brown piles as she sat alone.

I knelt beside her. 'What's your name?' I asked.

She looked at me. Her eyes were not quite empty.

I remembered something. Pulling the bottle from my pocket, I offered her an Immunol pill.

She shook her head vigorously.

'Just one,' I coaxed. 'Tell me your name, then,' I added, offering her an alternative.

'Wendy.'

'Where are your parents?'

She pointed down the beach.

'Why is everyone here, Wendy?'

'Because.'

'Because what?'

'The giving . . .'

'What?'

Suddenly the little girl looked at me very directly. She said, 'Get away from me, you stupid bastard. You're not one of us. You cannot attend the thanksgiving.' Her little fingers drew tense zigzags in the sand, destroying the castles. 'Get the hell out of Oldhaven. Go back to Earth where you belong, go build your boats somewhere else. We don't need you here, Kevin Moncrieff.'

One of the side effects of Immunol is a euphoric numbing of the senses, and the pill I'd taken a while ago was still with me. I smiled at Wendy and stood, riding down the terror which threatened to burst through the drug.

A line of Arcattle threaded their way through the bystanders, slow hooves sloughing through the sand, abundant turds dropping as they reached the shallow water and continued onwards without pausing, waves lapping at their slender legs as their hooves sank. The leader glanced at me as she passed: there was knowing recognition in those goatish eyes.

'How do you know my name?' I asked Wendy.

'You know it – so I know it. Now get back in your car.'

I backed away as she stared at me. The Immunol pills were still in my hand; I fumbled for one as a man fumbles for a cigarette in times of crisis. Yet I didn't take one . . . Somehow, it seemed that my hand would not convey the small white pellet to my mouth. I capped the bottle and slipped it back in my pocket.

Wendy was smiling at me now: a child's open smile but with something else behind it. 'Maybe you ought to stay, Kev,' she said.

And I thought, *maybe that's a good idea* . . . Maybe this is a good place after all. The sun was warm but there was a pleasantly cool breeze off the sea. People were beginning to paddle in the shallow ripples; further away, on the headland above the end of the beach, I saw Arcattle grazing. I wondered why they weren't down here with the rest of us. Out to sea, the other Arcattle were up to their necks, probably swimming. I saw their heads jerking this way and that as little puffs of quiet spray erupted about them, as they joined with the fish, as they gave themselves to the ocean of Arcadia . . .

Wendy was standing; she took my hand in her small, soft grip.

'Come on, Kev,' she said.

I held back.

'It's time now,' she said. 'If you don't come now you'll be left behind.'

She was right. Everyone was in the water now, walking steadily forward, eyes on the horizon. Everyone. I was wrong to think of holding back. I allowed myself to be drawn forward and the water slopped into my shoes, crept icily up my calves.

The zealot away to my right was yelling some prayer; part of my mind wished he would shut up. I needed time to think. I seemed to be getting myself into something I didn't understand.

'You don't need to understand,' said Wendy, dancing through the waves and tugging at my hand. 'Just give! Give!'

Others took up the shout. 'Give ... Give ... Give ...' It became a chant, monotonous and hypnotic, in rhythm with the pulsing of the waves as they rose to my groin, fell, rose higher, rose to my waist.

Ahead, someone was screaming.

A woman thrashed in the breaking waves, scattering scarlet spray as she fought with the black thing that was fastened to her right breast. A man waded towards her, then went under in a convulsive fighting.

'What the hell is going on?' someone shouted. 'What the hell are we doing?' He turned towards me, a thickset man in a dark, wet jacket, his eyes wide and his mouth twisted with fear. 'My *God*!' he howled, beating at the water with his hands as he fought his way back towards me. He staggered and paused, and his expression took on a dreadful knowledge as he jerked and kicked at something which seemed to be restraining him. The water around him began to well up crimson and he screamed in a continuous high tone which was almost a whistle – while he twisted and jerked, his arms upraised in the manner of a man avoiding a leaping hound.

Wendy stopped pulling me forward and began to cry.

Black sickle-shaped fins were slicing the surface all around; people were going down, squealing and thrashing. I found that I was running, a tramping, high-stepping run as I tried to get clear of the water, struggled to reach the beach. Once my foot sank into a pothole and I fell, and I swear I was screaming underwater before I sprang to my feet and clawed my way on, and found dry sand under me, and collapsed.

It was a long time before I could turn my head and peer over my shoulder at the water.

Nothing much was happening, now . . .

I sat on the harbour wall with a girl one night: in the confusion and collapse of the ordered sub-colony existence there were many such chance relationships until people found their niches again.

She said, 'They've known for fifty years that this was going to happen, and yet there were no preparations. The bastards . . .' All six of Arcadia's moons were in the sky and the night was almost like day, so that we could see a shapeless thing floating face down nearby. Behind us many of the dwelling units were empty burned-out shells: the acrid whiff of old fires mingled with the stink of death.

The harbour was small, compact and rectangular with a narrow entrance. Luminous trails glowed on the surface like the tracks of snails at sunset, originating at various points around the harbour wall, converging at the entrance. Billions of plankton made up those trails, countless tiny things which the Minds had given birth to, and which were now making their way out to sea. The girl watched them.

'The Minds are still there,' she said. 'Do you feel it?'

'Not now.' I took an Immunol pill and offered her one.

'The blackfish protected them while they gave birth,' she said slowly, ignoring the bottle, 'and in return they fed the blackfish. It was a square deal, so far as they were concerned. So why did we have to get involved? We wouldn't have harmed them.'

'I don't suppose they knew that.'

I was watching a patch of water which glowed with an eerie luminescence. Then a cloud obscured Daleth and the water broke into concentric ripples – and the thing was bobbing there, shining . . .

It floated less than ten metres away, a sphere slightly larger than a man's head. We watched it, fascinated, horrified, disgusted; the stench of rotting fish came faintly to us. The thing rotated with the wind then, startlingly, leaped into the air and landed with a splash, some three metres nearer to us.

'What the hell . . . !' The girl was on her feet.

Then we saw the fins of blackfish, circling and darting, and the sphere bounced and splashed, was pushed here and there as sharp teeth tore at its decaying flesh, noisily devouring...

And all around the harbour wall other Minds rose to the surface and floated, their glow fading as they died, their duty done for another fifty-two years.

# one

Arcadian scotch whisky is good for a reflective mood, but a lousy thing for creativity.

I didn't walk directly home from the Swindons' dwelling unit: instead I took a stroll along the trail which follows the north ridge, and whenever I caught a glitter through the trees I stopped and looked down the hillside to the water. There were four moons in the sky that night and their reflections were everywhere, dancing in the faster currents, swirling in the eddies, watching me like silver eyes from the backwaters.

Like the moons I reflected, and saw my childhood, the girls I'd known; remembered the jobs I'd lost, relived the frustration which caused me to emigrate to Arcadia a couple of years ago. The initial terror of the Relay Effect, my comparative success since.

I paused again at a place where the steep bank had collapsed some time in the past, crumbling and tumbling into the water at the inlet they call Anchor Pool. It was a mysterious and romantic spot, and I wished I had a girl with me to kiss. The moonlight glittered on a metal plate let into a rock.

IN MEMORY OF
The Reverend Emmanuel Lionel Blood
Police Officer William Clarke
Eric Phipps
Alan Phipps
Alfred Blackstone
'They died that we might be saved'

I passed on, still reflecting, still not creating.

Jane Swindon had said, 'A man ought to be married by the time he's thirty-two, Kevin. Or even twenty-two. There's something unsavoury about an unmarried man. Present company excepted, of course.'

Professor Mark Swindon had said, 'I mean, look at Will Jackson, for example. Weird. A woman can't hang her clothes out to dry within five kilometres of the guy. And Vernon Thrale – he does folk dancing. Last week I saw him prancing about in a smock. You must take a long hard look at yourself,

Kev. I saw you talking to Lucy Sung in the street yesterday. She can't be more than five years old.'

And so the old subject had received its periodic semi-serious airing, and been forgotten until next time...

Eventually I turned around and began to walk home. Sure, I got lonely sometimes. Doesn't everyone, even married people? But when a man has a business to build up, when he has to sustain it in the face of a trade recession, when in any case he lives in a small community which the younger folk tend to leave as soon as they are old enough – then there's not much opportunity for love.

Occasionally people like the Swindons can be a nuisance. Secure in their own united happiness, they have that desire more usually found in Jehovah's Witnesses and junkies, to convert everyone to their way of thinking.

The crowd on the wharf was silent. I saw children fidgeting; their parents admonished them absently, while they kept their eyes on that place where the silver ribbon of water disappeared behind the tall banks of dense trees. Near me stood members of the Regatta Committee. They were understandably nervous. Over five hundred people had made the journey to Riverside on this spring day: five hundred colonists seeking escape from the problems which were besetting our world.

These people wanted to be entertained. They expected to be entertained. And there are few people more unpleasant than those unexpectedly deprived of their fun. Step into the Riverside Social Club any evening and take Chill Kaa's beer away from him, if you don't believe me.

Mortimore Barker stood a few yards away, a vast figure in a brightly patterned shirt, pants sustained by a thick leather belt.

'What the hell's the delay?' I asked.

The publicity agent smiled expansively. 'Take it easy, my boy. Just waiting for a little sunshine. Ah ... Here we go.'

The sun slid from behind a cloud and dazzled us all, worrals chattered in nearby trees, tiny mewlers sparkled iridescent above the water with blurred wings as they picked plankton from the surface. In the distance we heard the bumping hiss of skitterbugs moving fast.

They swept around the corner and into view, in line abreast, nine of them, small dome-shaped boats squatting on a cushion of foam as they raced up the estuary towards us. I was conscious of a feeling of pride. I had built those bugs. They towed water-skiers, girls dressed in flowing white robes, feathers of white spurting from their skis.

Strapped to the back of each girl was a golden kite. When they were about two hundred metres away from us the girls rose from the water, the sun illuminating the fabric of their kites, the wind and wetness causing their gossamer white robes to cling to their bodies. I raised my binoculars – then dropped them quickly, not wishing to waste any time in focusing on the rapidly approaching vision.

I stole a quick glance at Mortimore Barker. He was smiling, confident of the success of his stunt. The crowd was ooohing and aaahing. I wondered why crowds love spectacle and colour so much more than individuals do. Maybe this is something good about us. Maybe we like to think that everyone else is enjoying himself.

Ralph Streng stood beyond Barker. His smile was cynical.

Fifty metres away the skitterbugs throttled back and sank to the surface in a sudden crippled wallowing. By now everyone was watching the girls, who had dropped their towropes. They soared above the water like angels. On either side of us the thick denseness of the trees rose up steep hillsides to the broad ribbon of sky, framing the angel girls.

I heard a chuckle nearby. It sounded like Streng.

The incredible thing was, those girls all looked the same: identically beautiful with curly golden hair, small smiling mouths and, I'll swear, dimples. As they soared above us their innocence took my breath away.

Then...

Then they snapped their hands across, peeling the cloth from their bodies, and underneath they were naked. The line wheeled, out there in the estuary, and came swooping towards us, nine naked girls suspended from golden kites, all breasts and plump thighs and golden hair.

And across the belly of each girl was painted a single letter, in bright scarlet.

The letters spelled R.I.V.E.R.S.I.D.E.

The crowd yelled.

Then the girls wheeled again, losing height, and I could hear the wind in their harness as they swept close overhead then out over the estuary again, upstream, alighting gently on the water like a flight of golden swans. They waded ashore a couple of hundred metres away, on the opposite bank where the estuary narrows and the road bridge crosses the water.

I said to Barker, 'Brilliant, Mort.' My eyes were on the girls. They had slipped off their wings: a team of men had appeared and were throwing cloaks around them, and escorting them to a large truck. There was lettering on the side of the truck: I was reminded of a travelling circus I'd once seen, back on Earth. I raised my binoculars and read the words HETHERINGTON ENTERPRISES. 'Where did you get them from?' I asked.

'An agency.'

'Are they coming to the dance tonight?'

He shifted uncomfortably. 'Uh, no. They're not allowed to mingle. They go straight back to Premier City after their performance.'

The name of Hetherington and the sight of those girls being herded away had turned the day slightly sour for me. 'Like circus animals, Mort?' I asked.

He blinked, then turned to accept the congratulations – and in a few cases the outrage – of the regatta committee.

Paul Blake asked me to take a look at his skitterbug. I knelt on the wharf, fumbling about inside the inspection hatch where the simple motor is. I found that the cable from the thermostatic damper control to the miniature reactor was crimped.

'I seem to lose lift at full power,' he was complaining. He was fidgeting anxiously: he was scheduled to take part in the second race. Around us the water churned with the bustle of other craft being readied.

'Have you been fooling with the cable?' I asked.

He avoided my eyes. I saw two feet arrive beside my face, large feet clad in expensive clothes. I looked up into the massive jowls of Ezra Blake, Paul's father.

'I paid good money for that boat, Moncrieff,' he said too loudly. 'And you gave me a year's guarantee. The goddamned thing's never been out of your repair shop since the day it was bought.'

'Easy, Dad, easy,' muttered Paul.

'See here, Paul, this guy calls himself a boatbuilder. He arrived here a couple of years back with nothing and now he's doing pretty goddamned well – and he's making money out of us. So he owes it to us to give us a square deal. Huh? What do you have to say to that, Moncrieff?'

People were watching us. It always seems to be my lot to run foul of the Blake type, and always in front of an audience. At one time maybe I'd have backed down, but over the past two years I'd gained some sort of standing in the community – not an easy feat in the rough-and-ready atmosphere of a planetary sub-colony – and I wasn't about to see it destroyed by the likes of Blake.

'This boat's losing lift because your son's been tampering with the minipile dampers, Blake,' I said loudly enough for everyone to hear. 'I always make a point of telling my customers not to fool with the engine, but your son chose to ignore the warning. I'll tell him again, in front of you. If he tries to get more than the designed power by souping up the pile he's liable to kill himself and anyone else within range.' Blake was staring stiffly past my face; his son shuffled his feet. I relented. 'I'll tell you what I'll do,' I said. 'I'll fix it now, with a new cable, free of charge. And Paul – you come down to my yard tomorrow morning and I'll show you what you *can* do to improve performance. Right?'

'Thanks,' said Paul. His father strutted away looking for someone else to attack. Paul stayed to help me thread the new cable. He is a tall, good-looking guy who has a way with girls; his very presence makes me think of the chances I missed when I was his age. Somehow I don't think Paul misses any chances, and good luck to him . . .

It is a strange fact that a small colony like Riverside – where I'd expected to find the outward-looking and freethinking adventurers – can become parochial and preoccupied with trivialities within three generations.

'Disgusting!' I heard a deep female voice booming as though to prove my conclusions. I looked up to see Mrs Earnshaw, committee member and worthy Riverside notable, haranguing Mortimore Barker. 'I never thought the day would come when our colony would find it necessary to display naked trollops in order to attract tourists to the regatta. Not only is it demeaning to our colony, but it's degrading to the girls themselves. I feel insulted as a woman!'

Barker is not the type to go on the defensive. 'Don't talk to me about degradation, Bernadine,' he boomed. 'When you've seen New China, where the men work in the fields like oxen because their religion forbids machines, then you can talk to me about degradation. When you've visited Utopia, where women are cloned from a base stock chosen to pleasure humans and aliens alike, then maybe you'll understand what exploited sex is all about. Until then—' He waved a huge hand, turning away and leaving Mrs Earnshaw spluttering, '– don't talk to me about degradation!'

Shortly afterwards I stood with the other committee members on the improvised platform, waiting for the start of the first race. Mrs Earnshaw was there, still fuming; Mark Swindon the marine biologist with his wife Jane; Ezra Blake, and the Reverend Enrico Batelli. I addressed the latter. 'What do you think of our publicity man's job so far, Enrico?'

His eyes were thoughtful as he watched a mass of coloured balloons, released underwater, expand enormously as they surfaced and rose into the air. 'Very good, I'd say,' he murmured.

I pressed him further. 'Those girls shook me up. I thought they were meant to represent angels, but then...'

He grinned. 'People have criticized me in the past because I can't tell them I definitely believe in their concept of God. But I can tell you this: I sure as hell don't believe in angels. I saw nine pretty sexy girls and I liked the sight. I see nothing wrong in that.'

Mark Swindon said, 'I'm with you there, Enrico.'

Jane Swindon disagreed, but not predictably. She is not a predictable woman: small and tough and very pretty, amusing too. Riverside would be a better place with more colonists like her and her husband. 'They scared me a bit,' she said. 'I mean, I would expect Mark to like them; he always was a dirty-minded bum. But I didn't like the way they looked identical. It was creepy, sort of.'

Something nudged the back of my mind. I found myself thinking of Mortimore Barker's remark a few minutes ago. '... Utopia, where women are cloned from a base stock...'

Then a murmur of surprise banished the unease from my mind. A huge, garishly decorated float had drifted out from a narrow backwater, just upstream from the starting line where the skitterbugs jostled. It was not one of the official floats depicting the history of Riverside and prepared by the Kindred of the Pioneers; those were all downstream. No, this float was an impostor.

‘Get that goddamned thing out of here!’ I heard Mrs Earnshaw roar.

The wind was blowing downstream and the strange vessel drifted with it, turning idly in the current, tassels and banners stirring in the breeze. It appeared to be unmanned. It was about ten metres long and three wide.

‘That’s one of my barges!’ exclaimed Swindon.

A makeshift mast had been stepped in the blunt bows of the scow, another in the stern. Between them a long banner drooped, bearing the words,

HANDS OFF ARCADIA.

‘It’s the Liberty Lovers, or whatever the hell they call themselves,’ somebody said. The float drifted among the skitterbugs, revolving.

GO HOME, HETHERINGTON read the banner on the reverse side. A group of skitterbugs surrounded the barge and began to propel it back upstream. Suddenly there was an explosion. The sides of the vessel fell away, smoking. The skitterbugs scattered. A large pyre stood revealed in the centre of the barge. Flames were already beginning to dart around the base and within seconds the entire vessel was ablaze.

Mounted on top of the pyre was the effigy of a man: a fat, toadlike man sitting in a wheelchair. As we watched, the chair tipped; the figure slid forwards and was engulfed in the flames.

A considerable proportion of the crowd cheered...

There was a report and a ragged burst of cheering. The first race was under way.

Six skitterbugs fled down the estuary with a roaring hiss, riding pillows of foam. At the bend in the river five veered wide, following the channel under the trees – while the sixth cut the corner, travelling for a short distance over damp mud left bare by the receding tide. A cloud of ochre spray arose. As the skitterbugs swung around the distant bend and out of sight, it was apparent that the sixth craft had gained a slight lead.

I felt a touch on my arm. Doctor Ralph Streng stood beside me.

Streng is the sort of man who dominates any group; the sort of man whom people don’t interrupt. Of medium height and heavy build, he possesses a huge head with weatherbeaten face all topped by a vast mane of silver-grey hair. He is a very impressive and somewhat daunting figure, the type that gets to be chairman of committees. A woman – not his wife – was hanging on to his arm. Ignoring her, he was considering me with his sharp blue eyes.

'You saw young Blake cut the corner?'

'Yes. It's fairly safe, up to a point,' I replied. 'There's enough superheated steam to carry the boat about ten metres, at that speed. So it can ride over the mud on its reserves of steam, then refill when it hits the water again. Of course, the intake will suck up a quantity of mud – but as soon as the bug regains the water, it should flush through.'

'So you recommend skipping that bank.'

Streng had put me on the spot. He was taking part in the next race.

'Well ... There are dangers ... You have to be travelling fast enough.'

'Hell, Moncrieff. Why do you people always bleat about dangers? I wouldn't be racing if it wasn't dangerous.'

In due course the skitterbugs came skimming back towards us, the red-and-white striped craft of Paul Blake holding a clear lead. He leaped the mud flat again and crossed the finishing line several seconds ahead of his pursuers. He made a slow wide sweep opposite the wharf and tied up at a float. A cluster of young girls cheered shrilly. He climbed out and approached the platform, grinning, his face wet with spray. His father met him and congratulated him, the control cable incident forgotten for the time being.

I found Jane Swindon standing next to me. 'Enjoying yourself?' I asked.

'Sort of ...' She was watching Paul Blake; he had removed his helmet and was talking to some girl. His father was discussing the race with Kli a' Po, the colony's non-human. I'm used to the sight of Kli around the place now, but when I first arrived in Riverside I found him unsettling. Curiously enough, the thing which threw me was the fact that he wore clothes. Had he been naked, I could have accepted him in the way I accept a worral, or an ape. But the sight of fabric against the reptilian hide gave the same impression of masquerade, of *wrongness*, that a chimp's tea party does. I couldn't take him seriously. It made me realize what a perfectly natural thing racial prejudice was, back in the bad old days on Earth. Antisocial, indefensible by any code of ethics – but natural.

'You don't sound very impressed by the regatta,' I said to Jane.

Her gaze moved over the skitterbugs tied to the float: the contestants were checking their craft for the next race. Streng sat relaxed in the cockpit of his green bug, distinctive mane of silver hair flopping about in the breeze. 'Maybe I'm getting old, Kev,' said the pretty dark girl. 'Or maybe Mort's stunt with those angels spooked me. But I'm just wondering what the point of all this is. Those guys are trying to beat one another, that's why they're in those boats. But why are we watching?'

'It's exciting, for God's sake.'

'Only because there's a chance of someone getting killed. That's why ninety per cent of the people here are watching.'

'It's a spectacle, that's all. Just like the folk dancers.'

I indicated the roped-off area between the wharf and the fisheries warehouse, where the Kindred of the Pioneers cavorted doggedly with stamping feet and fluttering handkerchiefs to the tune of Vernon Thrale's fiddle.

'You'll notice nobody's watching *them*,' Jane said, still in that subdued voice.

The platform was raised about two metres above the wharf: to our right and left the crowd buzzed expectantly. Beyond the warehouse and behind us, the road rose steeply up the hillside among the domed dwelling units to the rectangular structures of the Social Club and Mark Swindon's Marine Research Station near the forested skyline. The entire colony – numbering at present some six hundred people together with an equal number of outsiders – was absorbed in the events on the water.

I hoped it wasn't because they wanted someone to die.

'I think they get their jollies by identifying with the contestants, Jane.'

'Don't you sense a sort of desperation? As though people are thinking: everything's gone wrong with the world, and nothing matters any more? Don't the races seem more... *competitive* than usual? Be honest, Kev.'

'That's just Paul. He's a bit wild.'

'He means to win. And so does Ralph Streng...'

I started as the cannon boomed and belched smoke, and the next batch of competitors hurtled down the estuary in a pall of spray and condensing steam...

# two

There was a stranger standing a little apart from everyone else, at the back of the wharf where the grass and weed gave way to denser foliage, spike trees and sticker plants. He didn't look like a tourist. He wore a dark raincoat and, although binoculars were slung around his neck, his hands had remained stuffed in his pockets ever since I'd first noticed him. In profile his features were sharp; his cheeks somewhat hollowed and his nose hooked, his hair sparse and white. He looked like a bald eagle who had been told to cut down on the calories. I judged his age to be around fifty-five.

It was his sudden movement which caught my eye. As the skitterbugs flashed past him, he raised the binoculars and watched the boats all the way around the bend. There was nothing unusual in that: dozens of people were doing the same thing. It was the man's intentness which struck me, a solitary intentness like the marine bird he resembled.

There was the usual buzz of comment as the boats disappeared.

'Streng didn't skip the mudflat,' said Mark Swindon.

'He will, when he needs to,' Jane replied.

And in due course the boats came back, Streng leading; and again he skirted the brown arm of the mudflat, skimmed up the straight, and came in an easy first.

So the races went on, and I could feel the tide of excitement rising within the crowd, until all the preliminary rounds were through, and the big final event was upon us. I saw the Newspocket crew stamp out their aphrohales and switch on their cameras; and, childlike, I pulled the miniature receiver from my pocket and saw myself watching the screen. Around me were important-looking people.

I wondered if the Hetherington Organization's emissaries were watching the broadcast in Premier City, and if they'd seen me. I wondered if they'd recognize me when I was introduced to them, tomorrow. I wondered why seeing myself on that tiny screen made me feel so goddamned important.

'A determination to succeed at trivialities is often an indication of a record of past failures, and serious ones,' someone was saying in didactic tones. I looked around, and saw a dark young guy talking to an earnest-looking, bespectacled girl. 'I saw a sign once,' he said. 'It read: "In case of fire, remove extinguisher from bracket and invert. Approach fire with caution, playing jet upon base of flames. If fire is too big to handle—" And the rest was erased. Somebody had written in, "Go light a smaller one".'

The girl laughed. She said, 'Yeah, Phil. And I'd be scared to race in those goddamned little bugs, too.'

'There's really no danger,' said the young guy, stiffly.

Six skitterbugs were strung abreast across the starting line, their small auxiliary pumps puttering away, maintaining the inflow of water until they began to move forward and the ram effect began. Paul Blake was there, and Bill Yong. Al Sung moved up to the line, waved to somebody. Streng sat easily, watching the muzzle of the cannon. Probably he'd calculated that he'd get a split-second's advantage if he obeyed the flash instead of the sound. Chukalek, the cook from the Social Club, was an unexpected finalist to Streng's right, fidgeting nervously. Alicia Desjardins completed the line-up, her dark hair bowed as she checked the instruments, or maybe prayed.

They were all in their places, all correct and ready to go. This is the moment the fool in charge of the cannon usually chooses to goof off, and this moment was no exception. Nothing happened for an eternity, then there was a hurried consultation, muttered recriminations and a puff of smoke from the touch-hole.

The gun boomed.

The skitterbugs rose simultaneously and began to slide forward, steam and spray fountaining from their sterns. Within ten metres they were moving fast; the drivers cut the auxiliaries and the noise abated. Accelerating with ghostly quietness, the little bugs hurtled down the estuary.

Paul Blake skipped over the mudflat, gaining a slight lead as the craft wheeled around the bend and disappeared, leaving parallel silver arcs on the dark surface.

The hawklike stranger had joined the cameramen and was talking to them: I couldn't hear the words but I saw them nodding. The lenses probed among the crowd like inquisitive eyes while we waited for the boats to reappear. Bets changed hands. Mortimore Barker lumbered past thoughtfully, head down and heavy jowls oozing over his collar.

I heard a metallic voice grating, 'Blake's still in the lead. Streng's closing. Past Anchor Pool now, Desjardins last ...'

Someone held a transceiver: someone else was probably up on the ridge trail, overlooking the lower part of the estuary. The course was over fifteen kilometres long; the craft turned at the estuary mouth between the two tall headlands and just short of Mark Swindon's fish pens. They would return in about ten minutes.

Behind, I heard the endless jig of Thrale's fiddle as the Pioneers pounded determinedly on, singleminded in their endeavour to bring culture to the masses. Mrs Earnshaw, having forgotten Barker's shameless exploitation of the female body during the opening spectacle, hurried past me and caught up with the promoter before he reached the cameras. I heard her urging him to make sure the Kindred of the Pioneers' exhibition of arts and crafts at the Social Club was thoroughly publicized.

The minutes went by and the tension mounted. Conversation died; indeed, anyone who spoke was immediately hushed by his neighbours as everybody listened for the returning boats.

The transceiver crackled: 'Blake and Streng ... Blake and Streng ...'

Ezra Blake stood nearby, his face expressionless. Jane Swindon was chewing her lip; she and her husband watched the bend in the river.

The boats shot into view.

Two bugs held a clear lead over the others; they raced neck and neck beneath the overhanging trees, flinging a shower of spray clear up the bank. They seemed to be heading straight for the mudflat. The other boats were in a tight bunch, fifteen metres behind.

Somebody was muttering, 'Steady, boy ... Steady ...'

A rising din, a babble of comment came from the crowd, breaking into an untidy, excited cheering. The platform shuddered as people surged against the supports, craning necks, staring down the estuary.

The leading bugs arrowed towards the mudflat.

The rest of the field was nowhere now. Nobody was watching them. All eyes were concentrated on those two tiny speeding hunks of machinery, each with its frail human pilot, each pilot with his own inflexible desire to win ...

The crowd screamed.

Beside me a woman gasped, a man grunted, 'Oh, God ...'

One of the bugs, out there in the river, seemed to hesitate.

The second bug swept wide, paralleled the arm of the mudflat. The first bug skipped on the mud, raised an explosion of black spray, leaped, touched again and dug in, flipping over.

A small shape flew in a fast low arc, limbs waving puppet-like, and hit the water on our side of the mudflat with a small splash, a quiet splash.

The second bug rounded the mudflat, passed the subsiding ripples without slackening speed and raced up the calm water towards us, towards the finishing line. There were no cheers. Near me, a girl was weeping quietly.

A bug paused by the mudflat, wallowing while the pilot could be seen leaning over the side, pulling something inert from the water.

The winner flashed past the platform; the second, third and fourth bugs finished within seconds. The fifth boat was a long way off: this was the boat the crowd watched. Beyond, the capsized bug lay on the mudflat, helpless like an upturned turtle.

Soon Alicia Desjardins slid slowly to the float, the motionless form of Paul Blake draped across the snub nose of her skitterbug. Hands reached out, lifted him ashore, laid him out on the wharf. By the time I reached the group, Streng was already rising to his feet from beside Paul Blake. He wiped his hands dry on his thick sweater.

'He'll be OK,' he said briefly. 'Just a bit shaken up, that's all.'

Through the forest of legs, I saw Paul sitting up, shaking his head dazedly.

Ezra Blake broke away from the group and seized Streng by the arm.

'You bastard!' he yelled. 'You lousy bastard, you could have killed him, you know that? What sort of a fucking doctor do you call yourself, eh?' His heavy face was white, his thick lips worked.

Streng detached himself. 'I call myself a good doctor, if that's really what you want to know,' he said calmly, in that deep voice of his. 'And in point of fact, I didn't kill your son. You'll gain nothing by idiotic speculation.'

It was some seconds before Ezra Blake could speak. His fat fists shivered before his chest as he mouthed wordlessly. Maybe one of us should have stepped in, calmed him down, got Streng away: but nobody did. I think we were all a little awed in the presence of so much rage.

Ezra Blake finally said, 'You ... You knew he was going to jump the mud, and you...you pulled across his bows.' He stared at the rest of us; his rage was turning to tears, the futility – and maybe the relief that Paul was unhurt – was unmanning him. 'You forced him to...to slow down...so that...'

Paul was on his feet, coughing; he recovered and walked unsteadily towards his father. He took the older man by the arm. 'Come on, Dad,' he said. 'Forget it, huh? It's all in the game.' Then, because we're all of us human, he said, 'I'll get the bastard next time.'

His father stared at him, mumbling.

Streng said, 'You're quite welcome to try, Paul.' He turned away and walked towards the platform steps.

Mortimore Barker stood hugely there, face grave. 'In all my years as an observer of the human animal in all its guises, I have rarely seen, if ever, such an—'

'Let me past, man. Save your speech for a bigger audience.' Streng brushed past the press agent and climbed the steps.

'By Christ, I will, at that!' shouted Barker, charging after him.

There was a stampede up the steps to the platform where we found Mrs Earnshaw holding the trophy – a miniature replica of a skitterbug mounted on a bronze plaque – for once totally at a loss.

Barker snatched it from her. 'I'll present the prize!' he roared. 'By Christ, I'll present the bastard with his prize! Cameras!' He gestured imperiously and the Newspocket lenses swung his way, and the microphone boom extended like a gallows.

And Ralph Streng stood calmly before him, smiling ...

'Ladies and gentlemen,' began Mortimore Barker.

Even if he doesn't have to act, a man still thinks quickly during a crisis. A Mortimore Barker character study was flashing through my mind: why was Barker so incensed? Barker was a hard case. Barker was not particularly fond of the Blakes, father or son. Father was wealthy and overbearing. Son was opinionated and loud ... But over half the crowd were not aware of this. And there is nothing a crowd likes more than a butt, a scapegoat – it makes each individual member of that crowd feel secure, cosy in his anonymity. And Barker was a newsman, quick to sense public opinion, quick to take a convenient moral stand...

Ralph Streng, right now, was good copy. He was still smiling as Barker began, voice taking on sing-song tones of exaggerated sarcasm. He watched the speaker with interest and I wondered what was in his mind, with what cold logic he intended to destroy Barker ... Streng seemed to radiate an aura of power – not good, not evil – simply animal power as his very presence began to make Barker's words seem childish and naïve and wildly inappropriate ...

Barker stopped talking.

He was staring towards the cameras; one of the crew signified that they were switched off, and the hawkfaced stranger was there, beckoning. Barker shrugged, ambled across, and there was a quiet discussion. I saw the stranger produce a card, emphasize a few points with a clenched fist. Barker nodded. He smiled. He returned to the centre of the platform, glanced back at the cameras, then handed the trophy to Streng.

'Congratulations, Ralph,' he said in a perfectly normal voice. 'A fine race, skilfully won ...' He continued for a few moments with a very standard presentation speech with but few traces of sarcasm.

Then Streng replied in like fashion. Barker led the crowd in a burst of lukewarm applause.

Next, Barker seized Alicia Desjardins by the arm and drew her forward.

'And now, here's the real hero of the regatta!' he boomed.

I noticed the hawkfaced man frown in sudden exasperation; then he shrugged, smiled briefly and nodded to the cameraman who had asked him something. The cameras continued to whirr.

Barker was quickly into his stride. 'This beautiful young woman, the only female contender in the race – but mark my words, if we can judge anything by her performance, we'll be seeing a lot more of the lovely ladies in the Riverside regatta in future. Yes, sir – we men have had it our own way for too long! But that's beside the point. The point is, we have Alicia to thank for preventing a dreadful tragedy this afternoon. After all the men in the race had ignored the cries for help of their stricken comrade, Alicia alone sacrificed her chance of fame and glory. Singlehanded and showing a courage and fortitude which the other contestants might have done well to emulate, she saved young Paul Blake from a watery grave ...'

'God Almighty,' I heard someone groan. I looked round. It was Mrs Earnshaw. She winked at me grotesquely.

Barker had managed to procure Paul Blake from somewhere and was standing over him and Alicia like a priest at a wedding, bawling his platitudes to Paul's obvious discomfort. Nobody likes to be cast in the role of one who owes his life.

'Alicia, my dear. Say a few words to your adoring public,' said Barker eventually.

Alicia Desjardins stepped dutifully up to the mike. She is a tall girl with dark hair and a pleasant, if slightly equine face. She gulped and smiled toothily.

'I'm not beautiful,' she began surprisingly. 'Uh, we have an arrangement in races. The person lying last is the one who stops at accidents. There's nothing brave in leaning over the side of your cockpit and hoisting some guy on to the foredeck. It's hard work, but I'm a strong girl. And I'd rather not have any more women in racing. I enjoy being the only one around here. Uh, thank you.'

Now the crowd really cheered. Jane Swindon grinned at me.

'Oh God ... Oh God ...' I moaned into her ear. 'I love that girl. I love her strength, her honesty. I love her hair and her figure and her attitude of mind. I love her, Jane.'

She was watching me and her smile faded, just a little. 'Well, why... Why don't you ask her out, Kev? Maybe have a few dances with her tonight, at the Club. Huh?' She was serious.

'I couldn't be seen dancing with a girl who looked like an intelligent bay mare, could I, Jane?'

She frowned, she tried not to laugh; I don't know what she was thinking. 'You are the original dirty rat, Kevin,' she said at last.

Although numbers of tourists had departed for their home subcolonies, the Social Club was packed, the crowd spilling out into the street. Children drank pop on the fringes. The evening was warm. I stood against the yellow concrete wall, beer in hand, while the mob milled about, shouting and laughing and passing drinks out of the windows. Despite Streng's suspect victory in the skitterbug class the regatta had apparently been a success, the various other events having passed without untoward incident.

Streng himself drew near, propelled by a chance surge of the crowd. With him was the Reverend Batelli and Tom Minty, a somewhat wild youth who was, surprisingly, a member of the Colony Committee.

Batelli was saying, 'But there must have been other considerations in your mind, Ralph.'

Streng was smiling. Above his head a kite bug sailed, its luminous web floating like gossamer in the twilight. The bug dipped, touched his shoulder. Streng glanced sideways, reached up and squashed the kite bug between finger and thumb, dusting the web from his clothes.

'I was thinking of winning,' he said. 'That's all. That's what racing is all about. I knew Paul Blake was going to jump the mudflat again, and he knew I was right beside him. He knows me, so he knew the risk. He took it, and lost.'

Tom Minty chuckled. 'I bet nobody's ever called you chicken, Doctor.'

'Didn't you think of stopping to pull him out of the water, Ralph?' asked Batelli.

'Man is a social animal. My instinct – that which urges me to preserve the species – told me to stop. My intelligence – that which distinguishes me from animals – told me that I would lose the race if I stopped. It also told me that I would be unpopular if I didn't stop. It reminded me, however, that it's the duty of the last pilot in line to stop – therefore Blake was safe from drowning. By stopping, I would gain a certain grudging approval from the crowd, nothing more. I desired victory more than the crowd's approval. So I won.'

'It sounds reasonable enough, put that way,' said Minty uncertainly.

'I'm glad you think so, Tom,' said Streng gravely, but we knew he didn't mean it. Neither the opinion of Tom Minty or anyone else meant anything to Ralph Streng. He had no morals, no scruples, and was motivated purely by self-interest.

In case it sounds as though I despised the man, let me say that I considered him probably the most intelligent person in Riverside, and certainly the most honest. Over the past year I had drunk many a scotch in his company, in that neat little dwelling unit of his near the Research Station. I'd tried to find out what made him tick, probing away while he chuckled and confounded me, and his wife smiled vaguely from her chair opposite.

I suppose one particular remark summed up his philosophy concerning himself and those around him; he said it often, smiling pleasantly.

'We are all amoral – but only I admit it.'

That was Ralph Streng. He smiled at us now, confident and self-possessed, and moved away. The crowd parted automatically to let him through, as though he willed it that way.

Mark Swindon was near; he turned to us after watching Streng go. 'He's got away with it again, huh?'

Batelli said quietly, 'Ralph will always get away with it.'

'Don't be too sure of that, Enrico.' Swindon was serious. 'People can't be unpredictable – particularly in a small colony. I know ...'

Two years ago, at the height of the Relay Effect when half of Arcadia went mad, Professor Mark Swindon had been hunted down by the villagers like an animal ... They had intended to kill him; thanks only to good luck and the intervention of a few unusual people like Tom Minty and Mrs Earnshaw, he was still alive.

Swindon continued. 'This meeting with the Hetherington Organization tomorrow, Kev ... I don't need to remind you how important it is to the colony. I'm sure we can rely on you to get the best deal possible – but you're going to meet some hostility when you get back here, whatever happens. Uh ... I wish you luck.'

He meant it. I looked around at the revellers. A barbecue had been set up in the streets; colonists jostled around Chukalek as he flipped steaks with an expert hand, eyes vacant. Ezra Blake stood close by, his gross jowls quivering as he roared with laughter at something old Jed Spark had said. Jed laughed back, toothless mouth wide and slack-lipped, slobbering. I heard glass breaking, an uproar of shouting from inside the Club. Chill Kaa was disputing ownership of a steak with some stranger, his moon face red and vicious. The stranger yelled back, fists bunched, while Chukalek glanced absently at them both, flipping steaks with a glittering knife.

I felt a twinge of uneasiness ...

# three

I slept well – the drink ensured that – but when I awakened there was a shiver of apprehension in my chest like a cold hand. Today was the day when I bargained on behalf of Riverside. Sunlight brightened the drapes and, as I crawled out of bed, I found that the Arcadian scotch had exacted its penalty for the dreamless sleep. I had a pounding headache.

I took a quick dose of Immunol from my illegal supply, the euphoric glow of Arcadia's own wonder drug spread quickly through my mind and body, and I was able to face opening the drapes, which I did.

It was a fine morning. My dwelling unit is not the standard colony issue, but is the top floor of a converted fish storage plant at the north end of the wharf. Following the success of Mark Swindon's fish pens the industry has boomed, and an entirely new plant has been constructed downstream. I live in the old plant for convenience; the refrigeration equipment has been moved out and the bottom floor has been converted into my boatyard, which spills out on to the wharf. At the time I arrived in Riverside there was a housing shortage.

Now, however, half the units in the colony are empty . . .

Again I heard the hammering noise which had awakened me. A group of men were dismantling the regatta platform and other accoutrements, taking down the flagstaffs, hauling the temporary pontoons out of the water.

Later, dressed and moderately alert, I inspected the boatyard. I employ three men in my small business, turning out around thirty skitterbugs a year which I sell all over Arcadia. Or try to. In the last six months trade hasn't been so good.

'Hi there, Kevin!' Paul Blake was waiting for me.

He was fully recovered from his accident and ready to go. I opened the hood of a nearly-completed skitterbug and began to explain the workings in simple terms.

'You see, the whole boat is built around this minipile. It's an old model, from the days when the reactor's energy was converted into steam, which was used to drive turbines. It was a wasteful system. When the electron flow motor was developed, they began to sell these small reactors off cheaply. I bought up a shipment.'

In fact it had not been quite so simple. I'd practically bankrupted myself in buying two hundred of the minipiles and shipping them to Arcadia. I wasn't out of the red by a long way – and I was reckoning to get another loan from the bank within a month, to tide me over a few temporary problems . . .

Blake knew none of this, of course. 'And you invented the skitterbug yourself,' he said in tones of awe.

'The principle is much the same as the old hovercraft, but simpler.' I pointed under the hood. 'I stripped out the turbine equipment and fitted a straight-through jacket with an expansion chamber, much on the principle of the ram-jet. And I put in a pump to keep the water flowing when the bug is stationary.

'So what happens is this. Water comes in through the scoop there in the bows, under pressure. It travels along this tube, then into the expansion chamber where it hits the hot vanes of the minipile. It expands violently, vaporizing. Most of it is blasted out underwater through the tail pipe and some is tapped off at this manifold and directed downwards to form the cushion of vapour on which the bug rides.'

Paul said, 'I can't understand why the water vapour doesn't condense again as soon as it hits the cold water of the estuary or whatever.'

'It does – to a certain extent. But it's coming so fast out of the nozzles that it doesn't matter. I expect the jet effect alone is enough to keep the bug hovering. Remember, the minipile was developed to handle trucks and aircraft. Lifting a little thing like a skitterbug is well within its capabilities – even though it's an inefficient way to use a reactor.'

I spent the next few minutes explaining the various tricks of the trade, the wrinkles by which a little extra performance can be squeezed out of my standard model without overheating the reactor. The angle of the scoop, the proportions of the down-draught nozzles compared to the thrust nozzle, the positions of the directional vanes – all these things can affect the performance of a skitterbug.

Paul thanked me pleasantly and was about to go, when something in the covered boathouse caught his interest.

'It's a yacht . . .' I said, somewhat reluctantly. We moved indoors. The sleek form of my latest project occupied most of the length of one wall. 'I'm trying out a few new ideas,' I said.

He examined the hull. 'First time I've ever seen a yacht full of holes,' he observed doubtfully, running his fingers over the thousands of tiny pinpricks which marred the smooth surface. He glanced at the name, bright yellow against the black hull.

EASY LADY.

'I'll be launching her in a couple of weeks,' I said.

Paul stood back. He stooped and sighted along the mast, which lay on trestles nearby. Sails hung from the wall.

'I guess you know what you're doing,' he said uncertainly.

There is a thing which happens to me sometimes, a sad hopeless thing which would interest Jane Swindon. It happens to me in the street, in restaurants, in elevators, anywhere – but mostly on journeys because then I have time to brood about it, to build up card houses of imagination which never collapse but merely fade with time, with the ending of the journey. I think it happens to most men. It is a thing few women know about, or care about, as they go on their way with thoughts as well-guarded as mine.

It happens on these journeys, just sometimes, that I see the Most Beautiful Girl in the World.

It is a sad event because it's so futile. She is sitting there, a few seats in front of me; I've caught a glimpse of her face as she boarded and I renew acquaintance with her loveliness from time to time as she turns to talk to her companion – who is always male and always better-looking than I. She hasn't seen me. Maybe she never will.

So I watch her with helpless admiration which is not lust, just a wonder that she exists and a sorrow that she and I will never meet – because I am not one of those fictional Lotharios who can charm any girl into instant and intimate acquaintanceship. Neither, I suspect, are many other men. So I watch and she is oblivious, and after a while she is gone – and it seems she was not with that guy after all. She was alone. Why the hell didn't I get there first...?

And the sweetsad memory stays with me, a fading but recurrent image, until one day I am riding the monorail and I see another Most Beautiful Girl in the World...

I'd driven fast to Inchtown, caught the mid-morning railcar with seconds to spare, and was now suffering that terrifying acceleration as the linear motor catapulted the small vehicle towards Premier City. The ride was almost soundless: just a faint whine from the guide rails and a quiet chuntering from the compressor which keeps that thin, lubricating film of air between the base of the car and the smooth trackbed. Soon even this latter sound ceased as the ram effect built up and the vehicle's forward-mounted air intakes took over.

At last the acceleration slackened and I was able to free my head from the back of the seat and scan my surroundings. I glanced out of the window but soon looked away: the sight of a nearby landscape passing at four hundred kph makes me feel sick. There was some wind noise but not too much. Quiet music issued from the speakers; then they crackled suddenly. The metallic voice of our driver came across, grunting something unintelligible, then was abruptly cut off. The car seemed to be swaying unduly.

I fancied the driver had said, 'There's no cause for alarm, ladies and gentlemen,' and my heart began to pound. If the driver tells me there's no cause for alarm, then he becomes automatically a liar.

But the stewardess came smiling down the aisle with coffee and it seemed everything was all right. My imagination had let me down again. The driver had been announcing our ETA in Premier City.

Then a girl reached out to take a coffee, and my heart misbehaved again.

She was truly the most beautiful girl in the world.

I only caught a glimpse of her profile before she sat back again, hidden from me by her headrest, but that was enough. She had shoulder-length blonde hair, a firm, round chin and a wide mouth. She had blue eyes and a nice nose. That might describe a million girls. I can't describe her beauty, or the effect she had on me.

I leaned back in my seat and watched the top of her head, which was beautiful. I watched her right hand, which rested on the armrest, and I reckoned her hand looked pretty goddamned good, too. I began to fantasize about who she was and what she was doing on this railcar. Most of the other passengers looked like sub-colony representatives like myself: dull well-dressed men and women, consumed with the inward fear that they would let their side down at the conference.

I wasn't concerned about my side anymore. If that girl had got up, and turned to me and said, 'Perhaps you'd like to be my guide around the city today,' I'd have said, 'Fine,' and to hell with Riverside...

Of course, she might also be a sub-colony representative. But somehow I didn't think so.

So I daydreamed the journey away, and on one occasion had the inspiration to get up and go to the forward john, which meant that I could watch her as I returned to my seat. But she didn't look at me. She was talking to some smooth-looking bastard beside her.

When we arrived at the Premier City terminal she disappeared into the crowd. I watched what might have been the top of her head for a while, then she was gone.

'I will give a résumé of the situation to date,' said the tall woman who had been introduced as Althea Gant, Vice-President i/c Arcadian Operations, the Hetherington Organization.

About sixty of us sat in the large conference room of the Parliament Buildings. There were ten Ministers and the Premier, some forty sub-colony representatives and, at the head table, the representatives of the Hetherington Organization. The room was long and narrow; someone had drawn the drapes so that the sun could only enter in little shafts in which dust motes danced.

'Arcadia was colonized a little over one hundred and thirty years ago,' Althea Gant continued, 'sponsored by the, uh, now-defunct World Emigration Commission.'

At the mention of this body, smiles showed on the faces of the Hetherington people and they regarded us pityingly, as though we'd been duped.

'As is the way with Government projects, unexpected problems arose. This planet has six moons which describe erratic orbits but are normally distributed evenly. However, it was found that once every fifty-two years the moons clustered together in the sky for a short period, before scattering once more on their individual paths. During this period there were high tides and other phenomena.

'Various life-forms on the planet operate on a coincident cycle; in particular a type of plankton which undergoes regeneration every fifty-two years. The plankton congregates in tidal estuaries and, as a defence mechanism, has evolved an unusual power.' Here Althea Gant hesitated. 'The details are not entirely clear to us, but it appears that gatherings of plankton, known as Minds, were able to induce telepathic powers in human beings.'

At this point there was an interruption from the floor. A thin, dried-up man stood. 'That is not strictly correct,' he said precisely.

'Maybe you'd care to tell us,' said Gant with a hint of asperity.

'Certainly. Uh, I'm Francis Legg, from Oldhaven. Yes ... The Minds, as we called them, were able to relay emotions from one person to another. In fact, we called it the Relay Effect. It was a remarkably dangerous thing.' Legg smiled thinly, seeing private jokes all over the place, and I judged him to be a lawyer. 'Suppose you met someone you disliked. The Mind would relay your emotion to this person and he would react, hating you back, as it were. The emotion would reach you and you would return it, redoubled. Soon you'd be fighting. In the latter stages there were examples of actual visualized and verbal thoughts being transmitted from one person to another – but it was the hatred which was the dangerous thing: the Relay Effect. It's quite surprising how many hate emotions there are flying about at any given time. The Minds amplified them, if they were within range.'

'Thank you, Mr Legg. Now I understand this affected all the coastal sub-colonies – well over half Arcadia's population. And finally, the Minds gained possession of people to such an extent that they were able to force large numbers to commit suicide by walking into blackfish-infested waters ...'

Althea Gant spoke on, reminding us of the panic which had gripped the Government, with refugees arriving from all directions, and tales of mass drownings rife. The coastal towns had been sealed off by military blockades – I don't think the sub-colonies would ever forgive the Government for leaving them to their fate, although it is difficult to see what else could have been done ...

Althea Gant continued, 'However, it seems that there was an antidote to the power of the Minds. A drug was discovered during the later stages of the Relay Effect, although too late to be of much benefit. This drug, known as Immunol, is prepared from a root which grows in certain south-eastern regions. It induces a euphoric state which effectively blankets out the Relay Effect and, indeed, the later murderous commands of the Minds.'

Our Premier was quickly on his feet. A small man, he looked anxious, nervous. 'I'd like to say something at this point,' he said.

'Of course.' Althea Gant sat down.

'Immunol is, of course, a complete answer to the Relay Effect – which will not occur for fifty years, in any case. I, for one, will not be here to see it.'

'But what about our kids?' someone shouted. 'What about them?'

The Premier bit his lip; the interrupter was a sub-colony rep. 'As you all know, it is your Government's intention to issue Immunol to the people at the first sign of danger.'

'So why is possession of Immunol illegal, right now?'

There was a buzz of interest; the man had raised a good point. It appeared that the drug was not addictive, neither had any harmful effects been observed – indeed, Arcattle and other indigenous animals ate it all the time. But as soon as the danger from the Minds had disappeared, the use of Immunol had been outlawed.

'The drug has not been thoroughly tested ... It is your Government's duty to safeguard the health of the people against indiscriminate use of possibly dangerous and untried substances ... I can assure you, as soon as our laboratories have thoroughly evaluated the—'

'Argh, shut up!' the man yelled disgustedly. 'Immunol was banned because it's fun!'

'The so-called pleasurable effects of this crude—'

'And because it loosens your hold on the sub-colonies. You're frightened we'll all get stoned and tell you to go fuck yourself! That's why the Government banned Immunol!'

'There are signs of a definite correlation between the indiscriminate use of Immunol and the incidence of—' The Minister for Health was on his feet now, quickly shouted down. His voice was lost in a veritable chorus of questions and accusations from the body of the hall.

Meanwhile the representatives of the Hetherington Organization looked on, smiling faintly as we made their job easier for them...

'Self-rule for the sub-colonies!' someone was shouting, again and again.

And so the meeting developed into a battle between the Arcadian Council and the representatives of the sub-colonies. The Premier shouted and gave up, stronger voices in the Government tried, but were shouted down.

The Representative for Inchtown put our basic fears into

words. 'How the hell do we know the Government will issue the drug in fifty years' time?' he asked forcefully. 'How do we know who the Government will be? How do we know they'll stockpile enough Immunol for everyone? They didn't do it last time. Christ, we all know what Governments are. They'll leave it till the last moment, then blame the weather for a crop failure!'

Finally Althea Gant stood again, and at last there was comparative silence. 'I think our Organization is aware of the problems which face this planet,' she said. 'In view of your expressed lack of confidence in your Government, it is hardly surprising that over thirty per cent of the population of Arcadia has emigrated to other planets within the past two years.'

Then the shouting really started...

My neighbour turned to me and remarked, yelling to make himself heard above the din, 'It's like I tell them back at Sea Settlement. The goddamned planet's dying and the Government's doing nothing about it. Thirty per cent! And they told us there was no cause for alarm. Hell, you can't blame the people. Why stay here and raise kids, when they're going to die before they reach old age, and when they're going to be scared to have kids too? Goddamnit, I'd emigrate myself if I could afford it. There are plenty of safe planets in this Sector.'

And this was the view of the meeting, voiced loud and long, while the various Ministers tried vainly to make themselves heard, to contradict the statistic quoted by Althea Gant.

Eventually everyone was shouted hoarse and the Premier was allowed to speak.

'Right,' he said, pale-faced. 'You've made your views clear. It seems there's nothing more my colleagues or myself can say, so I propose that we move on to the vote. Certain proposals have been put to your Government by the Hetherington Organization concerning the future of this planet. If you feel we should consider them now, raise your hand...' He sat down quickly.

In effect, he resigned office from that moment.

'I want to make one thing clear from the start,' said Althea Gant. 'The Hetherington Organization is a business concern. It runs its planets like businesses and it expects them to show a profit. We're interested in Arcadia because of what we can get out of it, and if we succeed, you'll succeed too. Right now you're failing; by the end of the year you'll have lost half your population. And nothing collapses so fast as a planet with a falling population, believe me.

'We propose to put you on your feet. Firstly, we'll bring in immigrants and set in motion a big publicity campaign to attract more. We in the Organization think in terms of billions. Arcadia has the potential to make itself the biggest planet in the Sector.

'Secondly, we'll develop the agriculture and fishing industries. And when I say develop, that's what I mean. We'll bring in as much equipment as we have men to handle, and we'll make Arcadia the cornucopia of the Sector. Light industries too – but we'll leave the stink and pollution of heavy industry to the other worlds. Arcadia is a beautiful place. We don't want to spoil it.

'Thirdly, in order to put certain fears at rest, we'll lift the ban on Immunol, which will be made freely available to all who want it. Subject, of course, to a controller stockpiling for use in the future, when the Relay Effect hits again. In this way, you'll have your insurance.'

She smiled. 'That's the essence of our proposals. I don't like to waste time. I'd like to know whether you want to get down to the details or whether we all ought to go home.'

There was a roar of acclamation. The meeting, it seemed, wanted to hear more.

I talked with my neighbour as the Hetherington Organization passed round some sort of prospectus. It seemed his name was Erikson and he was a fisherman from Sea Settlement, on the north coast. We became involved in a discussion on the merits of skitterbugs as adjuncts to fishing fleets, while some other wrangle was going on around us. By the time we'd finished, it appeared that we'd elected a committee of six to examine the Hetherington proposals, and that we were committed to giving them a reply within seven days.

We both had a couple of hours to spare before our respective railcars left, so Erikson and I took a stroll around the city. If I hadn't noticed the effects of mass emigration before, I noticed it now. Stores stood empty, signs in windows proclaimed optimistic offers of leases on favourable terms. The hoverbuses looked run-down, the advertising matter fly-blown and peeling.

'Why the hell are people pulling out of Premier City so fast?' I asked Erikson. 'They're safe here. The Relay Effect didn't reach this far inland.'

He smiled grimly, pausing at one of the few recently decorated stores on Main Street. 'I understand you had it easy in Riverside. Sea Settlement lost two hundred people in the Relay Effect and over three hundred have quit since. You can't blame them. I can still see it myself; I dream about it sometimes. All those people walking out into the water, like zombies . . . And the blackfish taking them as they walked.' He shuddered. 'God knows why I'm still alive. I came to my senses when the water reached my knees. Ten metres in front of me there was a little girl. She went under while I watched. In a sort of crimson swirling. I didn't try to save her . . . That sort of thing affects a whole planet – not just those who were immediately involved.'

'I'd just arrived on Arcadia,' I said. 'I saw a little girl die at Oldhaven . . .'

We stood looking at the store window in silence for a few moments. Gradually I became aware that the place was well-stocked with imported goods: rugs, pottery, silverware, furniture. It seemed that at least one business concern had confidence in the future of Arcadia. Curious, I stepped back and looked up at the sign.

HETHERINGTON'S HOME STORES.

'They're moving in,' I observed, vaguely alarmed.

Erikson regarded me. 'When Hetherington takes over a planet, that's just what he does. He buys everything. He buys your land, your business. He buys you.'

I always feel a quick dislike for someone who tells me unpleasant facts; I was beginning to regret burdening myself with this fool for the afternoon. 'Nobody buys me,' I said.

'Then I suggest you catch the next shuttle out . . .' said Erikson.

# four

It was dark when I reached the brow of the hill where the road begins to descend to the estuary.

Lights moved at the water's edge. The trawlers were unloading the day's harvest from the ocean. Masthead lights glowed, reflecting from the water, swinging and gliding about in the darkness as the boats jockeyed for position at the wharf. There seemed to be some confusion.

I started up the turbine and drifted slowly down the hill, over the bridge, and turned left on to the wharf. I parked the car and walked through the chilly night air to the scene of activity. Kite-bugs floated past, glowing softly; here and there a quick scurrying indicated the presence of a worral. Although allegedly herbivorous, these small animals seem to find the fishery a place of some fascination.

There is something very bleak about the appearance of a large warehouse at night. The huge sliding doors were open and the refrigeration units humming – but the doors to the cold-storage areas were firmly shut. Two men were arguing in the harsh light.

'I tell you there's no room, Mr Walters. Really, there's nothing I can do, is there? I can't conjure up an empty cold-room out of thin air now, can I?' It was the piping voice of Vernon Thrale, the Pioneer, in his more normal guise of wharfinger and warehouseman.

'You're a goddamned fool, Thrale, you know that? There are six boats out there waiting to unload. Couldn't you have foreseen this?'

'Well, I did warn you, Mr Walters.'

'You mentioned the truck hadn't arrived yet. That's all you said. You never said the truck *wouldn't* arrive.'

'It might still come. You never can tell now, can you?'

'Oh, for Christ's sake,' muttered Perce Walters. 'If you spent time looking after your job and less time dancing about in smocks, everyone'd be a whole lot better off.' He wheeled away and came storming back towards me. Seeing me at the last moment he stopped and stared angrily from under bushy eyebrows. 'Do you have any storage space at your place?' he demanded.

'Hell, Perce. You know everything was dismantled when I put the boatyard in.'

'Maybe you shouldn't have been so goddamned quick to pull things apart,' he snapped. 'We've got a whole catch of fish here, and nowhere to put it. Let me use your phone, will you?'

He walked up the wharf towards my place, while the fishing boats surged about in the estuary. I poured myself a scotch while Perce stabbed the bisiphone buttons as though he bore them a personal grudge. I didn't pour Perce a drink. I figured if he wanted one, he could ask for it.

The face of a middle-aged, ineffectual-looking man appeared on the screen. 'Natatchski!' barked Perce.

The man blinked, peered back. He wore red pyjamas. 'Don't you know what time it is?' he asked querulously.

'Of course I know what time it is,' snarled Perce. 'What's more important is where is that goddamned truck? I have a warehouse full of fish here, and a day's catch brought in, and nowhere to put it.'

'Sorry. I can't help you. The trucking depot's all closed down.'

'Wait a moment!' shouted Perce as Natatchski made a move towards the Off button. 'When are we next scheduled for a pick-up, for Christ's sake?'

'Hold on, will you.' The man disappeared and Perce turned to look at me. He didn't say anything: he just looked, and his eyes told me his anger and bewilderment were abating, turning to anxiety. I raised my brows and glanced at the bottle. He nodded and I poured him a scotch, feeling suddenly sorry for him. He was a fisherman and all his capital was tied up in his boat – and I think we both knew that this current problem was not merely the result of a breakdown, or even a clerical error.

Natatchski returned with a print-out. He held it up to the screen and pointed, as though saying: *don't blame me, blame the computer...*

'Next pick-up Thursday,' said Perce heavily. 'Why's that, Ivan?'

'No storage space.'

They looked at each other in silence for a moment, then Perce said, 'Full up, huh?'

'That's right, Perce.'

Later Perce and I sat in my living-room overlooking the

dark water of the estuary, finishing our drinks. The boats were all moored now. Two moons glowed in the sky: Aleph and Gimel, I guessed.

We weren't talking much. After a particularly long silence Perce said, 'I'm sorry if I spoke out of turn, back a while. I was shaken up, I guess. You know—' He stared thoughtfully at the dark water '– we've lost a third of our population, but we're still producing the same amount of food. I used to think the most important thing for a colony to do was to grow enough to live on. But it's not like that, is it, Kev?'

'No,' I said. 'A planet must have a balanced output.'

'They tell me two of the machine shops in Inchtown have closed down. Labour problems, I guess. People wanting out. See – farming and fishing, they're individual things, almost one-man jobs. But heavy industry ... You've got to have buildings and machines and bank loans and union agreements and machinists and draughtsmen and management ... And if people start to pull out, where does that leave you? Your industry collapses, huh? But farming and fishing goes on. If the tractor breaks down, you hitch Arcattle to the plough. If your boat engine seizes, hell, you hoist sails. We're ingenious, we colonists. When we run out of fabric for sails, we weave them from leaves ...' He stared at me. 'You see what I'm getting at, Kev? We'll be going primitive, because there's nobody to buy our fish, to pay us money to buy parts to fix our boats and tractors ...'

I said, 'Hetherington's people said Arcadia's best suited to agriculture and fishing anyway. They have a group of planets in the Sector and they plan to integrate us. We'll grow the food, somebody else'll produce the machine tools, another planet will service the space shuttles, and so on.'

Perce said slowly, 'That locks us right in, doesn't it ...'

There was a long silence after that.

During breakfast the following morning I heard that irritating buzz from my pocket which signifies that the Newspocket people think they have an item worth drawing my attention to. Usually this relates to the assassination on a remote planet of a potentate of whom I've never heard, the conclusion of a trade agreement between two totally insignificant worlds, or the fact that my subscription is overdue. Today, however, the item was of immediate interest.

There was a staggeringly beautiful girl on the screen.

I was just congratulating Newspocket on having got their priorities right at last when I realized she was talking about the Hetherington prospectus, so I tried to concentrate on her words.

Basically, it seemed that the Organization was going to pay a sum of money 'for the planet Arcadia'. The sum was so huge that I forgot it instantly; you know how it is with rows of 000s. However, it aroused an immediate and intriguing question in my mind: Who was going to receive all this money?

The girl was smiling as though discussing her shopping budget. 'This sum will be paid into an escrow account with the Universal Bank,' she said, 'and will be released to the Arcadian Council in five years' time, when the Hetherington Organization will divest itself of many of its proposed Arcadian assets and the planet will revert to primarily private ownership.'

What would the Arcadian Council do with all that money? Spend it, presumably. I could guess who the earliest beneficiaries would be. A local artist would be commissioned to execute a huge statue of Hetherington, to be erected in the Council Square, Premier City. Next, the Hetherington Museum and Art Gallery would commence construction, and exceed its budgeted price by four hundred per cent. Following which Vernon Thrale and the Kindred of the Pioneers would receive a grant towards promotion of local arts and crafts, sufficient to keep them dancing for the rest of their lives.

The rest would go into general funds. Ordinary people would never see it.

I watched her for a while, my mind more on the girl than the proposed sale of the planet. She had a nice smile and she used it often – particularly when she had something unpleasant to say.

'Naturally the Organization does not lay out this kind of money without certain strings,' she said, smiling. 'For instance, we reserve the right to appropriate private lands where necessary for the public benefit – this right will be exercised rarely, I assure you. On the other hand, there will be jobs for all. I understand the falling population has already created problems in this area.

'Of course, in the early years while we fight our way back to prosperity, the rewards may appear small. The workers will be paid a living wage only – but a notional fund will be accumulated to their credit. This will represent a full, normal wage and in effect will be a repayment of the capital which the Organization has invested in your planet.'

She smiled brilliantly at that and I missed what followed because I was trying to work it out. I smelled a rat somewhere. What exactly was the Organization trying to pull? Were they saying that we would be compelled to work for a pittance?

I searched around for the printed hand-out which I'd been given at the conference, but I had mislaid it. By the time I got back to Newspocket, the girl had concluded her talk. I found that I mistrusted her now, and her smile seemed vapid and false. She was not half so pretty as I'd thought at first.

A meeting had been called at the Social Club for that afternoon. I decided to lunch there, at the same time trying to pick up a few pointers as to how public opinion was shaping up. When I arrived the place was empty, so I wandered into the kitchen. Chukalek was there, moving about. I enquired after his health – he suffers from unexpected bleeding – and commiserated with him over being placed fifth in the skitterbug racing. He glanced at me quickly and nervously, fingers working.

In addition to the bleeding problem Chukalek suffers from nerves. This is not immediately apparent as he moves about the kitchen in his languid manner, peeling potatoes, jointing meat with a dexterity which bodes ill for any hostile life-forms, chopping onions, baking bread . . .

But it is in this latter accomplishment that his unfortunate psychosomatic ailment manifests itself.

He kneads the dough with an expression of secretive joy one step ahead of actual gloating. A droning hum issues from his pursed lips, rising in tone as he works feverishly with pumping elbows – he never uses the excellent mixer the kitchen provides – until it becomes a paean of delight when Chukalek begins to slap the completed mix about the table in orgiastic frenzy. Then at last he pulls himself together, dashes a hand across his brow and commences to tear the pale formless thing into dinner-roll-sized balls. He lays them in neat rows on trays and slides them into the oven.

But he always keeps back one small ball of stodge. For the rest of the day, and all the following day, he keeps this lump by him, squeezing it constantly in his left hand like a grip-exerciser.

As the day goes on this dough becomes darker in hue until by the time of the next baking it resembles wholemeal, and is replaced. Chukalek is always overcome with embarrassment when strangers question his dough. He will open his fist and regard it, surprised. He mutters something about his nerves. Then he will jam his left hand out of sight, into his pocket. During the rest of the conversation he keeps it there, kneading in stealthy masturbatory fashion, while the stranger's eyes keep dropping to it in furtive alarm.

'What do you think of the Hetherington deal?' I asked him.

He blinked; his left fist bunched. 'I don't reckon it makes much difference, huh?'

'Well, you heard the terms. A lot of people are going to be unhappy.'

He smiled. 'Not me. So they may take people's land – well I don't have any. Ezra Blake does, though. And they'll pay us low wages, will they? Well, the Club doesn't pay me a fortune now. Ralph Streng earns plenty, though ...'

We discussed the matter for a while and I began to make a few readjustments in my assessment of the deal. There were probably a lot of people like Chukalek, whose motives in voting at the referendum would be dictated by mild jealousy rather than honest self-interest. There comes a point in everyone's life when they *know* they are not going to improve themselves in any way.

When that time comes, the only course is to drag other people down to their level.

Feeling depressed, I moved through into the lounge where John Talbot had just served drinks to a small group consisting of Ralph Streng and his wife, Alicia Desjardins of the equine features, and the Reverend Enrico Batelli. I ordered beer and joined them; they were discussing the regatta, which made a pleasant change from the Hetherington deal. Soon others joined us: the Swindons, Mortimore Barker and other drink-minded colonists.

Barker and Streng seemed to be on good terms again; the incident of the prizegiving was now regarded in a different light.

'Hell, it was good copy, that's all,' Barker was booming, his glass of beer dwarfed by his huge fist. 'Nothing personal in it, Ralph. The public saw what happened in the race, and you were cast as a bastard. It's my job as publicity agent to give the public what it wants. Following the accident to the handsome young hero in the finals of the skitterbug races, what the public wanted was a villain to hiss.'

Streng smiled. 'Don't ignore the fact that I may *be* a villain by your standards, Mort. Why did you let me off the hook, anyway?'

Barker took a long and thoughtful drink. 'I suppose it's all right for me to tell you,' he said. 'Listen, I believe in freedom of the press, right? And a newsman's duty to his public, right?'

Streng was watching Barker sombrely now, his deepset eyes clouded.

Barker said, 'A representative of the Hetherington Organization told me to lay off Ralph Streng, if I knew what was good for me. I objected, being a fine upstanding newsman who knows where his duty lies. Whereupon the Newspocket people, taking their cue from the Hetherington man, said they wouldn't cover the prizegiving unless I treated Ralph lightly.'

There was a moment's silence while we worked that one out, then Jane Swindon said, 'You have friends in high places, Ralph.'

'That's news to me,' said Streng evenly, and we believed him.

Enrico Batelli suggested, 'I expect Newspocket is owned by the Organization anyway. They have tentacles everywhere. The point is, Ralph, you were saved from unfavourable public exposure.' He grinned suddenly. 'Do you know, I don't believe you care what people think of you?'

Alicia Desjardins was sitting beside Streng: women always do sit beside him, or stand beside him – and probably lie beside him whenever they get the chance.

Streng said, 'I care a lot. We all do: it's a basic instinct closely allied to self-preservation, and consequently very powerful. More powerful, for instance, than the instinct which urges us to preserve the species – to which sex is allied, of course. I would go so far as to say that all aspects of self-preservation are primary instincts, whereas sex and its adjuncts are merely secondary.'

Often when Streng stops speaking there is a long pause, because people want to be sure he's finished: they don't care to interrupt him.

So it was a long time before Batelli said, 'Garbage! A truly primitive life-form has no concept of self-preservation – yet it can reproduce. Reproduction is basic.'

Streng turned to Alicia Desjardins. 'I'd like to conduct an experiment, my dear. I'd like to ask you certain questions, and I'd like you to answer them truthfully. You think you can do that?'

She looked flattered. 'Of course, Ralph.'

Streng said to us, 'Truly honest and logical reasoning never fails. I'm a successful man – and a contented one – because I'm honest with myself. I wish we could all be the same.' He glanced at Batelli, who is always something of a sparring-partner for him on these occasions, then turned back to Alicia. 'You were in love with Paul Blake until recently,' he said quietly. 'And it's common knowledge you had a violent quarrel with him a few weeks back. You also wanted very much to beat him in the regatta. Logically you detest the guy.'

Alicia nodded, saying nothing.

Barker said loudly, 'Look, Streng, this is a bit ... uh, don't you think?'

Streng said, 'So it was with conflicting emotions that you rounded the final bend and caught sight of Paul Blake lying unconscious in the water.'

'Yes.'

'At first you thought: It serves him right. Eh?'

'Yes ...'

'So why did you pull him out?'

Alicia said firmly, 'Because he'd have drowned if I hadn't.'

'But as we agreed, you detest the guy.'

'You don't just leave someone to drown. It's not right. It's near enough murder.'

Streng said, 'That's not specific enough, Alicia. You're talking in abstracts – things you've been taught to believe since you were a kid, without ever thinking why. Try again.'

There was a slightly desperate look on her face as she said uncertainly, 'The race rules state that the last one in line picks up the bodies.'

'Rules, rules. Who makes them? Someone who's frightened of getting hurt; it's the prime instinct again ...' Streng's voice hardened. 'Don't try to tell me that was your main reason for stopping, Alicia.'

Suddenly it wasn't a game any more. Alicia was trapped, Streng was closing in like a predator. The girl said weakly, 'I couldn't just leave him there, don't you understand? I'd never have got it off my conscience!'

Streng leaned back, relaxing, smiling. As though the heat was off. 'Nearly there, my dear,' he murmured. 'Just one more step, eh? Just one short step to the truth. Come on, now . . .'

Alica looked around the circle of faces; we must have looked like Inquisitors to the poor kid. I thought she might have broken down at that point: the thing had gone too far. But her jaw firmed; she looked at Streng and said carefully: 'I picked Paul out of the water because the whole goddamned colony was watching. If the accident had happened out of sight around the corner I'd have left the bastard to drown, so help me! Is that what you want to hear?' So saying she stood, and walked away in the direction of the ladies' washroom.

The various reactions were interesting.

Barker said, in comic dismay, 'So much for my little heroine. I thought she was a bit uncertain in front of the cameras.'

Hazel Streng said slowly, bitterly, 'Ralph was once pulled out of the water himself. I've often wondered what his rescuer's motives were.' We looked at her in surprise. It was the first time anyone remembered her speaking out against her husband, even indirectly.

I found myself saying, 'I don't see why the hell you had to upset the girl, Streng.' But then I'm not a deep thinker. I have no pretensions that way.

Batelli said, 'You're a little too anxious to find truth, Ralph. Almost as though you're scared of the very necessary fantasy all around you. You weren't on Arcadia during the Relay Effect. If you'd been here, you'd have known what truth can do. Then, every man knew his neighbour's innermost emotions – and the results were not pleasant. In any case, you're missing a possibility. A simple reason for Alicia pulling Paul from the river.'

'I don't think so.'

'Just a hypothesis, you understand? But just suppose she's still in love with him.'

And Streng said, 'You'll have to define love pretty carefully, before I'll go along with that, Enrico.'

This time it was Hazel Streng who plunged for the ladies' room.

Following all this drama, it came as something of an anticlimax to find the meeting had assembled in the next room and was ready to commence discussion of the colony's future.

# five

I am a born leader, but I have a problem in finding followers. My childhood was largely spent in founding gangs and secret societies and at this I was successful – although the societies never achieved a higher membership than four, including my spaniel Urge. A dissident would invariably come to the fore and provoke this typical conversation:

Self: 'Shut your mouth, or I'll throw you out of my gang.'

Dissident (smiling unpleasantly): 'What gang?'

Sure enough the dissident had organized a coup and set himself up as the new leader, and I was alone with my spaniel. Throughout my childhood, gangs were constantly being whipped away from under me, like tablecloths.

So it was that when the meeting settled down, it was Mrs Earnshaw who hammered on the table for silence, and me who was looking frantically for a chair. I found one eventually, carried it to the long table and sat down at the very end of the row of colony notables, facing the assembled multitude. The table was not long enough and there was no room for me behind it, so alone among those on the platform I was exposed to full and critical view.

When the coughing ceased, Mrs Earnshaw rose to her feet. She had placed herself in command in very positive fashion.

'Fellow colonists,' she began. 'We've come together to discuss the terms of the Hetherington proposals, bearing in mind that the referendum takes place next Friday. I don't need to emphasize the importance of this meeting. On the outcome of our discussions depends our future for the next five years – possibly for our whole lives. Now, Mr Kevin Moncrieff attended a conference in Premier City at which certain tentative decisions were taken. Perhaps you'd like to address the meeting, Mr Moncrieff.'

Somewhat surprised that she'd given me the chance to speak so early in the proceedings, I stood up. I outlined the discussion with Althea Gant and mentioned the appointment of the committee which was to look into the proposals.

'But it's the referendum that counts,' I said. 'All the committee will do is to make public recommendations on Thursday.'

Chill Kaa was on his feet, broad face intense. 'But a hell of a lot of people will vote according to what the committee say. Is that right?'

'I guess so, Chill. The recommendations are bound to have some effect.'

'Yes. So tell us this. Are the committee mainly large landowners or not?'

I thought about that one, not yet seeing his point. 'I guess they'd be landowners and businessmen like myself, Chill. Those are the sort of people who'd naturally be sent as sub-colony representatives.'

'I thought so.' He turned round and faced the meeting. 'You see what's happening? We're going to lose out. All these committee members, they'll be scared of losing their land and their lousy businesses, and they'll do their best to persuade the whole planet to vote against Hetherington!'

I regarded him thoughtfully. His attitude was the same as Chukalek's: he'd be happy to see a levelling downward. And I'd already made up my mind that the Hetherington way – although unfavourable in some respects – was the only way to go. Without financial support and new immigrants, the planet would fold.

Mrs Earnshaw quickly took charge again. 'Thank you, Mr Moncrieff,' she said. 'Now, I'd like to say something. I notice that everyone will be expected to work for a minimum subsistence pay. I, for one, cannot agree with that. It's not that I'm not accustomed to working – heaven knows, I've done my share in the past – but I consider that I've earned a rest now, in my twilight years. And I'm not the only senior citizen in Riverside.'

There were a few guffaws from the younger element at the back of the hall, but in the main she'd got her point across. I saw sympathetic nods.

Will Jackson, the colony's elderly sex maniac, was standing. 'Quite right, Mrs Earnshaw. And I'll tell you another thing. I didn't hear any provision for sickness. They say they'll pay us a lump sum at the end of five years to make up for all the time on short pay, right? But that lump sum's based on wages earned. If a man's sick, or too old to do what he's told, he's not accumulating anything. When the five years is up, he's lost his land and his business to Hetherington, and he gets nothing back!'

Mark Swindon said, 'You must understand one thing. The

Hetherington scheme is set up the same as all his new colonies – but those other colonies are naturally composed of young people. Arcadia has been going for several generations. A lot of people are going it hard. But as far as I can see, the alternative is a reversion to a primitive existence!'

I'd heard that Mark had a penchant for making himself unpopular on these occasions, and I could see why. He told the truth.

Eventually the meeting drifted to a close, the colonists evenly divided. The bigger landowners and businessmen were in the main against the proposals for obvious reasons, although some of them could see sense. The small men were in favour of the deal. There were other sub-groups: the old, who like Mrs Earnshaw saw a loss of security, and a fierce group distributed evenly among the colonists who desired independence at any price. They suggested that Riverside should opt out of the deal, even if the rest of Arcadia voted in.

It was to this latter group that the Reverend Enrico Batelli addressed his closing remark. 'Forget it,' he said. 'What Arcadia does, we do. With Hetherington it's all or nothing. I know. I've worked for the Organization before.'

When certain people – Ralph Streng is a good example – enter a bank, the manager springs to attention, offering loans. No collateral, no guarantees from wealthy relatives – for force of their personality is such that the manager will fall over himself to accommodate them. They have a magnetic air of reliability which attracts money to them. No questions are asked. They are, quite obviously, solid citizens.

But when I creep into a bank and ask for a loan, the inquisition is searching and thorough, and it pretty soon emerges that I am a bum.

So it was with trepidation that I entered the manager's office of the Universal Bank the following day. Riverside is not large enough to support its own branch, so a travelling bank calls twice a week. The manager, Guy Oppenheimer, is a large jovial man; he was smiling broadly as I entered and I hoped it would stay that way.

After the usual pleasantries he asked, 'How's trade these days, Kev?' He'd glanced at the small screen on his desk, so he knew my Christian name – in addition to my overdraft, the trend of recent transactions, my age, sex and marital status.

And many other details. Any question he asked was almost certain to be superfluous – unless intended to catch me out in a lie.

'I've sold eight skitterbugs so far this year,' I said loudly. 'And I have orders on hand for another six. Hell, I reckon in another year I'll have paid off the loan on the minipiles.'

'I hope so, Kev. I hope so. Successful businesses mean a successful bank.'

We talked some more; I asked after his family and he told me they were all fine – although an elderly aunt had died in Sydney, Earth. I commiserated. Eventually small-talk was exhausted and he asked, pleasantly, the purpose of my visit.

'I have something big coming up.'

'Uh-huh?'

'A new boat. This could be a winner, Guy. It's a sailing boat, a sloop – but with a difference. It's a real fun boat, Guy. I think I'm right in saying that it's the only one of its type in the Galaxy.'

He raised his eyebrows at this. 'Sailing boat, Kev? They're a bit dated, surely?'

'*Easy Lady* isn't just another sailing boat. She's the start of a new trend. Now, what would you say the main drawback of sailing boats is?'

'Nobody will buy them.'

'The problem is, they're too slow. But *Easy Lady* isn't slow – she's goddamned near as fast as an ice-yacht. You see ...' I took a stylus and writing frame from his desk and made a few rapid sketches. 'Your ordinary sailing boat is slowed down by friction between the hull and the water – it's a drag which you can't overcome except in a small dinghy, when you can plane.' He looked blank. 'You know, skim along just touching the surface, with the wind behind you. But a big boat can't do that. A big boat is too heavy to plane, so it has to reduce drag by other methods – hull shape, principally.'

I was watching his face as I spoke, but he showed no expression. I went on, 'But you still have that friction problem. Except on *Easy Lady*. When *Easy Lady* is sailing, there's no friction between the hull and the water.'

'I'm very pleased to hear that, Kev.'

'I got the idea from the grain conveyor at Inchtown. You know that chute – a long sloping metal plate? It has millions of tiny little holes in it. They drop the sacks on at the top, air is forced out of the holes at high pressure and the sacks ride on this lubricating film of air, gliding down the slight downhill grade all the way to the local distribution trucks.'

'And you can apply this principle to boats?'

'Certainly, Guy. *Easy Lady* has a double hull, and the outer one is perforated with millions of tiny holes, letting out air. Pressure is maintained between the two hulls with a small pump. So the water never actually touches the hull – there's always this thin film of air against the surface of the boat. And there's virtually no friction. The scale test model went like the wind.'

'*Easy Lady* hasn't sailed yet?'

'Not yet, Guy. I'm planning a big ceremony next week – Saturday, I'm hoping. I've hired Mort Barker – you remember him? – to handle the publicity. He thinks he can get Newspocket coverage. It's going to be a big event for Riverside, Guy. If I get plenty of orders, I'm going to expand. I'll need to employ more men. This could grow into the biggest business in the sub-colony. It's the sort of thing we need, another industry besides farming and fishing – it makes for a balanced community. What do you say, Guy?'

He looked at the screen on his desk. It suddenly occurred to me that he was just a front man; that my spiel had been relayed to some central computer which had been evaluating feverishly while I spoke, noting every loophole with devilish mechanical thoroughness.

'I don't quite see where the Universal Bank fits into all this, Kev,' he said.

'I need a small loan to tide me over,' I mumbled.

He sighed, took his gaze from the screen and regarded me sadly and tiredly. All the bounce seemed to have gone out of him. He removed his glasses and rubbed knuckles into his eyes. 'What a pity it isn't last year,' he said. 'Or even last month. Yes – last month I could have accommodated you with no problem, Kev. But today ... With all this uncertainty ... Hell, Kev, look at it from the Bank's point of view. There's a referendum on Thursday. By Friday, Hetherington may have impounded your business, for all I know. See what I mean?'

'I don't need much, Guy.'

He stared at me closely, as though assessing my sincerity.

'Tell you what. I have an idea, Kev. I'll have to put it to the Directors – but I think I can get them to see it our way. Here's what I propose. You go ahead and have your launching and your publicity and so on – then come back next month and show me your order book. I think I may be able to persuade my Directors to advance a sum equal to twenty-five per cent of all firm orders received. That way, you'll have your finance for expansion.'

That way, the goddamned Bank wouldn't have to take a chance on the boat failing.

'I'm not sure I care for your methods of supporting local industry, Guy.'

'Hostility will get you nowhere, Kev.'

'The hell with you and your goddamned bank,' I snapped, and stormed out, mortified.

In point of fact my launching ceremony was badly timed because the attention of the entire colony was focused on the upcoming referendum. Maybe I should have paid more attention to the referendum myself, particularly since I'd been involved in the earlier negotiations – but the matter was out of my hands. Arcadia would go to the polls on Friday and nothing I could say, do or think would influence the result.

Mortimore Barker's large face was grave as he met me on the wharf the following afternoon. *Easy Lady* had been rolled out of the boathouse and stood at the top of the slipway.

'Newspocket won't give us coverage,' said Barker without preamble.

'What the hell do you mean? You told me it was all fixed up, Mort.'

'I thought it was.' He grunted with effort as he hauled his vast frame up the ladder to join me. He subsided into the cockpit, mopping his brow. 'They assured me everything was arranged – they said they were very interested in promoting local events. Now they say they need the cameras elsewhere. I tried to pin the guy down, but he wouldn't talk. He said he wasn't at liberty to divulge the destination of Newspocket teams.'

'Why the hell not?'

'Don't take it too badly. We'll shoot the whole thing with 3-V cameras and I'll sell it around.'

I said, 'I'm running short of cash. If I don't get a bookful of orders I'll be bankrupt by the end of the year. This launch has to be a success, Mort.'

'You can pay my fee out of your first sale.'

That's what I like about Mortimore Barker. He may be a big phoney, but he's a big-hearted phoney. 'Thanks,' I muttered. 'Uh ... What do you have planned for the ceremony? I liked that idea of yours – you know, to have a girl in a bikini sitting on the foredeck as the boat slides down the slipway ... I reckon Jane Swindon might do it for us.'

He stared at me. 'Are you crazy? She'd go over like a lead balloon.'

'I reckon she's ... kind of attractive, huh?'

'She's too tough, and she's too pure, and she's too married. Your boat is a *fun* boat, Kev. It's not practical. It's not a workboat. You must have a *fun* girl draped over it. She must look as though she's *offering* herself – and by implication, the boat. Jane Swindon would look as though she were offering a glass of iced tea. What sells is *sex*, Kev. Keep that in mind and you won't go wrong.'

'Look, if there were any fun girls around here offering themselves, I'd have found out about it. This is a small colony, Mort. We must make do with what we have.'

'That's my problem. As it happens, I've already found a girl. I've rented her from an agency I use sometimes.'

'One of those angels from the regatta?' I asked, interested.

'Hell, no. That's altogether the wrong type of girl for the job. No – the girl I have is a real *fun* girl – pretty as hell, too. Makes me wish I were younger. And slimmer.'

'How much does she cost?' I asked, suddenly alarmed.

'Forget it. I'll add it to your account. Just make sure this goddamned boat doesn't go straight to the bottom of the river, huh?' He heaved himself to his feet and scrambled down the ladder, eased himself into his ostentatious hovercar and purred away in the direction of Inchtown, a big fish in a little pool.

As I worked away at the boat, screwing the stainless fittings to the deck, adding a touch of varnish here and there, I was speculating about the girl. I had to confess to a certain pleasurable anticipation. It isn't often a man gets to rent a real fun girl.

The last couple of days before the referendum were eventful and feeling in the colony ran high as the various factions put their views at a succession of impromptu meetings. All pretence at colony solidarity had been dropped, of course; our interests were too diverse for any sort of unity on such a complex issue.

On Thursday, Newspocket carried a special item – the findings of the committee appointed by the sub-colony representatives. As expected, the committee found in favour of the deal. It began to look as though the referendum was a foregone conclusion – which was a good thing for the colony as a whole, although individuals would suffer.

More than anyone else, I felt sorry for Kli a' Po, our alien. He is a wealthy creature with a fine herd of dairy Arcows; his wealth has been earned through unremitting hard work. He'd raised the money to buy simple machinery and cleared the bush with the aid of his myriad children whom he begat by some mysterious method of asexual reproduction. I'd never asked him how this was achieved, and I sure as hell didn't relish being around when it happened.

Streng once said, 'Kli a' Po could get away with murder. He could eat one son and produce another to replace it, and nobody would be any the wiser. Makes you realize how meaningless our social code is, eh, Kevin?'

But now Kli was in a vulnerable position. In two years he'd built up the derelict Blackstone ranch into a viable proposition, ploughing all his profits back. He had nothing to show but his land and his herd.

Now, he stood to lose the lot to the Hetherington Organization. Kli himself had no false illusions about it – a successful ranch would be a prime target for appropriation.

The pity of it was, some people in the colony seemed to enjoy Kli's plight, gleefully telling him he would have to live in a unit like everyone else when the Organization took over. I met him in the bar of the Social Club on the morning of the referendum and asked him about it.

'Of course I'll vote in favour of the Hetherington deal,' he said in his slow voice, clutching a glass of iced water in his scaly paw. 'The only alternative is starvation.'

'But you wouldn't starve,' I pointed out. 'You're self-supporting.' As I said this, Streng's disgusting cannibal image flashed through my mind; I couldn't help myself.

Sharp little teeth showed within the leathery muzzle. I think he was smiling. 'It would be a strange colony if everyone were self-supporting,' he said. 'The very thing I like about you humans is that you are *not* self-supporting. Humans are dependent on one another – unlike my people. I like it here. I didn't always fit in with my own people: they called me gregarious. As time goes by, I hope I shall be able to mingle with people even to the extent that you do, Kev . . .'

More people were entering the club. Streng and Alicia Desjardins were discussing racing with Jane Swindon. Tom Minty entered with his cronies Bill Yong and Jim Spark; they ordered cola into which they tipped a measure of Immunol. I saw old Jed Spark looking on with stony-eyed disapproval, as ever. Will Jackson sat alone, stiffly upright in his chair as though his back was in a cast, hard eyes flickering around as he selected a girl to stare at. Mrs Earnshaw was moving briskly around in the background, setting up a display of hand-crafted junk among which I noticed a slim, privately printed volume: 'We, the Pioneers', by Vernon Thrale.

It was the usual noon-hour gathering, but the arguments were louder, the voices more strident. John Talbot was laughing nervously and continuously as he served drinks.

The polling booth – in fact a small converted helicopter – was opening for business in less than an hour. From time to time everyone's eyes went to the window which commands a view down the hillside, over the tops of the dwelling domes to the wharf. The helicopter sat there like a scarlet beetle, flanked by two uniformed guards with laser pistols. The authorities intended that democracy should prevail in Riverside.

Streng strolled towards us, smiled briefly at Kli and sat down. Alicia Desjardins followed him – a common occurrence, these days. We talked boats for a while, superstitiously avoiding reference to the polling, when there was a sudden commotion at the door.

Streng's wife came in fast, knocking over a chair as she hurried across the room. She stood over us, face working, eyes bright. There was going to be a scene. I cannot take scenes. I half stood in order to get the hell away, but found myself hemmed in by the tightly packed chairs around our table.

'I expected you home an hour ago!' Hazel Streng informed her husband with controlled violence.

All eyes were on us now; I cringed back in my chair and met

Jane Swindon's gaze from the far side of the room. She made a face at me.

Streng said, 'As you can see, I'm drinking with friends, my dear. Would you care to join us?'

'No, I certainly wouldn't. Who the hell do you think you are? Sitting here drinking with ... this ...' She nodded towards Alicia Desjardins, lips trembling.

'Sit down, my dear. Alicia, would you like to make room for my wife?'

Alicia jumped up and ran for the ladies' room. Tears were in Hazel Streng's eyes as she watched her go. 'I said no,' she muttered.

'And I said sit down,' said Streng.

He took hold of her wrist, slowly, almost absently – and I saw flesh whiten as he applied pressure. His wife's face was tense with pain as she was gradually forced into the seat beside him.

'It's a normal instinct on the part of the female to protect the home,' Streng told us in conversational tones. 'My wife thinks our home is threatened by Alicia – so her outburst is quite natural. I hope you'll excuse her. Now, Kevin – you were telling us about your launching ... ?'

A strained discussion lasted until the polling booth opened.

They announced the results on the Saturday afternoon. At noon the Social Club was packed again, Newspocket subscribers surrounded by freeloaders as they scanned their tiny screens. There were shots of a huge room in which dozens of clerks were sitting at desks feeding the magnetized voting slips into counting machines. Overlooking all this, stood representatives of the Hetherington Organization and the Arcadian Council. The proceedings must have looked primitive to the former, who were probably used to the more refined electoral procedures, the inserting of cards and pressing of buttons by the voters which accumulates a simultaneous total in the central computer. On Arcadia we are not so advanced.

The authenticity of the counting having been established, the clerks locked their machines against the possibility of a recount. Sheets of print-outs were passed to an adjudicator on the platform. I caught sight of the redoubtable Althea Gant, craning over the adjudicator's shoulder to get a preview of the results.

She smiled.

Then a slip was passed to the Premier, who took the microphone. He looked old – pale and old and ineffectual.

He said, 'People of Arcadia, we have accepted the proposals of the Hetherington Organization. The votes cast in favour were—' And the rest was lost in the cheering.

There wasn't much cheering in the Social Club. People watched for a few minutes more, then began to drift away. Soon I, too, slid the slim portovee into my pocket and walked out into the afternoon sunshine.

By that time the election coverage was over, anyhow. The scene had changed.

On the screen were shots of giant agricultural machines being driven out of freight shuttles at the spaceport – as though they had only been waiting for the results before starting up.

They roared towards the cameras like stampeding elephants. There must have been hundreds of them.

# six

The week following the takeover of the planet Arcadia by the Hetherington Organization was something of an anti-climax. For two or three days nothing happened at all, apart from the belated arrival of the fish truck. As I worked on *Easy Lady*, ironing out the last-minute snags, I could see men further down the wharf, loading the cases of frozen fish under the supervision of Vernon Thrale. I sensed an almost visible lifting of tension. Later that morning the fishing boats set off down the estuary, back to business.

On the Tuesday a stranger arrived unannounced. I met him in the Social Club, talking to Chill Kaa.

'Sinclair Singleton,' he introduced himself. I'd already noticed that Kaa – normally suspicious of strangers – had bought the guy a drink, and soon found out why.

Singleton was one of the pleasantest men I've ever met. We seemed to hit it off instantly, despite that awkward moment when he told us that he was the local agent for the Organization. Anyone less like an Organization man was difficult to imagine. As the lounge began to fill with people he was busy answering even the most stupid questions politely and with good humour.

His worst moment came when he handed out the Organization identity cards – and even this perilous duty he handled well.

'Just what the hell is this?' asked Will Jackson, staring with deep suspicion at the small plastic card bearing his name and a number.

Singleton smiled, continuing to pass the cards around. He'd already memorized our names. 'The cards are to make things easier for all of us,' he said. 'I suppose their closest relative in non-Organization life is the credit card. We'll all be using them instead of cash. It's much simpler this way. All the stores in Arcadia will have an accounting machine. When you buy something, you just insert the card in the machine, the storekeeper taps out the details of your purchase on the keyboard, and away you go with your card. Your account is kept at the Central branch of the Universal Bank. Hell, you'll find it a lot easier than carrying cash around – and you'll get a permanent record of your purchases each month.'

'So will the Organization,' said Ralph Streng ...

But in the main Singleton went over very well, and the colony was relieved. We assumed he was now technically the colony boss – although he never made that fact obvious.

It seemed that our pay, too, would be dealt with by the Universal Bank, as a direct credit. We'd never get to hold the actual bills in our hand. In fact we'd never get to hold *any* bills in our hand, since all currency had been called in by the Bank who made it clear that it was no longer legal tender.

On that same day, Singleton received work assignments for us all. He called a meeting and read them out in his pleasant, informal style, answering questions and giving explanations as he went along.

'Kevin Moncrieff,' he said at one point. 'I see you're assigned to boatbuilding, Kev. This means you carry on as usual, like most of the colony. I told the Organization you had a big launching coming up at the weekend, and they've agreed to allow you to keep your profits – and bear your own losses, of course – for another month, before going on to the standard pay scale. Pretty good, huh?'

It was much better than I'd expected. It meant that if the

launch was successful and orders came in, I might be able to get some money salted away before the Organization closed in on me. And in any event they were not taking over my business: that much was clear. I was free to build it up out of surplus profits and, in five years' time, reap the benefits.

I'd come off better than some. About twenty colonists were conscripted to clear a large tract of land to the east of Kli a' Po's ranch. Our alien's eyelids flickered as he heard that the Organization would be farming right on his doorstep, although at least they hadn't appropriated his own land – not yet...

I was broiling Arcow steaks with mushrooms and french fries – I'm still very much an Earth man, and in any case I didn't want to risk the failure of a more exotic dish. I heard the hovercar arrive; heard the expensive clunk of a solid door closing which told me it was Barker. I put the steaks into a holding pattern and went to the window, taking a quick gulp of scotch. Below me, walking around to the steps, I saw the tops of two heads. One was Mortimore Barker, fat neck imprisoned within his collar.

The other was the fun girl, blonde.

I glanced at myself in the mirror, wondered why I always looked as though I needed a shave and a drink, and opened the door.

The most incredibly beautiful girl entered my humble home, followed by the gross figure of Barker.

'Susanna Lincoln – Kevin Moncrieff,' said Barker briefly. 'Is that steak I smell, Kev? Good. Hell, you seem to be the only guy drinking around here. What about the rest of us?'

'Hello, Susanna,' I said, trying to recover from cardiac arrest, which I usually find fatal.

'Kevin ... I like your place. Nice and boaty.'

I glanced around frantically, seeing things I hadn't noticed before, items from the yard which I'd forgotten to take downstairs – an oily sack of shackles in the corner, a piston on the mantelshelf, an anchor under the table. 'Oh God,' I muttered. I shrugged and looked back at her.

... her eyes were quite unbelievable, deep blue pools into which I looked and looked, forgetting the shitty mess the place was in, forgetting everything, wanting nothing except to look into those eyes for ever...

'Love at first sight is all very well for some,' said Barker loudly. 'But I need a drink. Hell, I've just driven from Inchtown.'

She was wearing a light blue dress with some sort of filmy white thing at the neck. Her hair was golden and shoulder-length. It was not easy to describe her accurately because she was surrounded by this emotional haze which was clouding my visual senses. There was a tiny smile at the corners of her mouth as she looked back at me steadily.

'Fuck you, then,' Barker said. 'I'll get it myself.' Somewhere there was a tinkle of glass on glass.

Susanna said, 'I'd better have one too, Mortimore.'

The spell was broken and we drank and talked and I tried to pretend that nothing had happened – that we were three ordinary people discussing a business deal. I told Susanna about the boatyard and the colony and the history of Riverside as far as I knew it, and some degree of normalcy began to prevail. Mortimore Barker occasionally looked as though he was enjoying some private joke, however, and Susanna didn't meet my eyes very often.

After we'd eaten, Barker said, 'Susanna can get changed in your bedroom, OK?'

I looked at her and my eyes were caught again. At last I said, 'I saw you before. The other day, on the railcar to Inchtown. I was on my way to the conference.'

'Yes. That must have been me. I didn't see you, though.'

'I was sitting behind you.' It was an idiot conversation.

'For Christ's sake!' Barker was pacing about impatiently. 'We have a ceremony in an hour's time. We have to get ready. Susanna has to get changed.' He strode to the window, stared down at the wharf. 'People are there already.' He flung open my bedroom door; fortunately the bed was made up. 'Miss Lincoln – get in there and get your things on, huh?'

Susanna picked up a small bag and disappeared.

Barker poured himself another drink and said, 'What do you say, Kev?' He eyed me piercingly, an irritating half-smile on his heavy lips.

'I'm not sure she's quite right for the job,' I found myself saying.

He stared at me incredulously. 'Are you crazy, man? Hell, every man will be panting for her! And by association, for your goddamned boat!'

I tried to put my misgivings into words. 'You said we'd sell the boat with sex. I'm not sure sex is what I think of first, when I look at her. There's something sort of . . . sweet about her, you know what I mean, Mort? I think maybe nobody will notice the boat, with her there.'

Barker was looking relieved. 'Hell, that's fine. You had me worried there for a moment. You haven't seen enough women lately, Kev, that's your problem. You think you're falling in love with the girl. Forget it. Trust me. Everyone will notice your boat, man.'

But when Susanna emerged from my bedroom a few minutes later clad in a skimpy bikini which barely controlled her full breasts, I had my doubts. The sight of a girl dressed in sunbathing attire indoors always has a powerful effect on me; it may be to do with the exotic alfresco look of the girl which contrasts so vividly with the everyday surroundings, or it may be some nasty lurking little fetishism in me which only a shrink could explain – whatever the reason, it's nice. I goggled at Susanna as she stood in the bedroom doorway for several seconds, realizing at last – with quick embarrassment – that she was standing there because she hadn't room to get past me . . .

Later on the slipway the cameras whirred, Mortimore Barker directing. I stood beside the boat for a few shots while Susanna explored on board. Jane Swindon arrived, holding the ceremonial bottle of champagne which she would shortly be pounding ineffectually against the bows.

'I haven't had a chance to tell you before, Kev,' she said. 'I really appreciate the honour.'

I grinned at her, feeling good. 'It was you or Mrs Earnshaw,' I said. 'But I had the feeling she'd insist on using dandelion wine, so you got the job. Where's Mark, by the way?'

Her smile faded. 'He's away trying to persuade the Organization not to harvest the plankton. He's really worried about it, Kev.'

'Let's forget all that for this afternoon, huh? We'll have a drink on board, after the maiden voyage. I've stocked *Easy Lady* with scotch for the occasion.'

She smiled again. 'I don't think you'll be needing me.' She indicated the deck above us, where Susanna sat between takes. 'Who is she? She's the most attractive thing I've ever seen. I'm glad Mark's not here, to tell the truth.'

'I'll never understand how one woman can ever find another

woman attractive. What exactly attracts you, Jane? I can't imagine the sight of all that sex sitting up there fills you with lust, like it does me.' I chuckled.

'Just who the hell do you think you're kidding, Kevin Moncrieff?' she asked quietly. 'Don't devalue your emotions like that – and don't devalue that lovely girl up there. She's no mindless sexpot, and you know it. I've seen the way you look at her – and I've seen her look at you, too. Stop making like a rutting Arbull and get to know her properly, huh? I have a feeling it might be worthwhile.'

I've found on previous occasions that Jane has a low flash-point, and there was a hint of fury in her pretty eyes now. 'Sorry,' I said. Then I made the ultimate confession. I said: 'Jane, I've only known her a couple of hours. I sort of can't believe how I feel. I'm scared sick I might blow it.'

She said, 'You'll be alone on that boat with her for most of the afternoon. The camera crew will be following – but they won't be picking up any conversation. Just try to act naturally with her, for God's sake. No leering and stupid empty remarks. Talk to her the way you do to me.'

There was a burst of ironic cheering from the somewhat sceptical crowd as Barker stepped forward and boomed a few platitudes. Then he handed the mike to Jane and the onlookers became comparatively silent. She is enormously popular in the colony; I couldn't have picked a better person for the job.

She spoke very well, boosting my image as a good guy and an asset to the community without laying it on so thick that the jeering started again. She touched briefly on the present situation in the colony, she told a couple of jokes which actually had people laughing, then she came to the point.

'I name this yacht *Easy Lady*, and good luck to all who sail in her.'

So saying she swung the bottle and – being Jane Swindon – smashed it first time on the prow without putting us through the embarrassing suspense of a second swing, and a third ... I kissed her carefully on the cheek and climbed to the deck as *Easy Lady* began to move. The crowd uttered a ragged cheer. The fishing boats blew their hooters.

Susanna was already coiling down the ropes as we slid gently down the slipway and out into the middle of the estuary.

*

The high forested banks glided past us as we headed seawards in the afternoon sunshine. I saw worrals among the trees, dozing in the mild weather as they clung to the branches. We passed Anchor Pool, that deep indentation in the hillside where the current forms swirling eddies and where the entire colony was once held in thrall by a Mind, during the Relay Effect. The estuary widened out just past this point and I began to think of hoisting the sails: at present we were puttering along on the tiny auxiliary engine which also powered the pump for the pressurized hull.

Even at this slow speed, the effect of the lubricating film of air coating the hull was noticeable. The boat rode very easily with a smooth unbroken wake.

I wondered what Susanna's boat experience had been; whether I could trust her with the tiller while I got the sails up. We hadn't spoken much since leaving Riverside, neither had we looked at each other. Right now she was sitting on the cabin roof, watching the trees.

The wind was blowing from behind. 'Come and take the tiller, huh?' I said in the most normal tones I could achieve. 'It's time we did some sailing.'

She stood carefully and began to move back towards me, stooping and holding the handrail as she came, so that I had a clear view of her breasts to the nipples and beyond. I extended a hand and helped her down into the cockpit.

The camera boat ploughed in our wake, aglint with lenses, the huge form of Mortimore Barker standing on the prow like a figurehead. I looked back at Susanna. 'Do they have directional mikes?' I asked.

'I don't think so. Were you going to proposition me?'

'I ... uh ... I wasn't thinking of that.' I swallowed and looked away, anywhere, away from those blue, blue eyes. A sticker plant was thrashing on the bank, drawing some small animal into its anemone-like stomach. My hands were shaking as I busied myself with the ropes. Eventually I got the mainsail and jib up and Susanna, proving super-competent, had them drawing perfectly. With the following wind we began to move fast; anticipating me, Susanna disengaged the propeller.

'You've done this sort of thing before,' I said, climbing down into the cockpit as she adjusted the mainsheet skilfully, taking full advantage of the wind.

Suddenly she wasn't smiling. 'It wasn't quite the same,' she said quietly, and I knew she wasn't talking about the unusual boat. 'Did you say something about liquor down in the cabin?'

I took the tiller from her. 'The cupboard on the starboard side. Make mine scotch and ginger, a big one.'

She went into the cabin, turning towards me to descend the short ladder and favouring me with a huge and unexpected wink.

*Easy Lady* ran on down the estuary, the pump maintaining hull pressure with a quiet murmur. We were moving fast – very fast – but still not as well as I'd hoped. I trimmed the sails, wondered about breaking out the spinnaker then decided it was too risky on a maiden voyage.

I decided the problem must lie in the limiting factor of the hull shape. No matter how smoothly the boat went through the water, it still had to shove aside the same volume of liquid as it went. With a displacement hull such as *Easy Lady*'s, there is a maximum speed which can be attained: I'd known that – but the maximum was a little less than I'd hoped. Absorbed in the problem, my mind began to move into the future.

The next boat must be a catamaran.

The twin hulls of the catamaran can be built long and narrow, avoiding the displacement problem while still maintaining stability. The pump would be situated in a central cabin with flexible hoses to the two sponsons. There would be no need for the double-skinned hull – thus effecting a saving in weight. The sponsons could simply be made airtight – except for those thousands of tiny holes below the waterline.

Hell, it would be simple. The thing could be built in a matter of weeks.

Susanna reappeared with drinks.

I glanced behind. We were outpacing the camera boat; as I watched, Barker waved a hamlike hand then gestured to his helmsman. His boat swung in a wide arc and puttered off back up the estuary, filming complete for the time being. They would be waiting to get shots of our return, but meanwhile we could set about the more serious business of seeing how the boat handled.

We were passing between the twin headlands which denote the beginning of the ocean; they rose high on either side of us, jagged and black. We met a slow swell but *Easy Lady* rode it well, heading out to sea. Away to our left were the buoys marking the limits of Mark Swindon's fish pens. A few blackfish fins cut the water nearby; the brutes were feeding on the falling tide.

I had to get on terms with Susanna. If I didn't, then she would go back to Premier City and never give me another thought. It would have been just one more modelling job for her. She was sitting quietly on the opposite side of the cockpit, watching the shoreline behind me. Our eyes met and she smiled very quickly, then looked away again.

'You work in Premier City?' I asked.

'Mostly. I haven't been in Arcadia long; just a few weeks.'

'How do you like it?' I asked lamely, wondering why convention forbade us to discuss sexual attraction.

She hesitated. 'I seem to have come in the middle of things. Honestly, Kevin, I haven't made up my mind yet. Ask me in a month's time.'

I said, looking out to sea, 'You won't be around in a month's time. And I hardly ever get the chance to go to Premier City.'

She grinned at me suddenly and moved her position, leaning back against the cabin top. I watched her breasts all the way, helpless and hypnotized as they shifted beneath the almost non-existent bikini top. Then I looked at her face and again my vision blurred as emotion took its place. Susanna was sitting in a lake of radiance, the sun sparking her alight like a lamp. 'Maybe you won't need to,' she said.

'Huh?'

'The agency told me they might have another job for me in Riverside...' She hesitated. 'For the Organization. They said I might be here for several months – if everything works out.'

'What sort of a job?'

'I don't know. It's still only a possibility. It depends on a lot of things, they say.'

'You'd like the job?'

'Yes,' she said simply.

I watched a giant scoopbill winging its way south with lazy beats, its head hung low, broad beak skimming plankton from the surface as it flew. I'd been scared of Susanna, scared of the outrageous sexuality of her appearance, scared of the effect she had on me. The whole thing was too violent, too sudden, too good to last.

But now she was saying it might last, after all. Now I had the feeling that we might settle down to some kind of understanding within the norm of accepted human behaviour. I was not expected to prove myself by raping her on the cockpit floor. Perhaps I was expected to love her.

I said, 'I'd like you to stay in Riverside for a while.'

Her eyebrows went up. 'Come, Moncrieff, you can do better than that. This isn't the Moncrieff that Mort Barker led me to expect.'

So that bastard Barker had told her I was some kind of sexual libertine ... The fish pens were quite close to our port side now; a few fins cut the water nearby as blackfish prowled, attracted by the scent and sight of so many imprisoned fatties, but unable to penetrate the nets. 'Look, what can I say?' I muttered helplessly. 'Oh, hell. Susanna, I think you're the most—'

The goddamned motor faltered and cut out.

I grunted in frustration and lifted the inspection hatch. While Susanna steered and chuckled I checked the plugs and the points and eventually checked the gas, and found there wasn't any.

'The old story, Moncrieff. I'd expected something more original. Why didn't you install one of your minipiles? I understand they run for months without refuelling.'

'Too big. Too expensive,' I said absently, trying to work it out. I'd filled up a couple of days ago and only used the engine for a short test run since. The tank must be punctured. 'This is a sailing boat, you know.'

'It's not sailing too well now.'

She was right. Without the lubricating film of air, *Easy Lady* was wallowing unhappily in the swell. The motion was even worse than I'd expected. 'We'd better go about,' I said. 'It's a long way home.'

Susanna descended to the cabin with the scotch glasses, then her face appeared suddenly at the top of the steps. 'Hey, Kev, you remember telling me about all those little holes in the hull? Well, did it ever occur to you that if the air isn't going out, then the water comes in?'

The wind was getting up, suddenly chill as a cloud obscured the sun. The boat lurched as I stood. 'There's still enough pressure in the hull cavity to keep the water out.'

'Then will you explain all this wet stuff in the cabin? It's up to my knees, Kev.' She came scrambling out.

I stared down into the small area. The water was already covering the berths, rising as I watched.

The *Easy Lady* was sinking.

'Where's the dinghy, Kev?' asked Susanna quietly.

'Uh ... We don't have one. I ... sort of cut a few corners. I ran out of money. We have lifejackets.' I leaned over the side, staring down into the water. A blackfish was passing; he regarded me with cold interest, jaws agape. I felt the beginnings of a shudder and straightened up quickly.

'Look out, Kev!'

Something hit me a smashing blow to the side of the head. A flash of brilliance exploded within my brain and I saw the cockpit floor coming up towards me.

That was all I saw.

Later there was something hard under me. I lay on my stomach and the coughing was painful, racking my chest, burning in my lungs and throat. Hands were pulling at me more roughly, rolling me about, rolling me on to my back. I was lying on the beach, looking at the dull sky. My head ached with returning consciousness, ached in intensifying waves until it seemed to be coming apart. A shape intruded itself between me and the sky; wet hair streaked across my face.

'You look like you're feeling better, Moncrieff.' The words held the familiar banter but there was an unaccustomed tremulousness in the tone.

I sat up carefully. Heroes and heavyweight champs come round instantly following a blow to the head, but not K. Moncrieff. I clutched my scalp and began to scream, but the effort hurt too much and I quickly became silent. I looked around. We were sitting on the small strip of beach at the base of the cliffs: before me the sea was criss-crossed with the fish pens, but there was no sign of *Easy Lady*.

'She sank, Kev. I'm terribly sorry.'

'How the hell did we get ashore?'

'I sort of lifesaved you.'

'Christ.' I regarded her. She was kneeling beside me, looking wet and lovely, but my head hurt too much to think about what I wanted to think about. 'What about the blackfish?' I asked. 'They were all around us.'

'I steered for the fish pens. *Easy Lady* stayed afloat just long enough for me to get you into the nearest one. Then I swam you from one to the next, and so on. The hardest part was pulling you over the nets.'

'Susanna, I love you.'

She looked taken aback, then said, 'Men always fall in love with their nurses. You'll feel better, soon. Let's think about getting off this beach, shall we?'

At least we would have no problem with the rising tide. The opposing gravitational pulls of Arcadia's six moons balance out most of the time – except during the period of the Relay Effect. I looked around. To the south, the beach disintegrated into rocks and foaming spray at the base of the headland. North, the sand continued unbroken for as far as I could see, but there was no visible way up the face of the cliff. As a last resort we could start walking, although by evening the colony would have become alarmed at our non-return and would be sending out trawlers to search for us. We were in no immediate danger.

'Look,' said Susanna.

Ropes trailed down the cliff nearby. There was a small shed among a heap of dislodged boulders. Against the skyline I could see the slender arm of a gantry. I stood, walked painfully to the nearest rope and pulled it. A rough platform began to rise from amid the rocks.

It was Mark Swindon's makeshift elevator for dropping equipment to the beach.

'It's several kilometres back to the colony along the ridge trail,' I told Susanna. 'We can walk, if you like – it'll be easy enough to get to the clifftop on this elevator. Or we can wait for rescue, which might be a goddamned cold thing to do.'

'One of the things you don't know about me yet, Kev, is that I hate waiting. Let's start right away.'

We were both exhausted by the time we reached the colony. I couldn't face walking up the main street in full view of everyone, wet and bruised and defeated, my boat at the bottom of the ocean; so I took Susanna into the Swindons' place near the bridge. Mark was still away, but Jane was there. I explained what had happened.

'Kev, I'm terribly sorry.'

'I'm only just beginning to be sorry myself,' I confessed. 'I was feeling goddamned glad to be alive, a while back. But things sort of hit me when I saw the colony and the boatyard. *Easy Lady* wasn't insured, you know. I was short of cash, so I thought I'd take a chance.'

I was wearing Mark's clothes by now, and Jane had lent Susanna a skirt and sweater. Jane is much smaller than Susanna, but even the sight of the amazing fun girl bursting out of her inadequate clothing couldn't help my gloom – neither could the scotch which Jane had thoughtfully provided.

Susanna said quietly, 'How bad is it, Kev?'

'I guess you could say I'm bankrupt.'

At this dismal confession the door opened and Mark entered, gave us a look of mild curiosity and said, 'Fix me a drink, darling, huh? I've had a lousy day. They're going ahead with the mechanical whales. I couldn't talk them out of it.'

Jane said, 'Christ, is there anything else that can go wrong?'

'Yes. There's trouble in the colony – I'm surprised you haven't heard. Did you see Newspocket this afternoon? They showed shots of hundreds of Hetherington's workers arriving. The rumour's going around that they're going to get all the top jobs. And it seems there won't be very many jobs in any case. Most of the agricultural machinery is automatic.'

'They knew that already,' said Jane. 'So what's bugging the colony?'

'Employment conditions, I reckon. They say the Organization will have to offer top pay to attract people here. The newcomers will be working side by side with our people, but they'll be earning much more – so the theory is. Personally I don't believe it. But try reasoning with the colony.'

'How serious are they?' asked Jane.

Mark said, 'The goddamned fools have gone on strike.'

# seven

The first strike meeting was generally acknowledged to be something of a triumph for Riverside. Although no clear leader emerged from among the colony's ranks – the natural leaders were sitting on the fence – the strikers were well represented by Chill Kaa of the lunar features and Ezra Blake of the vested interest. The Organization was represented in the early stages by Sinclair Singleton.

'I'm quite sure we can rectify this misunderstanding with a

minimum of delay,' he said gently, smiling at the small group of negotiators.

'All right,' said Kaa. 'Just tell me this, for a start. What am I going to do with my trawler when the seavesters arrive?'

Singleton's smile intensified. 'I'm not sure that fishing is an issue before this meeting. I understood we were to discuss the immigration question.'

'What we want to know, right now, are the details of the lands the Organization intends to seize!' snarled Blake.

'But I didn't think ...' Singleton's hands fluttered helplessly; he made a couple of quick notes on the pad before him, more to occupy his fingers than for any gainful reason.

'There must be guarantees of a minimum wage now that the planet is knee-deep in newcomers,' spat Kaa. 'The long-time residents must be taken care of first. We must have jobs!'

'You had jobs until yesterday,' observed Singleton mildly. 'But now you've stopped working. Really, Mr Kaa, you can't expect pay if you don't want to work.'

'Don't want to work?' Kaa was losing control. 'Of course we want to work. That's what we're striking for!'

'Striking?'

'For Chrissake, you know what I'm talking about!'

Singleton watched him thoughtfully; he seemed slightly puzzled. 'I'm sorry, Chill,' he said. 'I'm new here. I'm just an Organization agent from a planet called Marilyn. This word strike seems to have some significance I've missed. Maybe you'll explain and I'll see what we can do for you.'

He was serious. I tried not to laugh; I dragged out my handkerchief and coughed violently into it while Kaa stared at him dumbfounded and Blake uttered a snort of incredulity.

Enrico Batelli said quickly, 'To strike means to withhold labour until demands are met. It is a method commonly used by workers to stop production – so forcing management to make concessions.'

'But I don't see how it applies in Riverside,' said Singleton. 'Surely, if you refuse to work, the Organization will simply send in people who *will* work. That seems to me the logical step. I can't honestly see how this will help your demands.'

'You can't, huh, wise guy?' Kaa's face was blotched with rage. 'I'll tell you why the Organization can't send in men, for a start. Because they won't cross our lines, that's why. By Christ, we'll picket the entire region!'

Singleton sighed. 'Then maybe the Organization will find another region. It's a big planet. Anyway, I thank you for giving your views, and I'll make sure they're transmitted straight to Premier City. I hope everything goes well for you people – or should I say we people? I've only been here a few days, but... I like Riverside. I want to see the place grow.'

He was a disarming character, was Sinclair Singleton. He remained calm while all the old grievances were aired again: the rate of pay, the lack of sickness or old age provisions, the automation, the land appropriation...

At one point Mrs Earnshaw stood and said, 'We must seriously consider seceding from the Organization. We of Riverside can go it alone!'

People glanced at each other and somehow the feeling grew that the elderly woman's words had merit. There was a murmur of assent.

Singleton looked bewildered. 'But the Organization has bought this planet. How can you secede?'

'The Organization sure as hell hasn't bought the people!' came the predictable shout. I don't know who it was, but it doesn't matter. There is always some fool who prefers rhetoric to reason.

There was a roar of agreement, also predictable...

Afterwards, in the more relaxed atmosphere of the Social Club, Ralph Streng said, 'But the Organization *has* bought the people. Why should anyone trouble to deny it? They've bought us cheap, too – but there's nothing we can do about it.'

'I heard that!' The redoubtable figure of Mrs Earnshaw loomed over us. 'Now just let me tell you this, Dr Streng. Nobody buys me, and that goes for every man and woman of the Kindred of the Pioneers. We've talked the matter over, and we intend to draw up a petition for the independence of our colony. Not that I expect you and your weak-kneed friend Moncrieff to sign, but there are plenty who will. There are quite a number of good stout-hearted citizens about, I can assure you!'

Streng looked at her in mock bewilderment. 'I thought the Kindred were folk-dancers.'

Mrs Earnshaw's countenance took on a darker hue. 'That's the sort of stupid remark I'd have expected from Mr Moncrieff, not from an educated man like yourself.' She stared at me suddenly. 'And you needn't grin in that doltish manner!

Don't think I haven't heard what you've called the Kindred behind our backs, Moncrieff! The sarcastic remarks, the oafish guffaws at our displays. I tell you – it's a good thing some of us know where the true values lie. The Kindred are dedicated to preserving what is best in our lives – and that includes the freedom of the individual!'

People were watching, grinning. The old woman was making a spectacle of us.

Ralph Streng stood, slowly and deliberately, placing his glass on the table. The sniggers ceased. He said, 'Mrs Earnshaw. Neither Mr Moncrieff nor I have ever questioned the right of the Kindred of the Pioneers to prance about the streets in drag – distasteful though we may find it. So grant us the freedom to consider you a bunch of goddamned fairies, if you will!'

This was greeted with a murmur of agreement so general as to cause Mrs Earnshaw to flush and move on. She caught sight of Vernon Thrale, held a muttered discussion and left. Thrale gulped down his grape juice, adam's apple bobbing, and hurried after her.

Streng said, 'Don't let's kid ourselves. The Organization's only just taken over – but there's already a lot of support for Mrs Earnshaw's views. If she expressed those views in a more persuasive manner she'd have the whole colony behind her.'

I was about to tell him that wild Arcattle wouldn't drag me to Mrs Earnshaw's side, when the door opened and Susanna came in, wearing a white trouser suit trimmed in blue. My heart lurched as she saw me, smiled and sat down. I devoured her with my eyes as I asked where she'd been all day, if she'd had a good night, whether the stiffness from her swim had subsided...

She watched me with blue eyes wide and assured me that everything was fine, except – 'Just one thing you've forgotten to ask,' she said.

'What's that?'

'You haven't asked what I'd like to drink, Moncrieff you cheap bum,' she said, her eyes mocking me again.

By the noon of Wednesday I realized the full extent of my financial difficulties. Mark Swindon climbed to the deck of Perce Walters' trawler and peeled off his rubber face-mask. 'She's down there, Kev,' he said. 'I didn't have time to see too much. There were blackfish around. But she's damaged.'

The trawler rocked on the ebb tide; the anchor chain grumbled in the fairlead.

'Is it bad?' I asked.

'There's a hole in the hull, about four feet across. She's lying against a rock shelf; there's quite a swell down there . . .'

I could imagine *Easy Lady* slowly being pounded to pieces; I felt sick. Susanna was watching me in mute sympathy. 'I'm so very sorry, Kev,' she said.

'You reckon nothing can be done, huh?' I asked Mark.

'She could be raised,' he said slowly. 'But the cost would be out of all proportion.'

I looked at them: Mark Swindon and Jane, Susanna, Perce. 'I bankrupted myself to build that boat,' I muttered. 'I could have stuck to building skitterbugs but I thought I ought to diversify. And the idea was good – I know it was. It worked. *Easy Lady* was the fastest single-hull sailing boat ever built. I've taken out patents, I've borrowed from the bank right up to my neck.' I looked at the Arcadian sea, the slow swell rolling in from the east, pounding lazily against the foot of the headland, rising in plumes of spray. Mewlers danced among the ripples, picking the tiny shrimplike plankton in their pointed beaks, their wings a pale blur. 'I don't know what the hell to do,' I said.

Susanna took my hand, Perce started the engine and winched in the anchor. The trawler *Arcturus* shuddered as she began to head back up the estuary. I said, 'If I'd gone on to the Organization payroll when everyone else did, none of this would have mattered. The Organization would have taken the loss. But I thought I was on to a good thing.'

'Stop blaming yourself, Moncrieff,' said Susanna, and I looked at her in surprise. Her eyes were unnaturally bright. I squeezed her hand; she bit her lip and watched the banks slide by with determined interest.

Later Perce tied up at the wharf and we went ashore. The colony streets were quiet, ribbons of emptiness drawn on the steep hillside. I noticed Jane hesitate. 'The place looks deserted,' she said uneasily.

It occurred to me that this is what Riverside must have looked like at the time of the Relay Effect, after the Mind had lured the inhabitants to Anchor Pool . . . Then I heard footsteps and turned quickly.

Vernon Thrale stood there. He said, 'Everyone's gone up

over the ridge. We had word that the brontomeks were coming. There's going to be awful trouble.'

'Let's take my car,' said Mark briefly. Perce elected to stay with Thrale and the rest of us climbed in. As the hovercar rose over the brow and the trees gave way to the broad valley beyond, he slowed.

Giant machines were lined up on the Inchtown road, glittering in the noon sun. There were around twenty of them, each one at least ten times the size of the average truck. They occupied the entire width of the road and were halted at the point where the track to Kli a' Po's place starts. Here a crowd of people were gathered. As we coasted down the hill the leading brontomek began to manoeuvre to and fro, making space in which to turn off the road. The crowd surged towards it.

Mark parked nearby and we climbed out. About two hundred colonists were milling around the intersection; as many more sat on the grassy slopes of the hillside, watching. Kids ran about noisily, almost lending a carnival atmosphere – but not quite. Chill Kaa and Mrs Earnshaw harangued the Organization men, whose spokesman appeared to be Singleton, the broken reed.

'And you can tell your men to get right back to Premier City!' Kaa was shouting. 'You'll not cross our lines!'

The lead brontomek managed to jack-knife its articulated length and lumbered off, obviously intending to cross the ditch and cut across open country. A number of colonists rushed in front of it and the giant machine halted with a hiss of air brakes, rocking on its voluminous tyres.

Ralph Streng appeared with a group of people who seemed to be looking to him for a lead. 'It's dangerous,' he told us. 'If I were Singleton, I'd put those machines on automatic drive and set them loose. Nobody's going to block the path of a machine on automatic.'

'Listen – whose side are you on?' Will Jackson asked.

Streng regarded the elderly man coldly. 'I'm pointing out the possibilities. I leave taking sides to people like you. I'm a doctor, and I'd rather not see a bloodbath.'

'We'll die rather than see our land ploughed under by the Organization!' shouted Jackson.

'Then you're even more of a fool than you look,' snapped Streng, turning his back on the man who continued to rave impotently.

I moved towards the main body of the dispute. About sixty Organization men confronted the colonists. They were dressed alike in grey coveralls, and to my eye looked alike too. They watched us warily but without visible signs of alarm, while Singleton and Kaa argued.

Singleton said reasonably, 'We intend to start ploughing Government land, Mr Kaa. We're not touching Kli a' Po's ranch. We plough to the north.'

'That's not the goddamned point and you know it. We refused to work that land. You're bringing in outside workers to do the job. That's against all ethics of labour relations. You men!' shouted Kaa to the silent Organization force. 'Don't you have any regard for your brothers? What the hell are you thinking of?'

A bottle spun through the air and exploded against the nearest brontomek in a shower of foam and tinkling fragments. The driver climbed from his cab and stood quietly with his workmates.

Beside me a voice said, 'Hell.' An arm slipped through mine; Susanna was there.

Singleton was talking in his persuasive tones, '... so we have set the machines to proceed automatically to the point where we intend to start work. I told my men to do this because I'm confident the colonists will not commit suicide. I know it's in your mind to call me a murderer, Chill – but I'm not. I have a duty to the Organization and to Arcadia, and it's essential that the land produces. In around thirty seconds this brontomek will move away, followed by the others, and there's nothing I can do about it without climbing into the cab and resetting the controls. So I'll be glad if you'll advise the people not to lie down in front of the vehicle.'

In fact the small group of colonists were already scrambling to their feet and scurrying from under the wheels of the giant machine.

There was an immense grumbling roar from the geartrain of the brontomek as it lurched forward, wheels spanning the ditch as though it were a puddle, and thundered eastwards across the valley floor.

Kaa, white with rage, swung a punch at Singleton.

'Time we were moving out,' I said to Susanna, drawing her away as isolated scuffles broke out and the colonists moved forwards.

'Beat the shit out of the bastards!' Kaa was yelling. He had Singleton backed against a tree and was swinging wildly to head and body. The Organization man crumpled as a blow caught him in the stomach.

The brontomeks were wheeling with mechanical precision, following their leader across the scrub. The ground trembled to their ponderous passage.

'Get in there and fight for your colony, you coward!' Mrs Earnshaw was blocking our path, mastiff features quivering with rage.

Streng was there. He said dryly, 'I'll fight at your side, Mrs Earnshaw.'

'By God, I'll take you up on that, Doctor!'

It's the only time I can remember seeing Streng taken aback. He watched blankly as the elderly woman strode forward, halted before a bewildered-looking Organization man, and slugged him briskly in the stomach. The man blinked. She caught him a ringing blow across the side of the face and he staggered. He must have been ten centimetres taller than she, and heavily built.

'Let's get out of here,' said Susanna quietly.

The last brontomek turned and lumbered away across the valley. The rough gravel of the road was littered with unconscious figures. Nearby I saw a man heave himself on to one elbow, cough and spread a pool of vomit over the road. One eye was totally closed; blood poured from a slashing wound in his forehead. As I watched him, he was kicked squarely in the face and fell back to lie motionless.

The fighting was becoming sporadic now. As I moved away with Susanna I met Jane and Mark: they were pulling Bill Yong away from an unconscious figure whom he had been kicking mercilessly. 'What the hell's going on?' Mark asked.

Yong moved away, looking for someone else to smash, but it seemed the battle was suddenly over. Chill Kaa stepped back from the prone, bleeding form of Singleton. 'I reckon we've shown the bastards who's in charge here,' he declaimed, staring around belligerently. His men began to gather around him, congratulating one another. Mrs Earnshaw came stamping back towards us.

'That's what I call a good scrap,' she said.

Bodies lay everywhere, bleeding. Men were crawling to their feet, standing unsteadily, fingering their wounds and gathering into silent little groups. They began to examine their still-motionless comrades, bundling up clothing and packing them under the heads of those too weak to rise. From time to time they would glance our way. There was no anger in the faces, and no fear...

'I think we know where we stand now, Dr Streng,' Mrs Earnshaw continued. 'I didn't see you or your friends fighting for the future of your colony.'

Streng was silent. There were around twenty of us who had abstained from the battle, and I still don't know whether we'd done the right thing or not.

'There they are!' I heard Will Jackson shout. 'There are the bastards who were scared to help their own people!' He was secure in his age, in his phoney righteousness.

The victorious mob regarded us, began slowly to move in our direction...

It only needed one word.

They numbered almost two hundred and they couldn't all have been involved in beating up sixty Organization men – but the point was, they were there and we were here, and they were looking for another victory. The first one had been too easy. Too easy...

'Right, you can hold it there,' said Streng, stepping forward. And they stopped, as though he held a gun on them.

'Well, I think you'll be the first, Streng,' said Chill Kaa, moving towards us. Then he paused, finding nobody alongside him. 'Come on!' he called to his men. 'Let's show these yellowbellies what we think of them!'

'I said hold it, Kaa,' snapped Streng. He walked quickly forward and stood before the fisherman. They were about the same height but Streng was much broader. I noticed Kaa's hands fidgeting uncertainly at his side.

'I want to know why you chickened out, Streng!' he blustered.

Streng replied, 'You think I'm afraid of a man-to-man conflict?'

Kaa edged back a fraction. 'That's sure what it looked like!'

'Well, maybe you're mistaken, Kaa.'

'Well... Why didn't you help us then? We could have had the crap beaten out of us for all you cared!'

Streng shook his head slowly. 'I don't think so. I really don't think so, Kaa.' He scanned the mob. 'I'd like to ask a question, just to prove my point. You men! Anyone who was hit by an Organization man hold up his hand!'

The crowd shuffled about, glancing at one another in growing uncertainty. No hands were raised. Streng smiled slowly.

'Right,' he said. 'Now listen to me. What you people did, was to attack and batter unconscious sixty people who were psychologically unable to defend themselves. What sort of a victory is that, Kaa?'

'What the hell are you talking about, man?'

'I'm talking about amorphs, Kaa!' Streng indicated the Organization workforce, picking themselves up, still tending to their more seriously injured colleagues. 'These creatures aren't human beings. They're amorphs, from the planet Marilyn! The Organization often uses them; they're docile and harmless. They don't fight, Kaa. They can't. All they want in life is to make themselves as pleasant as possible.

'And you humans have beaten them up.'

So when Althea Gant arrived on Saturday she found a contrite colony torn by internal dissension. The Liberty Lovers – that mysterious group – had gone to ground, the Kindred of the Pioneers were practising for a Maypole dance, and Mrs Earnshaw was experimenting with egg tempera. Mention of the battle of Inchtown Road resulted in instant unpleasantness. Even among my small group, we found it difficult to refer to the dreadful affair. The image of our own people ruthlessly smashing to pulp a defenceless group of aliens was too painful to consider.

Streng had something to say, although it was brief.

'The Organization couldn't have found a better way of bringing the colony into line,' he said. It seemed he was suggesting that the Organization had foreseen the battle and its results, but we didn't ask his reasons for holding this cynical view. Maybe we were scared he was right . . .

Althea Gant appeared in the Social Club at noon. The reception committee consisted of Jane Swindon, Ralph Streng and myself, the remainder of the colonists having melted away from the club when word of her arrival reached them.

'Am I ostracized around here?' Miss Gant enquired, staring about the empty lounge.

'The colony is in a state of flux right now, Miss Gant,' said Streng dryly. 'I'm sure it's nothing personal.'

A reasonably pleasant discussion followed during which Althea Gant repeated the Organization's desire to attract colonists to the planet – firstly to replace those who had left, in due course as a planned programme of expansion. Arcadia, she said in short, is going to boom. During the later stages in the conversation Susanna came in, looking gorgeous, and sat at our table.

Althea Gant said abruptly, 'Where's Professor Swindon, by the way?'

'He's down at the fish pens,' replied Jane. 'But I'm not sure he'd want to meet you. He's annoyed at the Organization's plans to harvest the plankton.'

Althea Gant smiled thinly. 'Still the same old story, huh? Something nasty lurking in the sea. I tell you, Mrs Swindon – unless Arcadians drop this notion of the ocean being a source of danger, we're never going to attract new immigrants. If half the population is frightened enough of the sea to want to leave, outsiders might start thinking they have good reason.' Her cold eyes turned to Streng.

'Tell me, Doctor – are you scared of the ocean?'

'Of course not.'

'Then you'll be interested in our plans to publicize the planet. We propose to direct our publicity towards allaying these ridiculous fears.'

'How?' I asked.

She leaned back in her chair and took a drink of gin, watching us all the time, sizing us up. Something important was coming. She replaced her glass on the table very deliberately.

'We are proposing a circumnavigation of the Arcadian ocean by a solo yachtsman.'

Looking back on that noon-hour in the Riverside Social Club which was to affect the lives of all of us there, I find it difficult to recall exactly my reactions on hearing Althea Gant's proposal. I think at first I was sceptical. A man sailing alone around the world would prove nothing except to himself. However, after a while I began to realize the effect such a voyage would have on the people of other planets, as they followed our yachtsman across the thousands of kilometers in their imagination. Skilfully handled, the tension and interest would grip the whole Sector. And, since the Organization had such a stranglehold on the media, there was no doubt that the coverage would be extensive. The success of the voyage should allay – at least for fify years – the public's fear of the Arcadian ocean.

The more I thought about it, the better the scheme appeared – apart from one obvious drawback.

It would backfire disastrously if the yachtsman got himself eaten by a monster.

'Riverside will be the centre of this project,' said Althea Gant as she gathered together her things. We accompanied her to the church where there was to be a meeting.

# eight

Althea Gant stood on the stage beside a table. On the table was a large box which had required the efforts of two colonists to carry it in from her hovercar.

'... and as a result of such a concentrated publicity campaign we hope to attract the immigrants we need. And need them we do – for a planet cannot remain underpopulated without a gradual regression in living standards. Historically it is the planets with the larger populations which enjoy the highest standards of living. All manner of secondary industries will grow up around the primaries of farming and fishing. Building, light industry, repair shops, service industries, tourism and so on ...' She went on to describe the ideal agricultural planet and I had to admit it sounded good. Her audience – at least half the colony – was listening attentively with few of the outbursts of dissent which normally characterize Riverside gatherings.

Then she came to her main point. 'And as a temporary measure we have found it necessary to import help.' She lifted the lid from the box on the table, took away the sides and revealed a strange formless thing, a large pockmarked mass of shapeless matter.

'It's alive,' someone near me whispered. 'I saw it move.'

'Yes,' said Miss Gant. 'This is a living thing – an amorph, from the planet Marilyn. At present it's in its natural unformed state – but it has a very interesting defence mechanism. When brought into proximity to another living creature, it will change shape. Even the very make-up of its internal organs will undergo a transformation.'

The thing on the table was shifting, growing. Originally grey and amorphous like a giant version of Chukalek's ball of dough, it was now becoming paler, pinker. A waving frond extended itself, which grew as we watched it and became a tentacle . . .

'This transformation is achieved by rapid absorption of water from the atmosphere through the walls of the body cells, so that not only is the amorph able to alter its shape, but it has almost unlimited powers of growth. Its home planet has a very high humidity and abundant rainfall, but even here, on this fine day, I think you can see that the amorph is bigger than it was.'

The thing was flowing over the edge of the table, extending to the floor yet still leaving a part of its bulk behind, joined by a rapidly-thickening trunk. The audience was fidgeting apprehensively. I saw Kli a' Po's teeth bared in a grin.

'I said this was a defence mechanism. The amorph transforms itself into the object least likely to be harmed by whatever, whoever is nearest and possibly threatening it. If placed next to a dog, it will rapidly become a bitch. It has the capacity to extract information from the mind of the dog as to what that dog would most like to see. It becomes that thing, love object, whatever you like to call it. We call it the Te, from the Old Latin word meaning thou.'

The amorph had become a column, slightly taller than Miss Gant herself, pink and black at the top, multicoloured elsewhere . . .

'When confronted by a human being, an amorph will usually – but not always – become a person of the opposite sex who is attractive to that person. Often a husband, wife, lover. But sometimes, a person's Te is the last thing he expects . . . The amorphs represent *ideals*. They are what you most want them to be. But *you* don't always know what your secret desire – your Te – is . . .'

I shivered suddenly; Susanna grinned at me mischievously. 'I have a sort of idea what yours is, Moncrieff you lecherous bastard,' she whispered. I smiled back, feeling better.

And now there was a man standing beside Althea Gant . . .

He was fairly tall with indeterminate features and brown hair. He looked pleasant enough; he smiled at us and took

Miss Gant's arm. He wore – or had grown – clothes: nondescript grey.

He said, 'Hi there, colonists.' There were a few nervous sniggers from the audience.

Miss Gant said, 'In showing you this, I've bared my innermost feelings on stage. This man creature is all I've ever wanted a man to be, even if I didn't realize it myself. In fact he is a composite of two old acquaintances of mine, both of whom would be extremely embarrassed if they knew. But I can recognize them in him. He is kind and gentle and would never harm a living soul – and, I admit it, he is easily dominated by me.' Now the audience laughed outright and unkindly. 'I can duplicate him, again and again, merely by exposing a number of amorphs to my presence.'

'Why did the Organization bring those creeps to our world?' someone shouted. Someone else called for him to be quiet, but it was apparent that many of the audience were uneasy.

Althea Gant smiled thinly. 'I can assure you their presence is temporary only, to help keep Arcadia functioning until the immigration rate builds up.'

Mrs Earnshaw was standing. 'If all you say is true, perhaps you'll explain why the amorphs we met on the Inchtown road did not change shape into something a little more agreeable to us? I, for one, am not particularly interested in your concept of what a man ought to be, Miss Gant!'

The Organization woman explained. 'After amorphs have been in a particular form for some time, their ability for rapid change becomes diminished. In order that our human amorphs should stay human while engaged in agriculture, and not turn into Arbulls, for instance, we submit them to an intensive humanization programme. The creatures you saw are known as fixed amorphs: they've lived with men for weeks. They will change, but so subtly that you wouldn't notice. For instance – had you realized that Mr Singleton was an amorph? A complete transformation might take days – or longer, since the very fact that they are in the company of one another has a moderating effect...'

Later, in the interests of good relations, we took the redoubtable Gant to the Swindons' for a drink before she drove back to catch the evening railcar from Inchtown. She loosened up a little under the influence of Mark's gin. 'We're doing our best for you people, you know,' she said.

'I'm sure you are,' said Tom Minty who had tagged along for the refreshments. There was more than a hint of sarcasm in his voice.

'The hell with you,' said Miss Gant equably . . .'

Within a few days of Althea Gant's visit, several of us received official notifications of our appointment to the publicity project.

Mortimore Barker was to be in charge of promotion.

Susanna Lincoln was responsible for public relations in coordination with Barker.

Mark Swindon was retained as an adviser on marine biological matters.

I was commissioned to build the boat.

And Ralph Streng accepted an invitation to be her skipper.

No doubt the Hetherington Organization considered Streng the perfect solo yachtsman, with his imperturbability, his coldly logical methods of reasoning, his singleminded methods of pursuing his aims.

As for myself, I found the Organization's terms more than fair, considering my imminent bankruptcy. I was to be paid a huge figure for the boat which, I calculated, would show me a hundred per cent profit – enough to clear off all my debts. Financing of the boat was to be arranged by the Organization, free of interest. I would be paid one-half on delivery of the boat before a stipulated deadline, and the balance on successful completion of the voyage. In addition I would receive a great deal of free publicity. Barker even suggested that the boat's name be the 'Moncrieff Arcadian' and the Organization said they would consider it.

What pleased me most, I think, was the fact that a galactic corporation was displaying confidence in my ability, despite my financial troubles and the loss of the prototype *Easy Lady* . . .

Susanna and I started work clearing the slipway and preparing the yard the following day.

'Listen,' she said after a while, breathless from stacking innumerable paint cans against the wall of the boathouse. 'How big is this boat going to be?' She regarded the expanse of cleared concrete. 'You could set a shuttle down there, for God's sake, Moncrieff.'

'I reckon about thirty-two feet. I'm starting the drawings tonight. We're going to be as busy as hell, Susanna.'

'All the better for Mort's publicity,' she grinned. 'A race against time before the thing's even launched.'

'It's obvious your place is here, where the action is,' I said. 'I expect I can find you accommodation up above the boathouse.'

She raised her eyes, regarding the timber ceiling. 'If I'm not mistaken, there's some guy already living up there, name of Moncrieff, a notorious lecher. I may look like a dumb blonde ... but I majored in geography. Not to mention biology.'

I was watching the far side of the creek, where the road from Inchtown wound down the hillside. A hovercar was descending fast, swinging wide at the corners, fountaining mud and gravel. 'Somebody's in a hurry,' I remarked.

The car raced over the bridge, slowed at the right turn into Riverside's steep main street, then came straight on as the driver saw us.

Tom Minty flung open the door. 'Jump in!' he cried. 'There's trouble over at the Blackstone farm.'

'What sort of trouble?' I followed Susanna into the car and closed the door.

Minty accelerated, swerved violently so that the guide wheels squealed against the roughly paved road surface, and roared up the hill into the colony. 'We'll pick up old Mrs Earnshaw,' he said. 'And Batelli. That ought to do it ... Yeah – your friends the Organization have gone too far this time.'

In due course a full carload arrived at the Blackstone farm to find Kli a' Po sitting disconsolately on an upturned barrow, surrounded by at least a dozen miniature editions of himself.

'You must tell me how you begat those children of yours some time, Kli,' remarked the Reverend Batelli with simulated sternness. 'I'm sure it's not the way the good Lord intended.'

Kli eyed the priest with what looked like a half-grin. 'If they offend your Reverence's susceptibilities I'll dispose of them immediately.'

'All right,' snapped Mrs Earnshaw. 'Now what's going on around here?'

As if in answer Sinclair Singleton came around the corner of the old farmhouse, looking over his shoulder and beckoning. There was a deep mechanical roaring; a brontomek came into view, smashing down the ancient fence around the farm yard and drawing a broad pulverized swathe straight through the packed mud and on along the meadow beside the track to the main road.

'Mr Kli!' cried Vernon Thrale who had just extricated himself from the car. 'They're ploughing up your farm!'

'Singleton!' bellowed Mrs Earnshaw. 'What is the meaning of this wanton outrage?'

The Organization man approached diffidently. 'Why, we've appropriated this farm, Mrs Earnshaw. It's all quite legal, and Kli a' Po will get it back in due course.'

'In five years' time, you mean,' the old woman snapped. 'What the hell is wrong with all that land to the north, isn't that enough for you?'

'This is the best soil. We've ploughed all we can in the adjoining area. I'm afraid we cannot allow one man to hold such large tracts of land when the planet's productivity is so vital. It isn't as though he was utilizing the land to the full.'

'That was purely due to a temporary labour shortage,' explained Mrs Earnshaw.

'It was because those bastards in the village refused to work for an alien,' said Tom Minty heatedly. 'Kli couldn't get enough workers even before the big emigration started. He's not going to get much support from the village even now.'

'You!' Mrs Earnshaw stabbed a finger at Singleton, who backed away. 'You're an alien, I understand. You're one of these goddamned amorphs, huh? Some alien you've turned out to be. You refuse to back your own kind.'

'There are aliens and aliens,' murmured Kli mildly.

The brontomek had turned and was lumbering back, ripping soil and flattening trees. A sticker plant went under, thrashing tentacles and squirting juices. Worrals darted about, pausing to blink dazedly in the sunlight, dashing off again. A thin pencil of light stabbed out from a turret above the brontomek's jaws and fried a small bounding thing.

'This farm is a historic monument!' cried Mrs Earnshaw as more fences went down. 'It's original owned died during the Relay Effect, and later the buildings featured in other important events resulting in the defeat of the Mind!'

Singleton said carefully, 'But that was only a couple of years ago, Mrs Earnshaw. I'm sure the Organization considered those facts, but I hardly think they carried much weight when the decision was made to plough.'

Minty said, 'You're an amorph, Mr Singleton. I hear that

your kind don't offend folk. You go along with the wishes of whoever's nearest to you.'

The Organization man smiled. 'You must realize that I've been exposed to Organization people and policy for so long that it's instilled in me.'

'But can't you see these policies are wrong?' insisted Mrs Earnshaw.

'No. I know we must produce, and I know this farm is under-producing. I know that it's for the good of all of us that we plough the place under. That's all I need to know – that I'm doing the right thing.'

'For Christ's sake, Kli,' snapped Mrs Earnshaw in exasperation. 'Don't you have anything to say? This is your god-damned farm!'

The alien said, 'I agree with Mr Singleton. He's doing what he must. We all are. You had to come and try to defend me, Mrs Earnshaw, because you felt it was your duty. Tom came because he likes to play the part of the rebel. Vernon thought he might, just once, be able to assert himself. And so on. We all have our motives. My motive is peace of mind – and to achieve this I like to work hard. I need no possessions. I only bought this farm because it gave me the reason to work.'

As he spoke, the miniature replicas all around him were regarding us. Some of them mouthed silently, miming Kli a' Po's words in uncanny synchronization.

'Let's get the hell out of here, Tom,' grunted Mrs Earnshaw. 'There's nothing we can do for this fool.'

As we left, the brontomek's sensing devices swivelled our way and watched us all the way down the track.

I awakened the following morning feeling exhausted, having spent half the night working on the plans for the new boat and the other half semi-conscious in bed, having nightmares about those same plans. It is always disastrous for me to work late: I need time to unwind before turning in; time for a slow scotch and long thoughts.

By mid-morning I was in Inchtown, climbing aboard the railcar for Premier City. There was some slight improvement in the service: the dreadful old hag behind the refreshment counter had been replaced by a delightful young girl with curly golden hair. She looked too good to be serving coffee and, in addition, she was elusively familiar. I smiled at her as she handed me my drink and she smiled back, but it was a conditioned reflex. There was no familiarity there unfortunately.

It was not until I'd returned to my seat and spread the boat plans on the pull-out table before me that I remembered where I'd seen her before.

She had been one of Mort Barker's angel girls at the Regatta.

A few weeks ago I would have returned and struck up a conversation on this basis and we'd have chatted in futile fashion for the rest of the journey, and I'd have detrained at Premier City wondering why I'd been wasting my time – chasing what Ralph Streng cynically refers to as 'a lay in the offing'. This, he contends, is the only reason any man makes conversation with any girl: the possibility of future sexual intercourse. He says it's the Secondary Instinct at work – that which commands us to further the species.

And he could be right, the bastard.

However, that particular side of my driving forces was all taken up with Susanna, so the angel girl remained unassailed. Instead, I worked on the boat drawings all the way to the terminal.

Premier City had changed. The air of apathy and decay had gone. Already there seemed to be more people about, and I noticed several shop-fronts being redecorated. Premises which a few weeks ago had been vacant were now in visible occupation: counters were being installed, shelving put up, goods being inventoried and placed on display.

I caught the antigrav elevator to the top floor of the Premier City Gazette building. The cubicle rose smoothly and silently but I am never entirely happy in elevators and my confidence ebbed further when I saw the official-looking notice some wit had stuck to the wall:

'The Management regrets that it is unable to accept responsibility for injuries sustained by passengers not equipped with parachutes.'

Its zany improbability afforded me a nervous smile, and I continued to observe my invariable practice in elevators, always to stand with knees slightly bent. In the event of a sudden impact, I believe that this will prevent my pelvis being rammed into my chest cavity.

The editor of the *Gazette* was not cooperative.

'I don't think I can help you much, Mr Moncrieff. I understand that publicity for the circumnavigation has all been arranged.'

'That's not quite what I came for, uh, Kenneth. In view of the fact that the voyage will be of great value to our world as a whole – and in particular your publication – I feel that it's in all our interests to make sure the costs are borne as equitably as possible. Don't you?' I'd composed this spiel in the hovercar on the way to Inchtown and I watched the editor's face carefully, interested to see how it fared.

He glanced around as though seeking escape. 'Sure, sure.'

'Maybe your periodical could be persuaded—'

The visiphone buzzed and a face appeared on the screen, talking fast about some deadline. The editor listened for a few seconds then placed a palm over the scanner and turned to me. 'Perhaps you'll excuse me now, Mr uh, Moncrieff. Try the Arcadian Arcade, huh? I'm sure they'll be able to help with a few consumable supplies, maybe.'

I played my ace. 'But the Hetherington Organization feels that cooperation between—'

He trumped it. 'The *Gazette* is a subsidiary of the Organization, Mr Moncrieff. Now, if you'll excuse me . . .' He began to speak into the phone.

I fared little better at the Arcadian Arcade. The giant supermarket had also undergone a face-lift in recent weeks – and in this instance the name had changed. A huge crimson sign above the glassy expanse of the front read: HETHERINGTON ARCADE. Nevertheless I entered and, after some haggling, succeeded in divesting the manager of one case of quick-dried protein-plus balls – a complete meal in a mouthful, according to the packet. If Streng was to meet his Maker on this voyage, he'd meet him well-nourished.

I tried a few more stores but with growing despondency. I should have expected this: the Organization had bought Arcadia, therefore it had bought Arcadia's component parts – the land, the monorail system, the stores, everything.

The trouble was, it was so goddamned *obvious.*

The last straw came when I called in at Jake's Chandlery to arrange the fittings for the boat. Jake wasn't there, although the sign over the unpretentious door was unchanged. There was a young girl there: a pretty girl with curly blonde hair who took my order and smiled at me as she assured me that my requirements would be delivered within two weeks.

There was something about that girl.

She was the twin sister of the girl on the railcar.

She was an amorph. Like the other girl, she was the product of some unknown guy's dreams and longings, standing there in front of me and making like human.

Weeks ago, at the Regatta ...

The whole of that aerial troupe with their angel wings had been amorphs, and we hadn't known it. Had Mortimore Barker?

Did it matter?

Clutching my case of protein-plus balls, I made my way disconsolately back to the monorail terminal.

# nine

During the following week I completed the plans and layouts: working round the clock, delegating as much of the detail work as I could, sleeping when I had to. On the following Monday I approached Sinclair Singleton at the Organization office.

'Good morning, Mr Moncrieff,' he said pleasantly, showing no signs of the battering he'd received a week or two back. Quite probably amorphs had some built-in system of instant recuperation – after all, a creature that can change its bodily shape had no need to stay bruised.

'I'm ready to start construction on the hull tomorrow,' I told him. 'Maybe you could let me have a few amorphs, huh? There's a lot of unskilled work to be done in the early stages.'

I listened to the words as they left my mouth – you know how it is – and I realized that they were insulting. I was speaking of the amorphs as though they were some sort of beast of burden. I smiled broadly in an attempt to remove the sting.

'How many do you want?' Singleton showed no sign of outrage.

'Four should be enough.'

'Sure, I can arrange that. I'll have to confirm the price with Premier City, but it won't be any more than you'd pay a human, Mr Moncrieff.'

It takes a man time to adjust to circumstances, and I am no quicker than anyone else. 'What!' I shouted. 'Hell, I expected them free. There's plenty of them over at the Blackstone place. I thought they ... you could reproduce at will.'

'So can you, Mr Moncrieff,' said Singleton gently.

'You know what I mean, for Christ's sake.'

He was still smiling. 'You must realize that we have been imported to this planet at considerable expense and the Organization wants to see a return on its investment. We can't work for free, any more than a human would. I'm sorry, Mr Moncrieff. And as regards the reproduction, there is a certain amount of ... volition involved. An amorph wouldn't bud merely to fill a labour shortage. Would you?'

Round about this time I was pulling myself together and calling myself a bastard, and wondering how I could get myself out of this. I said, 'Look, I'm sorry. I guess I don't know much about amorphs. Maybe you'd like to ask four of your people to work for me, and the Organization can deduct the fee from my balance on delivery of the boat, huh?'

'Certainly, Mr Moncrieff.'

The amorphs arrived the following morning – four overalled men of nondescript appearance – and I set them to work on simple tasks. Instantly they proved themselves remarkably quick learners and neat, efficient workers – more so than my human employees. Soon they were involved in more complex tasks. I never had to repeat an instruction and, although they'd probably never seen a boat before, they were able to recognize the mistakes in my hurriedly drawn plans – instead of going blindly ahead and wasting time and materials, the way a human would. They seemed to have an instinctive grasp of what I wanted.

And of course, that was just what they did have. They picked it out of my mind, without realizing it themselves. Although they were comparatively permanent, 'fixed' amorphs and therefore unlikely to change shape into my Te without warning, nevertheless my proximity affected their defence mechanisms and they became, to a limited extent, my ideal of a boatyard worker.

So the days went by, and each day when quitting time came my human work force would down tools and go home, and my amorphs would continue working, sometimes for hours, until a convenient stage was reached and they could reasonably leave without abandoning some important component half-finished . . .

Susanna often said, 'You ought to take a day off, Kev. We're well up to schedule.' I remember one occasion: she was standing on the edge of the quay looking up at an amorph on the scaffolding, the low sun gilding her hair, outlining her strong body through the thin fabric of her dress. 'At least come up to the club for a drink,' she said. 'We could see Mort and discuss publicity, if you must work. Or maybe we could just go for a walk . . .'

If things were going well at the boatyard, such was not the case elsewhere. Ralph Streng often dropped by to see how things were coming along and after a while it became apparent that all was not well with him.

He had become quiet, almost morose, as he watched the amorphs at work. I knew he was having trouble with his wife, who didn't want him to undertake the voyage. On one occasion he said, 'You're goddamned lucky you're not married, Kevin. Hazel's giving me hell, these days.'

It was good to hear. It was good to know that someone so superbly efficient and self-confident as Ralph Streng could suffer from something so mundane, so degrading, as a nagging wife.

'It shows she loves you,' said Susanna.

He shook his head. 'There's no reason for her to love me. Our marriage is a business arrangement. No – it's the fear of being left alone that's getting to her. It's a selfish fear and I've told her so, but it does no good. Hell, the goddamned woman can't understand the simplest logic. What about me? I'll be alone too – a hell of a lot more alone than her.'

'You volunteered,' I said.

'I'm doing it for the money. It's for the good of us both.'

'Crap. You're doing it because of the challenge.'

He was staring at an amorph. 'Listen, Kevin, I don't think you ought to have those goddamned things working here. There's talk in the colony. People are saying you should have hired human beings.'

'How can I? Most of them are on strike.'

'I reckon the strike's collapsed. The only reason people aren't working is because there's no work to do. A few are back at the Blackstone place, working under the amorphs – get that, working *under* them. About fifty people have been employed down near the mouth of the estuary, building a deep-water dock for the seavesters. Christ, where have you been this last week or two?'

'Building the boat for your voyage,' I said irritably. 'I don't have time for politics.'

That evening Susanna dragged me up to the Social Club. The place was full and in general I enjoyed myself: it was good to get back into circulation for a couple of hours. But I noticed a certain amount of constraint in people's attitudes towards me. A large proportion of the colony were out of work, with no income – and I had hired amorphs to work at the boatyard.

Perce Walters joined us; he bore no grudge, of course: he's not the type. 'I'm laying up *Arcturus* for a while,' he said. 'Can you take her on your slipway?'

'Sure. Why aren't you fishing?'

He looked faintly embarrassed. 'There's no money in it any more, Kev. All I get is the standard wage, and my boat's depreciating all the time. Hell, if I need repairs, I have to go through Singleton and all manner of red tape. It's not worth it any more. Besides, the seavesters will be coming into service soon – and then there'll be no place for any fisherman.'

I said, 'I don't get it. I thought the Organization were out to expand the population. That's what all the publicity will be for. So how do you make a planet grow if there are no jobs?'

Mark Swindon had joined us by this time. He said, 'Growth follows a pattern. In time there will be a gradual drift to the larger towns and an increase in service industries. It's happened all over the Galaxy and it'll happen in Arcadia. The shift to urbanization. People will quit places like Riverside, leaving a few machines and caretakers behind. The big cities will get bigger.'

'But what about all that stuff they told us about the rural life, and Arcadia being the cornucopia of the Sector?' asked Jane Swindon.

'That was just stuff,' said her husband. 'They'll use this image to attract immigrants – and the immigrants will find themselves working as book-keepers and insurance salesmen and plumbers in Premier City. Meanwhile, the countryside and the open air, the hills and cattle and the rustic wheatsheaves will be looked after by machines.'

'It really seems a pity,' said Susanna.

'You can't blame the Organization,' said Mark. 'This is the way human society works.'

I glanced around at human society as represented by the drinking members of the Riverside sub-colony and I had to admit it wasn't impressive. Tom Minty, Bill Yong and Jim Spark were laughing uproariously in a corner, high on Immunol. Jed Spark and Chill Kaa were arguing bitterly over another table, faces close together and vicious. Will Jackson sat stiff and granite-faced, unable to find a young girl to leer at. Mrs Earnshaw was bellowing instructions into a visiphone on the far wall; from the screen the indeterminate face of her paid companion, Miss Cotter, peered back, nervously. I may have been tired and a little disheartened that evening, but it seemed to me that human society had all the direction, unity and purpose of an Arcadian Council meeting.

However, the following morning I received a surprise. I was helping an amorph fit a ply sheet to one of the hulls, twisting the flexible panel while the amorph screwed it into place, when someone spoke over my shoulder.

'Uh, Moncrieff.' It was Ezra Blake. I was surprised to see him; we hadn't exactly been on good terms since the Regatta. 'I need a job doing,' he said.

'Yes? I'm pretty much tied up, right now.'

He ignored that one. 'It's Paul's skitterbug. The intake's damaged.'

'That's what comes of driving over mud.'

'Don't think I haven't told him.'

We walked down the wharf and I inspected the small craft: Paul had it up on blocks and was standing by, looking embarrassed. 'It'll take me a couple of hours,' I said. 'Can you wait until later today?'

'Couple of hours,' murmured Ezra Blake thoughtfully. 'That's around six dozen eggs at Organization rate. Tell you what. You can have free eggs and milk for a week. How's that?'

'I never drink milk,' I answered, perplexed. 'What's wrong with your Organization card! Are you overspent?'

He flushed angrily. 'Overspent, me? Hell, Moncrieff, do you take me for a goddamned peasant?'

'You must admit it's pretty strange when you try to pay a bill in eggs, man.'

He stared at me. 'Of course. You weren't at the meeting. I might have expected that. Well, Moncrieff, we have a new system operating here in Riverside. Nobody uses their cards unless they have to. Why the hell should the Organization know everything that goes on?'

'You mean we've gone over to a system of barter?'

'Too true. Mrs Earnshaw suggested it – that old bird has quite a lot of sense. Since we're all paid at the same goddamned rate, all goods and services are related to the standard hour. The standard hour is the unit of currency, get it? This is the first step towards independence, Moncrieff!'

We agreed on a price and he stumped away, satisfied. The incident left me with a feeling of uneasiness, however. Far from being a step towards independence, the introduction of a system of barter seemed to me a step backwards.

As the days became weeks, the *Moncrieff Arcadian* began to shape up. At first there was not much to see, and the casual bystanders – of whom there were always a few, such was the shortage of jobs in Riverside – were openly cynical. Two slender sponsons lying on a slipway are unimpressive, when considered as a means of taking a man around the world. Their flimsiness contrasted unfavourably with the huge bulk of Perce Walters' trawler *Arcturus*, beached alongside.

However, in due course the sponsons were connected by substantial cross-beams, and before long the roomy cabin was under construction. *Moncrieff Arcadian* was beginning to look like a boat. Mortimore Barker brought a camera crew down one morning and they shot some footage in a mood of buoyant optimism, with Streng posing heroically in the unfinished cockpit.

Afterwards, Streng said, 'I'm not happy about those cross-beams.' We were crouching in the cabin while he checked the standard of workmanship – a habit which had become annoyingly frequent recently. I opened the watertight hatch which led to the tiny forecabin where Streng's sleeping accommodation was, and examined the forward of the two cross-beams. A massive member of imported hardwood, it ran across the forward bulkhead.

'They look fine to me,' I replied shortly.

'Those beams have to take the full twisting motion of a choppy sea,' he stated. 'Hell, they're the only thing holding this goddamned boat together. They should be laminated.'

'It's a bit late for that now, Ralph,' I said mildly.

'Listen to me,' he snapped, bulky and overpowering in the

tiny space, 'it's my goddamned life that's at stake. If you want a skipper for this boat, then you put in laminated cross-members. I have no intention of sailing around the world in a jerry-built tub.'

He was under a considerable strain, of course; more so than any of us. All the same, his suggestion would entail several days of extra work, and put us behind schedule. He persisted in his attitude, however, and in the end I shrugged and told my foreman to start dismantling the cabin.

And so the pace quickened, and I began to lose track of the passage of days. Susanna dropped by several times a day to force-feed me on coffee and protein balls – I had developed a perverted taste for these chewy morsels which were to sustain Streng for months. She told me that the dispute between Riverside and the Organization showed no signs of abating.

'It's getting worrying, Kev,' she said. 'There've been outbreaks of vandalism.'

'Like what?' I asked absently, wielding the power drill.

'Like savagely raping innocent and beautiful blonde girls named Susanna.'

'Too bad,' I think I mumbled through a mouthful of brass screws before the meaning of her words filtered through my brainful of forestays and keelsons and spinnakers. 'What!' I jerked out, nearly swallowing.

'Like plugging the outlets on Sinclair Singleton's hovercar, and jamming the remote-control frequency of the brontomeks,' she replied acidly. 'Are you going deaf, Moncrieff?'

'Do they know who's responsible?'

'The Organization doesn't know, but I'm sure the colony does. It's these Liberty Lovers again, or whatever they call themselves.'

This conversation often recurred to me as I worked away and, as a precaution, I posted a guard on the slipway at nights. Since the circumnavigation was sponsored by the Organization, and since I'd already heard mutterings about the project, it seemed a wise precaution.

News from elsewhere was sketchy. As Streng commented: with Newspocket in the hands of the Organization and individual travel limited due to lack of personal income, anything could be going on.

'But there's nothing we can do,' he said one night. 'So why the hell bother? All that stuff on Newspocket, all the news from elsewhere in the Sector – it's meaningless. It doesn't affect *me.* And the only news which is valid is that which affects me personally, and allows me to act on it. If it doesn't fall into that category, then I don't want to know.'

The Reverend Batelli was with us at the time; he said, 'That's a remarkably selfish attitude, Ralph. Don't you feel any regret on hearing about a spaceship disaster, for instance?'

Streng smiled. 'Not regret – the lives lost are of no consequence to me. Such disaster announcements must be made by the networks for a purpose. Tell me – what is the purpose? What am I *supposed* to feel? Misery? If so, then I'd rather not know. Why should my emotions be dictated by the media? Yes, Enrico, it's a selfish attitude. But what is wrong with being concerned with self? We all are.'

'But only you admit it,' grinned Batelli, quoting Streng to Streng.

That discussion revealed a flash of the old Ralph Streng whom we all knew, and put up with. But I was becoming increasingly concerned about Streng's general attitude.

He had taken to dropping in at the yard at odd times, trying to help and succeeding only in getting in the way, spending hours obsessively working at such small tasks as we could find to keep him quiet. He would strip off his shirt and sand down a rudder by hand, taking endless pains to achieve exactly the shape and smoothness which satisfied some inner artist. As to whether the shape was hydrodynamically correct, nobody knew or cared. It was not a critical factor.

But, to Streng, everything was becoming a critical factor.

I think it was a Thursday when the big row blew up.

'Look – there's no way this goddamned thing's going to be completed by the deadline, Moncrieff,' he burst out, tattered shred of sandpaper in hand, sweat eroding rivulets in the dust on his face.

'Get the hell out of here and leave the worrying to me, Streng,' I snapped back. 'You make me nervous.'

He suddenly became calm, forcibly so. 'I've been meaning to tell you, Moncrieff, and this seems as good a time as any. I'm seriously dissatisfied with this boat. Your planned sail area is much too large, for one thing. I'm running the risk of a capsize – either the sail area must be reduced, or the hulls placed further apart. Tell me this – how do you propose that I right her, if she does turn over?'

'For Christ's sake, Ralph, you know how it is with catamarans. If they capsize, they stay capsized. There's nothing you or I can do about it.'

'You stand there and tell me I'll die because of your choice of yacht design?'

'You knew the boat was to be a cat when you accepted. Just make goddamned sure you don't roll her, that's all.'

'I want to see an antigravity device on that masthead, Moncrieff. If she goes over, I want to be sure I can get her back the right way up.'

'But the mast's completed! That means making a new mast from scratch to take the extra weight, and redesigning all the rigging! We'll lose days. It's lunacy, Streng!'

'There's nothing lunatic in wanting to stay alive,' he said calmly. 'It's the primary instinct. Neither you, nor anyone else, is going to kill me, Moncrieff.'

After a few drinks in the Social Club Susanna and I walked down the main colony street towards the wharf. It was a mild night but cloudy: three moons were up but all were obscured. In the unaccustomed darkness I felt somehow conspiratorial, creeping through the streets with a beautiful girl.

'Feeling better now, Moncrieff? Has alcohol deadened your senses enough to allow you to face life again?'

'Hell, it was only that bastard Streng today. He got me down. He has his own problems, I suppose.'

As we stepped on to the wharf Susanna said, 'He owes you a lot. Around two thousand five hundred brain cells, I'd say.'

'Christ, what are you saying?'

'Each measure of scotch destroys around five hundred brain cells, Moncrieff. Alcohol is the most vicious drug known to man. Eventually the contents of your cranium turn to soup. The cells never regenerate, you know.'

We crossed the bridge; the water flowed sluggishly below. The colony blazed with lights, a few more showed at the water's edge, along the wharf. I hoped my watchman was awake. As we entered the forest, I paused to relieve myself. The relentless voice of Susanna followed me behind my tree.

'You notice it is a primitive instinct of man always to piss up against something, like a dog does. Women don't have this instinct – we're more civilized.'

'Built differently,' I said, trying not to laugh. 'Speaking of statistics, here's one which I've found very useful in life. Did you know that the average drinking man, in his lifetime, passes enough urine to fill a swimming pool?'

'What size swimming pool?' she asked carefully.

'Oh, family size, I guess. Nothing spectacular. Like the one Thrale has in his back yard.'

We walked on through the trees. 'I must remember never to use Thrale's pool,' observed Susanna thoughtfully. 'Where are you taking me, by the way?'

'I thought maybe we'd make our way along to the point and back. I feel like walking tonight, don't you?'

'So long as that satyriasis of yours is kept within reasonable bounds.'

I let that one go and we climbed on, following the winding trail through the trees, eventually coming out on top of the ridge which follows the estuary. In the valley to our north lights glowed.

'Seems we're not the only ones to be working around the clock,' I observed.

'What are they doing down there?' asked Susanna.

'Cultivating and seeding, I expect. You know the Organization. They want to squeeze every last day out of the growing season. That's why they ploughed Blackstone's place in – because the land was already cleared and it meant they could get a crop out of it this year.' We were directly above the old farmhouse now. Bright new aluminium sheds glittered in the floodlights. A few men walked briskly to and fro, and we heard the distant grumble of machinery.

I found I was holding Susanna's hand. 'Hell, what's this?' I said casually, regarding it.

'It's mine, Moncrieff, and you look after it. I'm not a girl to give my hand lightly.'

We stood above Anchor Pool.

I felt Susanna shiver, as she looked down. 'Hold me, Kev,' she murmured. 'It's creepy here. You're creepy yourself, but I prefer you to that place.'

I slid my arms around her, and held her to me, and we kissed. It was wonderful; her lips were soft and sexy, her body fitted against mine as though it belonged. 'Listen, Susanna,' I whispered, 'I love you, do you believe that? I need you with me, always.'

'You need a cold bath, Moncrieff,' she replied. 'What are

your hands doing there? I thought you used them strictly for handling power tools and scotch. Kiss me again, huh?'

We stood there, propped against each other, for ages. Somewhere in there she said she loved me.

'You said you loved me, didn't you?' I asked. I wanted to make sure.

'Well, yes. I felt it my duty to Jane Swindon. She's been very good to me, you know – and me without a home of my own. She seemed to think it essential that I fell in love with you, so here I am, doing it. It's rather nice, really. I can't think why I haven't tried it before. Hell, I'm over twenty.'

From that point on our rate of progress was interrupted by frequent pauses. The ridge trail was an ideal place for romance: its isolation was heightened by the valleys on either side where lights glowed and people went about their ways with no knowledge of what was happening on the skyline. The only sounds were the occasional scamper of a worral, the stealthy rustle of a sticker plant, the muted grumble of a brontomek in the distance. The last time Susanna and I had walked this trail had not been a happy one: I'd been trembling with reaction from near-drowning and sick with despair at the loss of my boat, and I hadn't been in the mood to take advantage of her presence.

Eventually we emerged from the trees on to the grassy slopes around the clifftop; the angular shape of the hoist was silhouetted against the sky before us. It seemed a good moment to drag Susanna forcibly to the ground.

'My God,' she wailed. 'He's going to have his way with me!'

I stole a furtive look around the empty scenery, saw no onlookers, and took hold of her. She sighed, turned her face to mine, and we kissed; the longest and most sincere kiss I've ever known. I squeezed her breast and she wriggled against me. A glittering kite-bug sailed overhead, turning in the light breeze. Not so far away, I heard machinery.

'You have a very short attention span, you know that, Moncrieff?'

I began to unzip things here and there. I could see her face in the dim light, pale and dreamy. 'I love you, Susanna,' I said quietly. 'I reckon I've always loved you. It's just that I never met you until recently.'

'You put it so nicely, Kev.' The bantering air was gone and

she was very serious. 'I love you too. I can't remember a time when I didn't. I feel it's going to be a terrible anti-climax struggling to get these pants off. You won't laugh at me, will you?'

I said no, in fact I offered my assistance, which was gratefully accepted.

But there are certain things which are not meant to happen. I could have continued, we could have made love then and there, and ignored the rapidly approaching roar of machinery, but it wouldn't have been right, not the first time. We were confident enough in each other's love to know that there would be other times, plenty of them. Nevertheless it was frustrating.

'Tell me please, Deus, why you chose this moment to send a machine along the goddamned trail?' Susanna asked the sky.

The rumbling roar was close, accompanied by splintering crashes as trees went down. We rearranged our clothing and stood, staring back into the darkness where the forest began. A couple of small creatures bounded past us, then the clouds parted and a moon shone through.

'There it is,' said Susanna. 'Down there, on the slope.'

The grassy hillside fell away into the valley to our north; now we could see a distinct boundary where the paleness of verdure changed to the black of ploughed ground. To the right were the cliffs; the sea glittered far below. Away to our left, the moonlight sparkled on a billion spiny leaves in the long, narrow forest which crowns the ridge. Near the margin of the trees a huge shape moved, heading diagonally up the slope towards us.

'It's a brontomek,' I said uneasily. A needle of light probed the ground a hundred metres to our right, causing a dull red glow where it struck.

'It looks in a bad temper,' observed Susanna.

'I think it's out of control.'

The machine drove on, veering slightly and passing within fifty metres of us. I pulled Susanna down behind a rock outcrop. The lasers with which brontomeks are equipped are programmed to home in on heat sources. Their normal target is small agricultural pests, but I had never trusted their ability to distinguish humans...

'It'll be turning back in a minute, huh?' said Susanna doubtfully.

The machine drove on seawards, relentlessly.

'It's not going to turn,' said Susanna positively.

With suicidal, robotic singlemindedness the brontomek lumbered towards the cliff edge, tilted, and fell from view. The engine screamed momentarily as the drive raced, then there was a dull concussion, then silence.

I said, 'Christ,' in a tone of awe and regret at the astronomical costliness of this inexplicable accident, but that was merely for the sake of my public image as a responsible citizen. Privately, I felt a satisfying elation at this free show, and my only real regret was that we hadn't been standing nearer the clifftop, so that we could have seen the thing hit bottom.

'What fun,' said Susanna.

And yet the roaring continued, redoubled. I removed my fascinated gaze from the point where the brontomek had disappeared, looking back up the valley.

A dozen more giant shapes were driving inexorably towards the sea . . .

# ten

We ran down the hill towards the oncoming machines, stumbling, picking ourselves up, running on while the brontomeks approached steadily, their lasers quiescent. Unlike their leader, they were not in the mood for frying – merely mass suicide. As we ran the going suddenly became more difficult: we were now in the ploughed area and my feet were sinking up to the ankles in pulverized soil. I saw Susanna fall. I paused and helped her up.

She said, breathlessly, 'What the hell are we hoping to achieve, Moncrieff? You'd better have some good ideas.'

'Maybe we can save a few of them before they go over the edge.'

We stumbled towards the nearest machine; at that moment another moon emerged from the cloud cover and the scene leaped into sudden brilliance. The brontomek lumbered towards us like a rogue elephant, sensors twitching, huge jaws mindlessly agape. I allowed the brute to come close, stepped aside, jumped for the steps as it passed, grabbing the handrail. I shouted to Susanna to try to stop the next in line, and began to climb towards the tiny cab far above me.

I reached an intermediate platform and paused while the great machine throbbed beneath my feet. A conveyor belt ran nearby; small pieces of some propagating root crop slid past me and disappeared amid a glitter of plunging pistons at the rear of the machine, which seemed to be engaged in a mad planting spree.

I climbed on, entered the tiny cab. The controls were few. The machine was accustomed to operating under its own volition: human drivers were employed only under difficult manoeuvring. I looked around for the light switch but couldn't find it. Taking a quick glance out of the window I saw Susanna climbing to the cab of the brontomek to my right. The ground sped by, far below. Ahead, I could see the ocean, pale silver in the moonlight.

There had to be a stop control which overrode the automatic pilot. I pushed buttons, pulled levers without any visible effect – until I noticed giant cutters extending in front, chewing at the air. I had switched the computer to a harvesting programme. I pressed more buttons. I pulled at a long lever.

The brontomek lurched.

I dragged back on the lever and the huge machine began slowly to turn to the left. I found the lever's counterpart on the other side of my seat and pushed it forward. The brontomek slowed, began to spin slowly in its own length. I saw another vast bulk approaching head-on and aimed for it. Satisfied that I had set a collision course I left the cab, climbed quickly down the steps and jumped the last ten feet to the ground.

Nearby, a roaring machine reached the clifftop, paused for a second as it tilted and sprayed the air uselessly with fertilizer, then plunged from view. I felt a sudden terror. Was that the machine Susanna had been driving?

I saw her, running towards me. A brontomek passed between us, fountaining pulverized soil.

Then I heard the impact, and swung round.

The two machines had met at an angle and both had halted, balloon tyres spinning and churning dirt. The attachments around their jaws had become entangled – which was fortunate, otherwise they might have glanced off each other and continued on their way. As it was, they would stay like that and presumably run down, in time. At least I had saved two machines.

Susanna arrived painting at my side. 'I'm sorry, Kev. I couldn't seem to stop the goddamned thing. In the end I had to let it go.'

We looked around. About half of the brontomeks had disappeared over the cliff by now and the others were rapidly following, like gargantuan lemmings. There was nothing more we could do. There was not time to board a machine and climb to the cab before it went over the edge. Our only course was to do nothing and, absolved of all obligations, enjoy the scene.

A brontomek passed within metres, grunting and lurching, and reached the clifftop at an angle. A chance lie of the ground caused it to swerve and hang there, one giant wheel over the edge, the other churning air as the machine teetered on its belly, screaming. Then there was a gigantic crash as another brontomek, hastening to its death, collided with its struggling comrade. The two went together. By this time Susanna and I had been drawn fascinated to the cliff edge and we watched them fall, completing a half-roll each before they struck the base of the cliffs and scattered themselves over the beach in a mess of shattered steelwork.

'Look at that!' cried Susanna, suddenly.

The collided brontomeks still heaved mightily at each other like bulls, but now a new element had entered the contest. Due to some malfunction in the computers, they had commenced stabbing each other savagely with the lasers. Sparks showered in the moonlight. Behind us, the remaining machines tumbled to their destruction, but our interest was focused on the battling giants. As a needle of fire probed the ground nearby it occurred to me that we were in danger ourselves.

'Come away!' I caught Susanna's arm, pulling her back up the hillside.

'Do you really think you can show me something more fun than this?'

'I don't want you killed, stupid.' We crouched behind an outcrop of rock and watched from a safe distance.

A mad pattern was emerging as the machines fought to the death. The left-hand brontomek was firing in staccato bursts, raising crackling fountains of sparks from its opponent, but in a random manner, never concentrating its beams for long enough to do much damage. I was reminded of a dazed boxer who swings a wild flurry of blows with little weight, little effect. The right-hand brontomek, however, was employing a different tactic.

It was carefully and systematically cutting its opponent to pieces.

A turret fell, an ear sensor heeled over and dangled uselessly from its supporting gantry. One of the wheels slowed in its churning, stopped. The stabbing of its lasers became wilder, rays being aimed uselessly at the sky or raising puffs of smoke from the ground. The cabin caught fire; sputtering electrical flames darted from severed cables. The lasers winked out, one by one. A gush of fertilizer erupted from the rear. The tyres jerked spasmodically, then stilled. The machine was dead.

The other brontomek continued the butchery, slicing its motionless adversary into bite-sized pieces. Then, slowly, it began to move forward again, relentlessly pushing aside the shattered heap of scrap metal which was barring its path. Suddenly free, it lurched forward, accelerating, and raced across the valley, making for a small group of grazing Arcattle in the moonlit distance.

Minutes later, we saw the flash and thrust of lasers . . .

Susanna said shakily, 'That thing's gone mad, Kev. They're programmed to burn nothing larger than field pests. We were lucky it didn't come for us. How much fuel does it have?'

'Singleton told me they operate on minipiles. That means it could be months before it runs down.' I thought. 'They'll just have to hunt it down by air and bomb it to pieces. Otherwise it'll wipe out every animal in the area.'

'Every human being, too,' said Susanna.

We reported the incident to a watchman at the new deep-water harbour over the hill. The watchman – I think he was an amorph – called Sinclair Singleton and the two of them conversed for a while, alien to alien. The watchman relayed Singleton's questions to us and relayed our replies back; and somehow I began to feel like a schoolkid being interrogated about some misdemeanour. As a human being I felt in a secondary position, if not actually subordinate to the aliens, and I began to wonder who was running the planet, and what we Arcadians had got ourselves into, when we voted for the Hetherington takeover.

Then the watchman dismissed us and in his mild, friendly manner I detected the unspoken criticism: somebody must have caused those brontomeks to run amok, and it sure as hell wasn't an amorph...

As we left the place a vessel was slipping in between the headlands: the first of the seavesters. It was impossible to judge the overall size of the craft, since at least three-quarters of it must have been underwater – but it looked huge. A streamlined control tower projected above the surface and the disturbed water for hundreds of metres bore testimony to the vessel's displacement.

On the following morning I was on my way to Barker's dwelling unit when a high-pitched buzzing from my clothing announced that Newspocket had an important item. I slid the portovee from my pocket to see the angular face of Althea Gant on the screen. It was a fine early-summer morning and I sat on a nearby wall to find out what the hell she had to say. A few passersby paused, looking over my shoulder.

'This broadcast is for the benefit of the Riverside sub-colony only,' snapped Miss Gant, her expression not pleasant. 'And it is being transmitted to that area only – so if you people think you're getting any goddamned publicity for your criminal irresponsibility last night, you're mistaken. It's time you realized that the Organization has an investment in this planet which it intends to protect – and in such circumstances a group of dissident sub-colonists represent small fry.

'Last night some of your morons cut the power line to the Blackstone Agricultural Station and caused a black-out. Under cover of the confusion you tampered with the brontomeks and caused their destruction. Now, that takes more than one person – my guess is that twenty or more of you were involved.

'I want you to realize this. We can just as easily cut off supplies to you. That means food, fuel for your power plant, spare parts for your machinery – every goddamned thing you need. We can reduce you to a primitive existence – and we will, if there is one more repetition of this vandalism.

'And while you're fishing with your rotting nets and dug-out canoes, trying to gather enough food to keep yourselves alive – then we'll move in and possess your land, as we have every right to do.'

Althea Gant stared impassively from the screen. 'So what's it going to be, you little sub-colonists of Riverside? Cooperation – or slow death?'

I put the portovee back in my pocket. The onlookers had melted away. The street looked suddenly empty. There was a buzz from my pocket; I took the instrument out again. The face of Althea Gant appeared.

'This broadcast is for the benefit of the Riverside sub-colony,' she snapped. 'And it is being transmitted to that area only . . .'

And it would be, no doubt, over and over again. Until the Organization judged that Riverside had got the message . . .

The informal meeting at Mortimore Barker's dwelling unit was attended by Susanna and myself as persons directly involved with the circumnavigation, Mrs Earnshaw and Vernon Thrale as representatives of the Kindred of the Pioneers, and Tom Minty and Mark Swindon of the Colony Committee.

'I can only deplore the actions of these lunatics who have placed our entire project in jeopardy,' Barker began, standing huge and impressive in the small living-room, puffing at a rank cigar while the rest of us sat looking up at him. From this angle, his jowls resembled dirigibles.

'Yeah, well don't look at me when you say that,' said young Minty.

'Listen to me, you fool,' boomed Barker. 'There are just a few people in this colony capable of perpetrating last night's fiasco, and they're all friends of yours. Don't think I don't know who tried to foul up the Regatta by producing that ridiculous effigy of Hetherington. Let me tell you this: our jobs – our very lives – depend on putting Arcadia on the map. This will not be achieved by wanton destruction!' Unconsciously Barker had struck a pose: he stared sternly at a point one metre above Minty's head, his chest inflated. 'The Organization way – unpopular though it may be in some respects – is the only way.'

'You might be said to have a vested interest,' remarked Minty coolly. 'Perhaps you'll tell us how much above the standard wage they're paying you.'

As Barker's face reddened in huge outrage, Mrs Earnshaw snapped, 'Were you responsible for that goddamned effigy, Tom?'

'Kindred, kindred,' said Thrale helplessly.

Mark Swindon met my eyes; he shrugged. The meeting was off to a bad start.

Minty then attacked Mrs Earnshaw too, since she held a small tract of land to the south of the colony. Thrale sprang to Mrs Earnshaw's defence, adam's apple bobbing as he shrilled denials. Swindon and I kept out of it. Eventually accusation and counter-accusation ceased to sustain the meeting's interest, Tom Minty denied all connection with the Liberty Lovers, and as we began to sink into a state of exhausted apathy Mort Barker reintroduced the purpose of the meeting – his plans for the big launching date.

These exchanges were typical of the uncertainty which gripped Riverside during the succeeding weeks up to the date of the launching. In essence there were three factions.

There were those whom it suited to go along with the Organization; these included myself, Ralph Streng, Mort Barker. I also included Susanna in this group – although anyone less politically minded would be difficult to imagine. On the fringe of this group were Jane and Mark Swindon. Despite Mark's feud with the Organization regarding the seavesters his opinion was that Hetherington's way was the only way, at present. His was the common-sense outlook. Quite a number of colonists including the influential Enrico Batelli went along with him.

The second faction sat nervously on the fence, not wanting to offend the radicals, yet not wanting to lose their possessions in Organization reprisals. On that fence sat the Kindred of the Pioneers, led by Mrs Earnshaw. Ezra Blake and other property owners together with the fishermen also wobbled in unhappy alliance with this polychotomous group – which constituted the majority of the colony. They would not speak out against the Organization, yet from within their ranks came such surreptitious schemes as the Bartering Pool – which by now almost everyone had joined.

Finally we had the Lunatic Left, also known as the Liberty Lovers. Their members were unknown, but probably included a number of the ostensible fence-sitters. I suspected Tom Minty of being their leader – which meant that his friends Bill Yong and Jim Spark were among the followers. Chill Kaa was probably there, too.

It was a dangerous situation. It needed only one false move by the Organization – a mass confiscation of property, for instance – to turn the fence-sitters into rabid Liberty Lovers. Then all hell would break loose.

In this atmosphere of uncertainty, the preparations for the Great Voyage continued.

'Of course I know Streng can't climb into a boat that was launched five minutes ago and sail round the world,' Mortimore Barker said. 'All I'm saying is – we must give that impression to the Galaxy. The *Moncrieff Arcadian* slides down the slipway, the gallant skipper leaps aboard, takes the helm and sails away into the sunset, for Chrissake. Is that too much to ask?'

He was edgy. We were all edgy. 'Okay,' I said hastily, as Streng looked about to dispute something, 'After the trial runs I'll haul her back up the slipway, then you can have your goddamned show.'

Barker said, 'It's our show, not my show, Kev.'

Streng said, 'I want to make this perfectly clear. I'm not setting out on any goddamned voyage until that boat is completely checked out.'

In this manner the days went on, each of us trying to contain our personal worries in the context of the overall picture. By early Daleth the *Moncrieff Arcadian* was beginning to look like a ship. The mast was installed, capped by Streng's ridiculous anti-gravity device; much of the interior work was done, the sails had been delivered and the deck fittings mostly installed. With three weeks remaining to the launch date I decided it was time to get her into the water.

This time there was no ceremony. Susanna was there, of course; Barker, the Reverend Batelli and a few colonists watched from the wharf; Streng fussed about like a mother hen.

I was becoming increasingly concerned about Ralph Streng. His manner still held that inherent confidence – arrogance, almost – with the result that I found it difficult to disagree with his irrational suggestions, particularly when there were others present. The bastard always sounded as though he knew what he was talking about. This made it appear that I was trying to cut corners whenever I refused his outrageous requests.

On one occasion I had an unexpected ally.

'Listen to me,' Streng had said. We all listened, bystanders, boatyard staff, amorphs and all. 'If all that 3-V equipment goes at the mast-head it's going to cause excessive leverage in choppy seas. The rigging will be strained, liable to failure, and the boat top-heavy. You'll have to find some other way, Kevin.'

The onlookers nodded wisely.

Not for the first time, I thought fast and frantically, but my brain was already exhausted by the weeks of worry and frustration – not to mention the knowledge that we were a week behind schedule. 'I don't know,' I muttered uncertainly. 'We must have that overhead 3-V coverage. It was in the original agreement. I don't quite see how—'

'Well, I sure as hell can't help you,' snapped Streng. 'I'm not the goddamned builder. Just see it's done, huh?'

Barker suddenly made his presence felt. 'The 3-V gear goes at the top of the fucking mast and that's an end to it. We've lost enough time. You were hired as a skipper, Streng, not a fucking prima donna.'

Instantly Streng said, 'You're quite right, of course, Mort. Stupid of me. Maybe I'm trying to think of too many things at once, huh?'

And he smiled at us all, and apologized to me, and everything was all right until the next time.

So we slid *Moncrieff Arcadian* down the slipway and she travelled gently across the water until brought up by the rope. She bobbed there in the middle of the estuary looking good. The knot of colonists cheered with faint irony.

Mortimore Barker strolled up, wearing a brilliant patterned shirt in deference to the heat, his voluminous pants sustained by a huge, brass-studded belt. 'A fine sight,' he boomed. 'A credit to you, Kev.'

I said, 'I'll have to get the name painted on.'

Barker suddenly looked embarrassed. 'Don't be in any hurry. I don't think the Organization have finalized that, yet.'

'Well, tell them to hurry up, huh? We can't leave everything to the last minute.' We pulled the boat to the wharf.

Streng, Susanna and I climbed on board, descended to the cabin and for a while we discussed the stores needed, while Streng made lists on bits of paper. Recently he'd been noting down items such as dry cells, rice, matches, accumulating pockets full of scraps of paper and, in some cases, chips of wood, on which he'd scrawled reminders – which only he could decipher.

Weeks afterwards, picking an offcut of ply out of a pile of random pieces, I discovered a scribbled list on which I could make out only the word 'gauze' in Streng's characteristic doctor's scrawl. I've often wondered if he ever did take the items on that list, and whether any of them were useful...

But on that Gimel afternoon we were more intent on finding fault, and we soon persuaded Streng to start doing something useful – which, in this instance, was to test out the compressor and other mechanical gear. All this stuff had been tried on dry land: now we had to see whether it stood up to working conditions.

The compressor fired with a throaty roar, then died down to a mutter as Streng throttled back. I examined the water around the sponsons, and saw the disturbance of a million tiny bubbles rising to the surface.

'All correct, skipper,' said Susanna in relief, giving Streng a mock salute. He grinned back, the lines of tension easing for a moment. I found time to wonder about his wife. For several weeks now, she hadn't been seen around the colony. Kli a' Po with his alien sense of values had suggested that Streng had assimilated her, and it had taken us a moment to realize the creature was joking. Then Will Jackson let slip that he'd seen her at the window of her dwelling unit, and we relaxed.

I said, 'Tomorrow we try the sails out. We might make the deadline yet, eh?'

I'm older now, and I've learned the stupidity of such statements. Instantly there was a roar of escaping air and we were engulfed in wet fog.

I heard Streng yell something and grabbed at the compressor lever, throttling it back. The engine petered out, the hissing stopped. The mist cleared and we stared at the starboard sponson.

The problem was minor. The clip which secured the pressure hose to the intake had loosened and the hose had come off.

'Nothing serious,' I assured the others. 'We'll soon fix that.' I selected a screwdriver from the tool box.

'Nothing serious?' echoed Streng. 'By Christ, the boat's crippled and the man says nothing serious?'

'It's only a clip, Ralph,' said Susanna.

'Only a clip? For Christ's sake, my life depends on that clip! Just suppose it'd come off during a storm, where would I be?' He was staring at the dangling hose as though it were a hostile tentacle. 'Moncrieff, I'll have no clips on that pressure line. From now on, we use welded joints, you hear?'

I tried to reason with him. 'We've been through all that, Ralph. We reckoned with the flexing motion of the boat in a heavy sea, metal tubing might fracture. That's why we used rubber.'

'Flexing motion?' he yelled. 'There had sure as hell better be no flexing motion on this boat!'

He swarmed over the cabin roof, descended to the sponson and began to jump up and down, gauging its motion in relation to the rest of the craft. Susanna caught my eye; she raised her brows. I tried to smile back reassuringly at her.

By now Streng, apparently satisfied that the boat was not going to twist itself in half, was feverishly undogging the sponson hatch. He lay down, thrusting his hand through the hole. 'There's water in here, Moncrieff! The goddamned thing's leaking like a sieve! I can feel it coming in, for Christ's sake!'

I've launched many boats, before and since, but that was the worst launch I ever remember. Everything seemed to conspire to diminish Streng's already low fund of confidence.

'It's leaking because you've opened the hatch, Ralph,' I called. 'You've released the pressure which keeps the water out.'

'We'll capsize!' he shouted, frantically screwing the hatch back.

'No, there's foam buoyancy in there.'

He glanced across at me, red-faced as he worked. 'What good is that in a heavy sea, with a sponson half-full of water because the goddamned compressor's failed or something?'

'The sponson wouldn't fill. There's a one-way valve on the hose intake.'

'My God.' He scrambled back and rejoined us in the cockpit. 'My God. This is a frightening arrangement, Moncrieff. Everything depends on that compressor. You'll have to install a back-up machine, man. It's crystal clear to me why your other boat went to the bottom.'

A crimson cloud of insanity seemed to invade my brain and I stepped forward prepared to pulp his goddamned arrogant face. Suddenly Susanna was there, between us, holding on to me.

'Don't do it, Kev!' she cried as I tried to get around her. 'That's what they want to see!'

My vision cleared slightly and I looked up, and saw them grinning down at us from the quay: Will Jackson the sex maniac, Jim Spark the dotard, Chill Kaa, and others. Barker was there too, great face a mask of alarm, ponderously trying to climb down into the cabin.

I relaxed with an effort.

'All right, Streng,' I managed to say. 'You'll get your extra compressor, but we'll have to forget the goddamned deadline.'

One week before the launch was scheduled Althea Gant visited the colony and I tackled her on this subject.

'I'm sorry, Mr Moncrieff,' she said coldly, 'but you made a deal. The Organization has geared its entire campaign to a launch on the first of He. There's no way we can agree to a postponement.'

'But surely, on the basis of Streng's safety – which might mean the success of the voyage . . . ?'

The visiphone buzzed. It was some underling of hers, and when she returned to me I felt disinclined to pursue the subject. If the boat wasn't ready in time, there was nothing I could do about it. By the time I'd implemented a dozen or so further detail modifications insisted on by Streng, I calculated that we would be ten days behind schedule.

Meanwhile the final preparations were made in an atmosphere of frenzied activity bordering on panic. Everybody helped: Susanna, Streng, Barker, the Swindons, Batelli, Walters, all the good guys – while the rest of the colony grinned sceptically from a distance.

I'd had to order Streng away from the boatyard: the alternative would have been a strike by my men. Since the short fitting-out trials were complete – the boat had not performed quite as well as he'd hoped – Streng had been breathing down our necks constantly. The moment a man stepped back from his job Streng was there, checking on the workmanship. He turned up with weird devices which he insisted we install. He wanted a stainless railing fitted on the sponsons in case he needed to stand there: we fitted it. When he began to complain about the self-steering gear and demand dampers on the tiller, I called a halt.

'Get the hell out of here, Ralph,' I said, 'and don't come back until the launch, huh?'

So he busied himself with the stores and provisions. He

began to accumulate a pile of stuff down by the warehouse, constantly driving to Inchtown and further for items he suddenly deemed essential. Finally, bewildered by the multitude of things still to be done, he became obsessed with the one field which was within his personal experience – medicine. He began to stock up with splints and bandages, ointments and antiseptics, hypojets and antibiotics. I saw inside his instrument case once: he could have performed open heart surgery on himself, there was so much stuff there.

'It's probably the most important single factor in any lengthy voyage,' he told us one night when, utterly exhausted, we'd all repaired to the Social Club to drink ourselves unconscious. 'Health. More lives have been lost at sea through the failure to observe the simple basics of medicine, than through any other cause – and I include shipwreck, collision, typhoons, anything.'

And the onlookers nodded wisely...

'A slight cut on a man's finger, if left unattended, can turn septic in a day, gangrenous in two. I will not jeopardize our venture for the sake of a bottle of antiseptic...'

The alarming thing was, he'd said all this before, almost word for word, a few days ago when a camera crew and Mort Barker had interviewed him...

So the preparations dragged on in a haze of alcohol and haste. The deadline was two days away and the men were still working on board; they'd be working for days. I called Althea Gant.

'The Organization is quite within its rights in withholding payment for your work, under the terms of our contract,' she said icily.

'So I take the boat out to sea and sink it, huh?'

'There's no call for that attitude, Mr Moncrieff. To tell the truth, I was expecting this delay. I had already postponed the Organization's plans until next week. But the fact remains that you have not lived up to your contract – consequently you will not be paid; not yet.'

My mouth was dry; I stared at the screen, at that thin, harsh face. 'When will I get my money?' I asked.

'The full amount will be paid on successful completion of the voyage. Put Mr Streng on, will you? I wish to speak to him.'

I found Streng and went back to the boatyard, slightly

numbed with forebodings. If the voyage failed now, I would lose everything. I'd be even deeper in debt than I was before I took on the deal. And even looking on the bright side, if the voyage went well, I'd have to stall all my creditors for another few months; all those people to whom I'd promised payment within days...

And then it occurred to me. It was the Organization I owed that money to. They'd taken over the yacht chandlers, the lumber yard, the supermarket...

And they'd taken over me.

# eleven

Launchday minus two.

The final coats of paint and varnish were applied. A team of amorphs began cleaning up the slipway, stowing away the half-empty paint cans and offcuts of hard Arcadian timber, preparing the area for the ceremonial equipment: the 3-V cameras, the platform, the seats. These workers were paid for by the Organization. As they completed their task another force arrived in a truck with prefabricated timbers and started erecting things. Megaphones roared out instructions, cameras whirred through dummy takes. In this atmosphere, we tried to complete the boat.

Barker directed the installation of the boat cameras. 'That one on the bracket at the mast-head – it won't quite have a 360 degree field because of the thickness of the mast.'

Susanna paced across the cabin roof, stood on the forward edge. 'Which means you can pee into the ocean from *here*, if you must. Careful how you turn round afterwards.' She grinned at the lone yachtsman.

'Goddamned invasion of a man's privacy, these cameras,' Streng muttered.

'And another on the afterdeck, just above the rudder.' Barker indicated the place. 'That covers the cockpit and the main cabin, which should be enough. I think we can do without a camera in your bedroom, Streng. I'm sure the Sector won't be interested in whatever the hell goes on in there.'

'And the microphones?' I asked, wondering how else Barker could ruin the lines and the finish of my boat.

'We'll bug the main cabin, the cockpit – and the forward decking, I think, so that Streng can lie there and philosophize, with the boat on automatic pilot. That will give a nice suggestion of relaxation, of security.'

'Be sure to remind me to philosophize from time to time,' said Streng sarcastically.

Barker glanced at him. 'Uh, we can't do that. Communication is strictly one-way, I'm afraid.'

'What the hell do you mean?'

'I mean no radio, no receiver of any kind on the boat. This is strictly a lone voyage, Ralph. Which means you hear nothing, see nothing of humanity until you get back. Otherwise there's no point. We can see you and hear you – but, as far as you're concerned, you're on your own. Every attempt is being made to convince the Sector of the authenticity of this voyage. There'll be observers at the launch and they'll check the whole goddamned boat for hidden aids, like a propeller driven off the compressor or anything like that. Your trip is on the level, Ralph.'

'I would hope so,' murmured Streng calmly, with a sudden return to his old manner. 'I'm undertaking this voyage because of the challenge it presents me, and I certainly wouldn't countenance any faking.'

He wandered off and we saw little of him for the rest of that day. Later Susanna and I had to go to Oldhaven Aerogeographical Institute to pick up the satellite photographs which were to serve Streng as charts. We left yet another list of items for the Swindons to buy in Inchtown, jumped into my hovercar and moved briskly off.

Later we walked hand in hand along the road behind the beach. It was two years since I'd seen Oldhaven and the place hadn't changed much. People lay on the sand, watching the waves lapping at their feet, and a name came into my mind . . .

Wendy.

There was a little girl just like Wendy sitting with her parents on the beach nearby; she was tracing patterns in the sand with a chubby finger. Her hair was fair and drawn into a pony tail, her cheeks were plump and she caught my eye and smiled. She looked about nine years old.

I hoped she lived to be a hundred.

Susanna had stopped walking; I stopped too. She said, 'Huh?'

'I was here when the Minds made the people walk,' I said.

'Would you rather we went home now?'

'No. I'm OK. There was a little girl . . .'

She grinned me out of it. 'Hell, Moncrieff, don't you ever draw the line? Isn't there any age at which a woman can say: I'm the wrong age for Moncrieff? You even like old Mrs Earnshaw, don't you.'

'I guess so. She's an old bastard, though. A likeable old bastard, I reckon.'

She sighed in despair. 'Just my luck. I had to run into a guy who loves all women of all ages.' She sat down on a low wall, pulled me beside her. 'And I thought he loved only me. Now I find the only reason he loves me, is because I'm a woman. Hell. Moncrieff, is there *any* woman that you'd draw the line at, for God's sake?'

I thought. 'I can't stand a stupid woman,' I said at last.

'Not even if she's as beautiful as the ocean, Moncrieff?'

'Not even then. Women ought all to be beautiful and smart and funny and strong like Susanna Lincoln – or even ugly and smart and unhappy and angular like Althea Gant – but a stupid woman is an abomination and I don't want anything to do with her. The thing isn't confined to sexes. I can't take stupid men, either. Chill Kaa, for instance.'

She regarded me gravely. 'We all have to live, Kev.'

'Maybe that's what my problem is. Maybe I feel that these people wouldn't have survived under a more basic system. In early Earth, for instance, a woolly mammoth would have stamped on Streng's pathetic wife within minutes – but there are no carnivores on Arcadia. Or Earth, for that matter. I think I'm frightened that there's nothing to prevent fools from multiplying any more, they're so well protected. Natural selection has no effect on the human gene pool and I'm frightened we're on the way down as a race.'

Susanna said, 'Okay. You know it and I know it, and politicians and insurance companies and salesmen and publicity men like Mort Barker capitalize on it. But you can't do anything about it and the crunch won't come until long after we're dead. And you've forgotten one thing.'

'What's that?'

'The process is reversible. Some day an alien race will arrive which is genetically compatible with the human race.'

'That's a long shot,' I said gloomily, regarding the humans lying in animal mindlessness on the beach.

'You think so, Kev? That's because your concepts aren't flexible enough. Now – just think about the implications behind the amorphs...'

Once I'd asked Susanna what she'd worked at before she came to Arcadia, and it turned out that she'd been a research assistant at a laboratory involved in temporal studies on Earth. 'It closed down,' she said. 'We established the existence of parallel worlds due to a lucky coincidence – and then there was nothing more we could do. The Director got himself killed and the thing folded.' So she'd come to Arcadia as a scientist, and found her niche as an agency model. She must have been the smartest model in the Sector.

'Tell me about the amorphs,' I requested.

She stood, pulling me to my feet, grinning. 'I don't want to raise any false hopes in that pessimistic mind of yours. Ask Mark Swindon, huh? He's the biologist among us. Now talk about something else. Oldhaven isn't good for you; I can see that.'

As we left the coastal city a seavester was moving majestically out to sea, trailing a faint haze of pale smoke.

We arrived back at Riverside in the late afternoon. This lateness was due to an uncontrollable need for physical activity which came over us some five kilometres short of the sub-colony, and resulted in our leaving the vehicle, climbing up a grassy hillside among Arcattle droppings and sleepy ground-worrals, and abandoning our senses to a passion almost frightening in its intensity.

There was an air of buoyant optimism at the boatyard, for a change – despite the fact that Althea Gant was there. Jane Swindon took one look at us and grinned knowingly. What is this strange aura that surrounds two people who have recently had sex? I felt as though Susanna and I were enclosed in a giant fuzzy pink cocoon which was blatantly visible to all those excluded from it. Fortunately Jane was the only one who noticed: the others were grouped around Althea Gant's News-pocket.

'...And so Arcadia strides ahead,' the commentator was snapping. 'And the future for this once-beleaguered world looks assured. Every planetfall brings new immigrants, new equipment ...' He raved on while the screen showed huge building machines rolling across an endless concrete plain. Space shuttles stood like militant giraffes in the background. It might have been anywhere, but then I recognized a landmark and knew that it was indeed Premier City Spaceport.

But there were new buildings around the perimeter, many of them, gleaming silver rectangles and domes. The audience murmured its appreciation and, stealing a quick glance at Althea Gant, I saw that her lips were slightly parted, a glow of excitement transforming her plain face...

So the pictures were for real. Arcadia really *was* striding ahead. Martial music blared from the little portovee and the camera zoomed in on a uniformed man, standing at ease with laser loosely held.

'He's not an amorph,' somebody said quietly. 'You couldn't get an amorph to carry a gun.'

'I told you the amorphs were only a temporary measure,' Althea Gant said reprovingly.

'How much are they being paid?' said the same voice; I looked around, and saw it was Mrs Earnshaw, a rare visitor to my boatyard.

Althea Gant didn't reply, and in the suddenly constrained atmosphere I looked around and saw that the name had been painted on the bows of the boat.

*Arcadian.*

I said to Miss Gant, 'They've left off half the name, haven't they?'

She regarded me coldly, her lips pursed. 'I don't think so,' she said...

'It was part of the goddamned deal!' I insisted, as we sat in the Social Club that night, indulging in a pre-launch party. 'My name was to be used on the boat as publicity for me.'

'Hell, it doesn't really signify,' boomed Barker placatingly. 'Everyone knows you built the boat, Kev.'

'Do they know on Aldebaran, for Christ's sake? Do they know on Earth?'

'You were the first to be in breach of contract, Mr Moncrieff,' said Althea Gant precisely. 'In any case, the Organization feels that the impact will be lost, if the boat's name is cluttered up with extraneous matter. It is Arcadia which is our prime concern.'

Streng said, 'She's right, of course,' and the others nodded...

'I trust your wife will be at the ceremony, Ralph,' said Miss Gant, changing the subject.

'Of course. Hazel has been unwell lately – a serious allergy which affects her at this time of year, and always seems resistant to any of the antihistamines. She's always reluctant to show herself at these times – the vanity of women is a curious thing, but fortunately Hazel can overcome such foibles.'

I watched Streng carefully during this stilted little apology, but he seemed sincere enough. Nobody seemed about to pursue the matter and a strained silence began, which was broken by the arrival of Mrs Earnshaw and a group of people who sat at the next table. Vernon Thrale was there, Tom Minty and his henchmen, Elsie Cotter and a couple of the Kindred – and a stranger.

This group sat in a significant silence, watching us in the way people do when they await comment. They watched us and we watched them, and I wasn't the only one who was wondering what the hell it was all about. At last Streng spoke, rising to his feet and approaching the stranger.

He held out his hand. 'Ralph Streng,' he said.

The man took it. He was an indeterminate-looking guy, pale of face with mousy hair and there was something just a shade effeminate about him. 'John Doe,' he said.

Althea Gant said abruptly, 'All right. Who the hell is that man?' She stared belligerently at Mrs Earnshaw.

The old woman smiled back calmly. 'You heard him. He says his name is John Doe. Are you denying him the right to a name?'

Suddenly we understood...

Althea Gant was on her feet. 'That creature is an amorph! You've stolen it from the Agricultural Station!' Her face was pink with fury. 'Unless you return it immediately it will be confiscated. Proceedings will be taken against you and your accomplices!'

'Tell her, John. Do you want to go back?' asked Mrs Earnshaw.

'No,' said the amorph firmly. 'I like it here.'

'You see?' crowed the old woman triumphantly. 'John is a member of an intelligent species and therefore entitled to freedom of choice, under Galactic Law. He stays with us. In due course he'll be asking his friends to join him. I think we know what the answer will be. The Organization's days of slave labour are over!'

'Hold it there, before you get in deeper than you know.' Miss Gant had regained control of herself. 'Let me tell you this. The amorphs are not an intelligent species, and the Organization owns them. Just as you, Mrs Earnshaw, own that goddamned goat of yours. Any appearance of intelligence on the part of the amorphs is illusory, since they have no free will. Every thought they have is planted in their minds by humans – and can be amended by us too, if necessary. The whole question's been fought before. Forget it and put the thing back where it belongs, and I'll say no more about it.'

'Batelli!' snapped Mrs Earnshaw to the priest. 'You set this woman right.'

Batelli looked thoughtful. 'Intelligence has often been defined,' he murmured at last, 'but I don't see that it affects the issue. Nearly all creatures are intelligent to a greater or smaller degree – and plenty of them are the subjects of more intelligent species. It's in the natural order of things. I find I'm unaffected by emotional words like slavery. If Miss Gant has the power to take and control that amorph, or to force Mrs Earnshaw to give it up by whatever means at her disposal – then that is simply a fact, nothing more.'

'Listen to me, Batelli,' snarled Mrs Earnshaw. 'I've known for a long time that you were a pretty goddamned strange priest. Only a freak could hold his morning service on the goddamned wharf tomorrow because a publicity agent told him to!'

There was a moment while we assimilated this rapid change of subject, then Batelli said in mild tones, 'Mort Barker told me it would look good, publicity-wise, if I held tomorrow's service around the boat. He was quite frank about it. In his own words, he said that a shot of religion would give the junket class.'

'It's goddamned irreverent, for Christ's sake!' spluttered Mrs Earnshaw.

Batelli regarded her calmly. 'Irreverence is meaningless in any context. My God has no pride. Pride is a sin, but God is good. On His behalf I do what is best for the greatest number.'

Mortimore Barker chuckled. 'Tell it how it is Enrico, that's my boy.' He turned to Streng. 'You hear that, Ralph? Surely, for a guy like this, you'll agree to be filmed praying tomorrow at the launch? Seriously, it'd go over big in the Sector.'

Streng smiled slowly. 'I appreciate your concern for my spiritual welfare, Mort. But for me to be seen by a group of colonized worlds doing anything so illogical as praying is more than my pride would stand. I'm no God, you realize.'

And so the evening wore on, and the arguments continued. They were bound to, with so many different views, so many different interests present. The occasion was intended to be a party, but at times it more resembled a civil war. Nothing was decided, of course. Views were aired, insults bandied – and afterwards, everyone felt a little worse about everyone else.

Around midnight there was an event so totally unexpected that it was spoken of for weeks afterwards, whenever the drinkers gathered in the Club. There was something of a commotion outside: the slamming of doors, the yapping of authoritative voices.

A group of men entered, dressed in white coats. They talked together absorbedly as they walked through the door; they hardly glanced at the roomful of people. They were strangers to us. Following closely behind came four women, also dressed in white. They parted like theatre curtains to reveal a wheelchair.

Swathed in blankets, his huge head protruding above them like a giant toad emerging from a swamp, was a man. His eyes were bulbous, his lips thick and slack, his complexion florid. Apart from his face, only his feet could be seen, neatly shod in shiny black shoes, the right foot beating a continuous tattoo on the footrest of the chair. A doctor bent forward, dabbed a bead of froth from the corner of the shapeless lips; another checked the dials and gauges on a console which occupied the entire left side of the chair...

And so we watched in horrified, fascinated silence the arrival of Hetherington, the armless tycoon who owned half the known Galaxy.

As they wheeled the dreadful thing to a position of prominence, a thread of muscle twitched on the cheek, a bloodshot eye rolled and regarded me with globular intelligence and the lips mouthed something faintly – but not so faintly as to elude the tiny microphone before that loathsome face...

I'll never know what Hetherington said. But I think it was something about me.

'I name this boat *Arcadian*,' pronounced Althea Gant shrilly. 'And may God bless the man who sails in her.'

So saying she swung the bottle which caused a visible blemish on the paintwork but failed to shatter. Barker lumbered forward, grasped her thin hand in his huge paw, and together they swung, and this time foaming liquor cascaded wastefully down the prow.

The crowd cheered. There were a few derisive noises.

Slowly the *Arcadian* slid down the slipway – this effect a miracle of electric motors, wires and pulleys – and plunged into the brown water of the estuary. A band began to play, 'Forward Arcadia'. A rope tightened and the catamaran moved in a broad arc, finally coming to rest against the wharf, where the rest of the performance was to take place.

'All right so far,' commented Mark Swindon in my ear.

Susanna was posing tastefully against the cabin roof, presumably to remind the Galaxy of the sacrifices a lone yachtsman was to make. My part in the public proceedings was over. I'd answered a few short questions from Barker concerning the boat's structural soundness and he'd sabotaged my efforts – in the interests of highlighting the dangers Streng was to face.

'But the point is that he'll overcome them, my boy,' Barker placated me afterwards, 'thanks to his unquenchable courage and the stalwart construction of his doughty vessel, built by Moncrieff. We have months to get that point across. Right now, what we want is drama.'

Earlier on, we'd had drama in plenty. While Batelli had held his service on the port side of the boat, we'd worked on the starboard, loading the last-minute stores, attaching the sails to the rigging, fuelling up, checking lists, trying to ignore the ominous silence of Streng – whom everyone had expected to go totally and reassuringly berserk at this point. But he said nothing as a helper ripped a sail, as a search of the slipway failed to uncover a missing case of liquor, as the fuel pipe broke and filled the cockpit with diesel fuel. The panic increased, the rest of us grew more jumpy, more incoherent: but Streng stood silently by, watching expressionlessly.

We'd have liked to think he was calm and confident, but in point of fact I think he was stunned into a state of catalepsy by the magnitude of his task, by the unpreparedness of the boat and by the incompetence of those around him.

But now he stood beside the floating *Arcadian*, his right hand gripping the shrouds in the rehearsed pose. Susanna withdrew tactfully as the cameras picked up the dumpy form of Hazel Streng, approaching from the left.

'She doesn't have much of a presence,' Barker had admitted to me earlier. 'In fact, I'd thought of using Susanna for his wife. But this is a big scene and it was too risky.' He nodded towards the impartial observer who had arrived that morning and was examining the boat for hidden aids.

I glanced at the monitor. Hazel Streng was in close-up, and I'd have sworn there were real tears on her cheeks as she moved towards her husband and they kissed with every appearance of sincerity. Off camera, Barker was gesticulating like an orchestra conductor, mouthing instructions, raising his eyes skywards as some little detail offended his sensibilities. He was the master artist, intent on extracting maximum impact from his canvas. I noticed the impartial observer – a professor of law on sabbatical from Earth – smiling in reluctant appreciation.

Barker hurried past me. 'My God,' he muttered, mopping his brow with a large white handkerchief. 'I thought Ralph was going to retch when his goddamned wife kissed him.' He approached the podium where the dignitaries were grouped, murmured a few words to Althea Gant, nodded to the enigmatic form of Hetherington in the wheelchair, and came back. Together we watched Streng and his wife saying whatever people say to each other in such circumstances. 'The sound is off,' Barker explained reverently. 'This moment is too precious for public ears.'

Finally the Hetherington entourage slid into the scene from left, Barker stepped up with the microphone and made a few introductory remarks, then gave way to Althea Gant.

There is no need to dwell on Miss Gant's address: it followed the expected pattern dealing in turn with Streng, the lonely sea, God, Hetherington and the Organization's future plans for the planet Arcadia. It was not in any way inspired, but it was probably exactly the right speech for the occasion. It finished on a note of mawkish sentimentality as one of Hetherington's attendants placed a box on the table before the wheelchair. The great man nodded slightly, as though giving the box his blessing. Althea Gant lifted the lid.

She took out a medium-sized, Earth-type Siamese cat.

'The ship's cat is a tradition from the earliest days when Man ventured forth on the mighty oceans of the planet Earth,' said Miss Gant, her thin face contorted into a fond smile as the animal struggled in her arms. 'And who are we to deny our courageous pioneer this one little companion? Ralph, I give you Melissa, and may she be company for you on this historic voyage.'

Streng, obviously taken aback, took hold of the cat gingerly and tucked it under his arm, freeing his hands because Barker had now stepped forward bearing a further gift.

'My contribution also has long been known as companion for lonely men on the high seas,' the publicity man intoned. 'I hope that this gift provides you with as much pleasure, food for thought and comfort in time of need as it has done me.'

So saying, and with a perfectly straight face, he handed Streng a black-bound Bible with a conspicuous cross on the cover.

'Thank you,' mumbled Streng, wrestling with the cat.

'There is an inscription inside the cover,' said Barker, his voice beginning to choke up with emotion. 'Please don't read it now, my boy. Wait until you're over the horizon.' He took out his vast handkerchief and made play with it.

Meanwhile Althea Gant was making a similar gracious presentation of the cat's mate to Mrs Streng, with fulsome remarks designed to ensure that the Sector did not miss the symbolism of the gift. It was those left behind who played the most difficult role, she said – a sentiment which I privately doubted.

Streng dropped the item into the cockpit and paused uncertainly, aware like all of us that an anti-climax was to come. However, Barker had allowed for this. In unison, the assembled fishing fleet blew their foghorns and columns of water sprang skywards from their hoses. Streng swung himself on deck. The ropes were cast off, the sails hoisted. The cat leaped to the cabin roof and stood watching in alarm as an expanse of brown water opened up between itself and safety.

We climbed into a launch and joined the flotilla of trawlers, skitterbugs and other craft following Streng and the *Arcadian* down the estuary. Mixed noises came from the crowded wharf, but the microphones by now had been switched off.

'He's on his own now,' remarked Barker, standing beside

Susanna and me in the spacious cockpit of the launch. A monitor on the seat showed a split image: to the left, Streng's back could be seen as he bent down, working at something in the cockpit. The other image was an overhead view: we saw him jerk his head up, correct his course, and return to unravel what appeared to be an orgy of copulating snakes on his cockpit floor.

'You goddamned fool, Moncrieff!' Streng's voice yelled and I looked up from the screen to find that we'd drawn alongside him. 'Couldn't you have sorted this out before the launch?'

There was a puff of wind and he pulled rapidly away from us, sails drawing well. I wheeled round on Barker. 'Did that go out to the Sector?' I asked savagely.

'Of course, Kev. Nothing is censored from now on; that's the deal. He's on the air continuously, except for a few hours in the middle of the night when nothing will be happening anyway.'

'What sort of advertisement is that for me? He called me a goddamned fool!'

'Take it easy. It's good copy and it shows that our yachtsman is human. We have months to sell your product, Kev. Let's make the most of our moments of excitement. Most of this voyage is going to be pretty goddamned dull.'

Streng was well ahead now, trailing neat parallel wakes as he moved into broader reaches of the estuary. The skitterbugs buzzed around him like mosquitoes, but the rest of us were dropping behind. I glanced up at the north headland: there was something a little out of place in that familiar skyline. I put the binoculars to my eyes.

The rogue brontomek jumped into focus, crouching there like a squat sentinel, watching the waters and the doings of Man with timeless, mechanical indifference.

Susanna said, 'If anyone can make this trip, Ralph can.' She gazed beyond the opening between the headlands, at the glittering ocean beyond. 'Just one man, alone for thousands of miles.'

'And a cat,' I said. 'Don't forget the goddamned cat.'

'That's no cat,' said Barker briefly.

'What do you mean?'

The publicity man smiled. 'You don't think I took the chance of having our man go insane with the solitude, did you? Hell, there's too much at stake to allow any chance of failure. No – that creature with Streng is an amorph.

'In due course, I trust it will transform itself into Streng's ideal of what a woman should be.'

'You goddamned crook, Mort,' I whispered in admiration. 'Does he know?'

'Hell, no. You know Ralph. He's stubborn. He wouldn't have accepted it.'

Susanna said, 'Suppose it begins to change shape in front of the cameras? The whole sector would know what you've pulled. And you can't warn him to get it out of sight. He has no radio receiver.'

Barker roared with laughter, a huge fat laugh of delight at his own cunning. 'What the hell do you think was written in the flyleaf of that Bible?' he boomed gleefully.

There was silence after that. By the time we reached the gap in the headlands *Arcadian* was a small neat shape in the vastness of the ocean. Above us, the brontomek stared down, ear sensors bent our way. A tentative needle of light probed the water, raising a little puff of steam.

# twelve

The circumference of the planet Arcadia is around thirty thousand kilometres and its single equatorial continent roughly rectangular in shape and occupying one-tenth of the planet's surface. Riverside is situated at the extreme east of this land mass, some fifteen degrees south of the equator.

Along the whole of the southerly shore of the continent the prevailing winds blow west, due to the rotation of the planet. There are a few local variations to this rule, caused by the lie of the land, the time of day, and the season of the year. Similarly the ocean currents south of the continent flow from east to west. Nine-tenths of Arcadia's surface is covered by water with comparatively small ice-caps at the north and south poles. Across a wide band to the north of the south pole, both wind and current flow in the opposite direction, west to east.

Streng's circumnavigation was therefore planned in a westerly direction. He would skirt the southern edge of the land mass at a distance of around one hundred to two hundred kilometres offshore, to take full advantage of the prevailing tides and wind, while minimizing the effect of local variations. When he reached the westward extreme of the continent he would keep on going at a latitude of around twenty degrees, eventually turning northwest and arriving back in Riverside to a carefully staged and tumultuous welcome.

At the rate of 300 kilometres per day – a conservative estimate, I thought – he would be home in a little over three Arcadian months, arriving approximately the fifteenth of Cheth.

Against this background of careful calculation, and with Streng himself safely over the horizon and by now running south-west, I was able to relax. My part in the affair was over. In the course of the next few days I visited my various creditors in Premier City; discovered, as I had suspected, that they were all now agencies of the Organization, and laid my cards on the table. They agreed to wait for payment. They had no option.

Even Jake of Jake's Chandlery accommodated me. 'Sure, Kev,' he said jovially. 'Your credit's good with me.'

'Since when?' I asked suspiciously. Nearby, the angel-faced amorph was stocking the shelves, displaying a length of strong thigh, a heavy curve of breast.

Jake watched her possessively as he spoke. 'Since the Organization cleared you.'

As I left I glanced at the sign above the door: it was changed, now. It read HETHERINGTON CHANDLERY. I caught sight of Jake back in the store: he was swinging the girl down from the stepladder and running his hand up her leg in the process.

He'd been bought out. This was no case of a temporary takeover with a return to original ownership after five years. The price? Enough cash to live comfortably despite the low standard wage – plus the girl of his dreams. It made me wonder. I wondered just how many lands and businesses would be returning to private ownership, in five years' time.

Nevertheless it seemed that my own situation was comfortable, and I had no intention of selling out. I spent the next few days cleaning up the yard and planning the production of my next run of skitterbugs – I was through with sailing vessels, for a while. I laid off my rented amorphs, who drifted into the colony in various capacities, and quickly proved popular.

Since the launch, Sinclair Singleton had temporarily lost control of his charges. Mrs Earnshaw's original amorph, John Doe, had been used to persuade other agricultural station workers to join the colonists, and all of them began quickly to assimilate the independent outlook of the rest of us. It would take some intensive indoctrination by Althea Gant and her assistants to get them back to normal. Even their appearance began to change, proving that they were not so permanent in form as the Organization had led us to believe. An amorph who Will Jackson was using to repaint his small dinghy even began, gradually but unmistakeably, to change sex...

We discussed this one day on the wharf. Mark Swindon was there, Kli a' Po the dispossessed, and Susanna, looking gorgeous.

Kli's snout was bared in a leathery grin as he watched two small replicas of himself swimming in the muddy water. 'You see, there?' he pointed with a tentacle. 'That one, that's an amorph.'

I stared at the little creature as it scrambled to the wharf and shook itself, then kicked water in the face of its companion with a croak of laughter. 'Isn't that the damnedest thing?' said one of my men, who happened to overhear.

'Such is the vanity of the human race,' observed Kli. 'They see nothing strange in an amorph assuming human form – but let one take the shape of Kli a' Po, and they point the finger of amazement.'

Mark laughed. 'That's not quite fair, Kli. It's the concept of an amorph resembling a known person which is surprising. Usually they take the shape of some indeterminate love-object. Some sort of ideal. In the case of a man, this would likely be a composite of all the qualities he'd ever admired in a woman. But he might be so single-minded in his love for one particular woman that she alone would constitute his Te. Any amorph, exposed to him, would take the shape of that one woman. Idealized, of course. All the little faults that the rest of us might have noticed in that woman would be missing. The amorphs around here are not representative. They've been exposed to humans for so long that their ability to change shape has become limited – so their defence mechanism tends to operate on a mental level. They assume pleasant personalities. No, the amorphs in Riverside would have to be exposed to one person only, for several days, for a physical change to be significant.'

'You had contact with the amorphs in Premier City, Mark,' said Susanna. 'Don't try to tell us you haven't discovered what your Te looks like.'

He laughed. 'Okay, okay. If you must know, my Te looks very much like Jane, thank God. But not quite exactly like her. There's just enough difference for her to start asking questions, if ever she saw it.'

There was a thoughtful silence. It was apparent that we hadn't yet realized all the implications of having amorphs living among us . . .

'How's Streng?' I asked, wondering about the Siamese cat.

'Fine, so far,' Susanna told us. Significantly, Newspocket were not broadcasting the progress of the lone yachtsman on the Arcadian channel. Our only news came from the temporary studio at the back of the marine Research Station, where Barker was presiding over a small team of technicians, blending the scene with his own brand of dramatic expertise before relaying it on to Newspocket headquarters in Premier City. 'He's around a thousand kilometres south-west, still tidying up the boat. She seems to be performing well.'

We watched a number of covered trucks glide over the bridge and climb the hill into the colony. 'At least the Organization hasn't cut off supplies yet,' I observed.

'Mort Barker's been getting some calls from Althea Gant,' said Susanna. 'I think there's going to be trouble unless those amorphs are sent back. Apparently the Agricultural Station's empty now; they've all been recalled to Premier City until harvesting time. Except the dozen or so that the Kindred are holding on to. Gant's asking them. And she's got wind of the Cooperative bartering system too. The Organization doesn't like it.'

'They'll find it difficult to stop the Kindred,' said Mark. 'Old Mrs Earnshaw has the bit between her teeth. I think the Organization might easily underestimate the power of the culture bug.'

He gazed across the estuary pensively. 'Colonists have no real history, no real background – and they're very conscious of it. Every intelligent being carries a terrible memory of that time before birth, when it fought its way from Nil to the consciousness of Self. Our primary instinct – self-preservation – is based on that memory; that fight must not have been in vain.

'And the absence of a history, of a background, is symbolic of Nil. It is a terrible nothingness like the time before birth. It is to be avoided at all costs.

'Now – culture is comforting, in that it represents history in tangible form. When a person weaves a basket according to ancient skills, it can be seen, and touched. Although not a historic item, it is *of* the past and therefore reassuring. Even replicas of historic monuments and reproductions of ancient art are valid from this point of view – even more so, if the viewer believes they are genuine. A history book is not so valid, however, because the events it describes cannot be seen or touched and are quite obviously second-hand and transparently susceptible to faking.

'So the Kindred of the Pioneers weave their baskets and dance their traditional dances, screen-print their fabrics and sing their folk songs. It's reactionary, it's a re-living of the past by people who are scared of the future. It's a desperate clinging to a Something by people who are scared of the Nothing all around them. If you like, it's a substitute for God – who Himself is a substitute for logic.'

We stared at Mark and he looked back at us, smiling faintly. There was an eerie familiarity about his words.

'Ralph Streng ...' murmured Susanna at last. 'That's pure Streng.'

'It just popped into my head,' grinned Mark. 'A relic of a drunken evening in our yachtsman's unit a couple of months ago.'

'For a moment I thought you really believed all that slick crap,' I said. 'Hell, I wouldn't give much for the future of colonization, if Streng were right.'

Mark said, 'Maybe I do believe it. Because it's slick, it isn't necessarily crap, you know. Slickness is also a characteristic of simple truth ...' he hesitated. 'There's a rumour going around the colony that Streng's gift pussycat is actually an amorph. Do you know anything about this, Kev?'

'Maybe,' I admitted guardedly, wondering what this had to do with anything. Chukalek appeared at the other end of the wharf, hurrying towards us with his jerky gait, a legacy of past attacks of bleeding.

Mark watched the approaching cook absently. 'Because if this is true, then it could be dangerous. An amorph will change into a normal person's ideal. But would we call Ralph a normal person? Remembering what we know about his philosophy, would you even say that he had an ideal, animate or abstract? In my opinion, Ralph is so logical, so unemotional in his outlook that the amorph won't know what to change into. And since the transformation is an instinctive defensive mechanism – what other method of defence might the creature be forced to employ?'

As we sat considering this one, Chukalek arrived, breathless. One hand was deep in his pocket, while the muscles of his forearm flexed and relaxed, flexed and relaxed.

'Maybe you'd better come up to the colony,' he panted. 'There's trouble. The Organization men have arrived. They're searching for their amorphs.'

The Organization team consisted of a dozen armed men and Althea Gant. They'd ridden concealed in a supply truck and had emerged at the Social Centre. 'Like goddamned genies,' Chukalek had told me, kneading frenziedly at his handful of dingy dough.

And now they were in possession of the colony, standing in the street outside the Social Club while Althea Gant addressed the cowed populace. It is quite amazing, the daunting effect a show of uniforms has on a group of civilians. He was a clever man, who first found out that a mob is beaten if each member thinks that he, personally, is outnumbered. The laser rifles were quite secondary.

'Right,' shouted Althea Gant. 'You've been warned often enough. Now we're moving in. Troops will be stationed here to ensure there are no recurrences of the recent outbreaks. The amorphs will be repossessed immediately. I'll urge you to give them up now, otherwise the search will continue. Furthermore, all private land is confiscated – under the terms of our purchase of this planet. We've been lenient long enough. Now you are going to pay for your fun.'

As the roar of protest died, Chill Kaa said to me bitterly, 'You see the sort of people your bosses are? They waited until after their goddamned launch ceremony before moving in. They didn't want their publicity spoiled – but now Streng's safely on his way, they can do what the hell they like.'

'I'm not so sure about that, Chill,' countered Mark Swindon. 'I think the main reason they're here is to prevent us interfering with the transmissions. The satellite's beaming its pictures here, and we could wreck the whole stunt if we wanted to.'

Two more armed men pushed their way through the crowd and joined Miss Gant; one of them said something and she nodded. Then she faced us again.

'My inventory shows that I am twenty-seven amorphs short, and a brief search of the colony has not revealed them. Somebody has taken them into the bush. Right – so I want them produced *now,* otherwise future supplies to this colony will be cut off. And you needn't think your pathetic bartering system will help you – because you won't have anything to barter! No tools, no food, no boats, no vehicles. A sub-colony cannot go it alone: this has been proved time and again. You – Kaa, is that your name? Now get out there and tell whoever has those amorphs to bring them here right now. You've already lost your land. Do you want to lose your lives?'

Kaa began to climb the hill.

I examined the faces of the crowd. There were no strangers – but neither were the leading lights of the Kindred there. There was no sign of Mrs Earnshaw, Vernon Thrale, Tom Minty and his henchmen.

We waited. The sun was hot and the guards restless, fingering their laser rifles, wiping sweat from their faces as the heat reflected from the concrete road and the bright dwelling domes. We heard a noise from up the hill near the Research Station: a vehicle starting. Everyone stood quietly, looking up the slope.

Then a truck came into view from around the back of the Social Club. Its guide wheels were down as it passed the front of the building, turned and headed towards us. It was the big delivery truck; there was a puzzled murmur from the crowd.

'Look out!' somebody shouted.

A man leaped from the cab of the truck, rolled over, jumped to his feet and ran among the units. When I looked back at the truck I saw that its guide wheels had been raised...

Riding on a cushion of air which sprayed dust all around, with the propeller a pale blur behind, with wheels up and no brakes, the hovertruck skimmed down the hill towards us.

Rudders flapping uselessly as it gathered speed, it began to rotate on its axis, spinning slowly, sideswiping a dwelling unit and demolishing a lamp post, plunging towards the crowd. People scattered, running for the side-streets. Susanna and I climbed the concrete steps of the bakery. For a moment the hovertruck seemed to be driving straight for us, then it spun off a bollard in a shower of sparks and rebounded to the other side of the street. A guard hurled himself behind a unit as the truck passed within inches, the side-draught ballooning his clothes.

We watched the truck accelerate as its course straightened, then it raced down to the wharf, bucking uncontrollably as air escaped from gaping rents in the fabric of its skirt. It reached the wharf, leaped four metres to the water, struck in an explosion of spray and skittered over the surface like a flat stone. It smashed into the far bank and exploded in a brilliant crimson and yellow fireball, spraying flames into the trees. A second later the roar of sound reached us. A couple of trees tilted, blazing and fell slowly forward into the estuary, raising a cloud of steam. The flames climbed up the bank, crept in a spreading pool across the water.

It was a curiously satisfying sight. 'Oooh,' murmured Susanna like a child. I felt her hand in mine and hoped I hadn't been squeezing too tight. Some hypocrite swung round and stared at us, began to yell that there was nothing amusing in the destruction of public property and that Susanna was no better than that goddamned murdering driver – when the growing general clamour was suddenly stilled.

The troops were slowly reassembling. But this time there was a difference.

Each soldier was guarded by an amorph – one of the colony amorphs, who had appeared from nowhere during the diversion caused by the hovertruck.

Mrs Earnshaw appeared, together with other Kindred. She confronted Althea Gant.

'You will notice that my ideal man is not a lily-livered punk, Miss Gant!' she roared in her powerful voice, while the colonists chuckled.

Most of the colony amorphs were large, aggressive-looking types; possibly replicas of the old woman's late husband, the Admiral. It shows how wrong a man can be. I'd always visualized Mrs Earnshaw's husband as a frail guy, dominated by her forceful personality, revenging himself on his junior officers. In fact, their marriage must have been a tumultuous affair of vigorous give and take.

'And where do you think this will get you?' asked Althea Gant.

'It'll get us free from your goddamned Organization, that's where!' snapped Mrs Earnshaw.

Later Susanna and I joined Mortimore Barker in the studio. The publicity man received news of the revolution with some dismay, although I explained that the Kindred had expressed their intention not to interfere with the project.

'Mrs Earnshaw still feels it's for the good of us all,' I said.

'You mean we're letting that old trout decide what's good for us?' boomed Barker, outraged.

'For the time being. Right now the Kindred are deciding what ransom to demand.'

Barker muttered something and returned to his job. There were large 3-V alcoves in adjacent corners of the room; a few technicians sat before consoles. The left-hand alcove was fed by the camera at the rear of *Arcadia*'s cockpit; Streng could be seen against a background of choppy blue sea, fixing something on the boom. He glanced over his shoulder at the camera, grinned briefly and returned to his work. Above him the sail strained; the mikes picked up the creak of ropes, the murmur of water. It was an incredibly realistic sight.

The right-hand alcove was even more spectacular. The view here was from the controversial camera mounted at the masthead. The vertical viewpoint translated into a horizontal image produced a hypnotic effect, as though the viewer was falling forwards into the scene. The whole of the cabin roof, the full length of the sponsons and much of the sea could be seen. I looked down at the broad shoulders and grey head of Streng as he worked away at the gooseneck. The waves heaved all around, tilting in the weirdest fashion as the boat heeled. The sail was a glowing diagonal curve, strung with the graceful arcs of ropes.

Streng was talking into the camera. '... really no problems at all: just a small boil on my leg. I'll deal with that tomorrow, I expect. And that goddamned gooseneck – it's no more than you can expect, with a rush job and an inexperienced builder ...'

Barker rested his huge hand on my arm. 'Easy, Kev. Any publicity is good publicity – and everyone knows that long-distance sailors always gripe about their boats.'

'... a few blackfish,' Streng was continuing in that goddamned suave voice of his. 'Nothing to worry about, unless the boat falls apart under me. And a few problems with the overhead camera. I hope that's functioning all right now, because the view should be quite something.' He looked up. I glanced at the other alcove and saw his face, peering up beside the mast. I also saw fins of blackfish patrolling the area just aft of the port sponson. For a brief instant, I hoped the bastard would overbalance, as the ocean heaved about the pendulum of the mast.

The cat paced past, across the roof and down into the cabin in a lithe bound. It still looked very much like a Siamese cat. I wondered if Streng had seen his instructions, or whether his pride had forbidden him to open his Bible.

We sat in the studio while Streng chatted away with the cameras, all sign of previous strain washed away in the joy of being at sea, away from incompetent, inconvenient humanity.

'One of the interesting points which nobody had thought of,' said Barker, while Streng was opening a bottle of beer and telling the Sector what he'd eaten for lunch, 'is that half the viewers are hoping he won't make it. Hell, we've all got to admit that his personality is controversial. But it's all to the good. The ratings are an all-time high, I'm told.'

'For this crap?' I asked sourly, watching Streng demonstrate how to tie a running bowline.

Later the Swindons arrived with bottles of liquor from the Social Club and we settled in to make a night of it. There was a feeling of siege. Although nobody said as much. I think we were all concerned that the Kindred might, after all, decide to storm the studio and foul up the one useful contribution Riverside was making to the planet's economy.

'It's fairly quiet right now,' Jane told us deftly pouring scotch. 'They're all in the Club, arguing about the ransom demands.'

'Supposing the Organization decide they don't want Gant and the troops back,' suggested Susanna thoughtfully. 'I mean, you couldn't blame them ...'

It became dark outside; the talk slowed. Susanna and I sat on cushions against the wall, Mark and Jane occupied a couple of collapsible chairs, the technicians drifted off duty and Barker brought in another armful of liquor.

Eventually it was midnight by Streng's time. The scene in the left-hand 3-V alcove was peaceful: Streng had been writing up his log for the day with a glass of gin at his elbow.

From time to time he read out interesting snippets for the viewers, and Barker filled in with a few comments for those who had not been watching earlier.

Then Streng shut his logbook with a snap.

Barker twisted a switch, and the broadcast to the stars was over for the day.

Streng approached the camera. The light from the cabin was behind him and his face in shadow, but I could see that his expression was unpleasant.

'Right, you bastards,' he snapped. 'I happened to open that goddamned Bible today, Barker – did you see that? Or were you sitting on your fat ass drinking in the club, as usual?'

Barker said to us, 'We needn't put up with this. We could just go away and leave him to rave – or better still, switch him off. But there's a sort of fascination about it. You wonder what crap he's going to come up with next. Of course, it would never occur to Streng that we might not be listening. Everybody listens to Streng.'

So we listened to Streng.

'. . . could have wrecked the whole fucking project. The cat could have metamorphosed in front of the whole fucking Sector, and shown up Hetherington for what he is – a goddamned swindler. Luckily it's still a cat – luckily for you, that is. It will, however, soon be a dead cat. The blackfish are hungry, Barker – so I'm going to throw them a tasty morsel. And tomorrow I'll spin a sad seaman's yarn about the tragic loss of my dear fucking Melissa. I may start laughing in the middle of it.'

Susanna stirred against me. 'He wouldn't do that, would he?' she said. Outside, I heard voices, shouting.

'. . . but don't let this distract you all from the other problems. Item one, this goddamned boat's leaking like a sieve. Last night I bailed twenty gallons from the starboard sponson while the customers weren't looking, but I can't go on shielding you for ever, Moncrieff. I need my sleep. Maybe tomorrow I'll start bailing out right there in front of the Sector, and show you up for what you are – a grasping crook who cashed in at the expense of ninety per cent of the planet. And I have a few things to say to you, Barker, you fat swine . . .'

Susanna was hugging me. 'Don't pay any attention, Kev,' she said softly. 'Streng's scared and he's hitting out. He's taken on too much. There's nothing wrong with the boat.'

I don't remember what I said. I suppose I was still mumbling something, embarrassed by my own fury, when the door opened and light flooded into the gloomy scene.

The unmistakable shape of Kli a' Po stood silhouetted there. Around his feet were several miniature editions.

'I think you all ought to come,' he said. 'There's a mob of people on their way to burn down my farmhouse, that they now call the Agricultural Station. It seems that the Organization turned down the Kindred's terms for release of the prisoners – called their bluff, I think you phrase it. Please come.'

His agitation was obvious even to human eyes. And there's a curious thing about Kli a' Po that I've noticed – I think he has a defence mechanism nobody knows of. The more alarmed he is, the more replicas he seems to be accompanied by – as though he is hedging his bets on survival.

We hurried out of the studio and into the main clubhouse. The only person there was John Talbot the steward, who glanced at us unhappily as we passed. John likes to sit on the fence: his job depends on it.

Then we stepped out into the street, and saw the mob.

# thirteen

There followed a brief argument with the women who seemed to relish the idea of exposing themselves to danger.

'Listen, are you trying to tell me I can't take care of myself?' Susanna asked hotly. 'Hell, Moncrieff, I've been going around with you for a couple of months and come to no harm. What can I fear from a ravening mob?'

She looked longingly down the hill, where the domes flickered luridly in the light from dozens of blazing torches. Riverside, at this moment, resembled a vampire hunt in Transylvania.

'The scene bears the Lovers' trademark,' remarked Jane. 'Remember that effigy at the regatta? This looks like fun, Mark.'

There was a sudden roar from the crowd, and the torches

began to bob downhill as the journey to the Blackstone farm began.

Kli said, 'I'm not going. I feel the sight of me may incite them further. I regret the loss of my farmhouse – the Organization would have handed it back to me in five years, but the colonists will now make that impossible. You people deal in strange values.'

'Jane and I will stay with you,' said Susanna, seeing a way out of her impasse with me.

Mark Swindon and I hurried down the street to catch up with the tail end of the mob. I don't know what we had in mind; it was obvious that there was nothing we could do. A mob led by Chill Kaa and Tom Minty would not take kindly to opposition.

By the time we caught up with the stragglers the main body of the crowd was surging over the bridge, their torches casting an eerie luminescence over the dark waters. I was passing a small, grimly plodding figure and recognized Mrs Earnshaw.

'What are you hoping to gain by this, Mrs E.?' I asked. I think the attitude of Kli a' Po had brought home to me that somebody always suffers when a crowd gives itself over to violent enjoyment. And that was this crowd's purpose – enjoyment. They were like kids who see the chance for fun and games while their parents are away.

'It will demonstrate to the Organization that we of Riverside will not tolerate any further interference in our affairs,' the old woman said breathlessly.

'Even you must see that's a goddamned pointless thing to demonstrate,' Mark snapped.

'I can't take responsibility for the way in which the Organization has provoked our people.'

'In other words, you're not in charge of this?'

'For God's sake, Professor Swindon, do I look as though I'm in charge?' Mrs Earnshaw turned to face us, and to my amazement I caught a glitter of tears in the old woman's eyes. Ahead of us, the crowd were beginning to climb the hillside.

Mark said quietly, 'Remember the Relay Effect? Hell, that was over two years ago – but people don't learn. Feeding input to a mob is an entirely different matter from feeding the same information to a number of individuals. For one thing, a mob will not reject the inconsistencies, neither does it have the capacity for foreseeing the consequences. It's a strange thing, but when men come together their capacity for rational action diminishes in proportion to the size of the gathering. A mob like this could be compared to a moderately intelligent gorilla.'

'Spare me that,' Mrs Earnshaw said. 'Tell me what the hell we're going to do about it?'

'Who's in charge of them?'

'Who the hell would think of a thing like torches, when we have vehicles with headlights – and plenty of flashlights in the commissary? Who can make enough noise to carry a mob with him on a stupid mission like this – and wreck any chance of a deal with the Organization, huh? Mr Chill goddamned Kaa, that's who. Listen, Professor Swindon. I was a fool to kidnap the Organization people – I see that now. But at the time, when they were threatening us with rifles, I saw red. And now the whole thing's got out of hand.'

We stopped, the old woman panting for breath again. Mark said, 'I'll take you back. You'll kill yourself trying to keep up with those people...'

He glanced at me enquiringly.

'I'll carry on. I may as well see it through.'

By the time I caught up with the main body of the mob, the leaders had already reached the farm. The rectangular shapes of the buildings were picked out in glowing crimson against the darkness of the trees opposite, and a few flickered around the eaves. The farmhouse was timber-built of post and beam construction, clad in ancient shingles; the flames were spreading fast.

I found I was walking beside Will Jackson. The elderly man glanced at me from under the brim of his hat. 'Not thinking of trying to stop us, are you?' he asked coldly. His eyes were drawn back to the flames as irresistibly as they were normally drawn to a young girl.

It was dark on the rough, scrub-lined track. Everyone was watching the blaze as they hurried forward with intent faces. The mob was spread and numbers were silhouetted against the flickering background of the farmhouse; they ran about excitedly, throwing flaming torches.

In the unreal environment which was almost primeval I thought this: *I could kill you now, Will Jackson, and nobody would ever know, and Riverside would be a better place...*

Instead I said, 'Fuck you.'

He replied, 'And fuck *you*, too.'

The flames had got a good hold on the roof, and a minor blaze had started around the bottom of the walls. Over to the right little flames began to trickle caressingly over hay stored in an open barn. From time to time I recognized people as they moved about, intent on ensuring that no vestige of the Agricultural Centre remain to insult the freedom of Riverside. I saw Kaa and Thrale, Minty and Yong, Jackson and Blake.

I saw the Kindred of the Pioneers...

I saw them gleefully consigning to ashes the very buildings which – two months ago – they had been ostensibly revering as a historic monument.

A gout of flames surged skywards from the roof with a crackling roar as the ridge sagged suddenly, the shakes blackening and disappearing. The watchers cheered. There was celebration in the air, but for once I was not enjoying a scene of destruction. To me, the cheering sounded very much like jeering; the simple pleasure of watching a good blaze was tainted by the unpleasant flavour of triumph.

There was a shrill hysteria to that cheering.

The wall began to fall towards us – the whole of one side of the farmhouse, opening slowly outwards like a drawbridge, finally thundering to the ground in a rising cloud of sparks, revealing the inferno of the interior. The crowd were screaming and my distaste for the affair became outright repugnance. It was only a poor inanimate building. Only a fool could become excited by the symbolism of its ownership. It meant little to the Organization: the only person to suffer would be Kli a' Po.

Some woman was squealing in my ear and I turned on her irritably...

She was not even looking at the flames. She was staring the other way; more heads were turning. Her squealing was not delight, it was fear. Others were shouting too, people were scattering, running for the open fields, scrambling for the cover of the forest...

A hundred metres away, its sensors trained attentively on the leaping flames, crouched the huge shape of the rogue brontomek.

Experimentally it directed a bolt of slender light into the holocaust, but the effect was barely perceptible. The machine paused, cogitating. Although the size of the heat-source was attractive, it did not compute as prey.

But there were other, smaller heat-sources around, becoming more distinct as they separated themselves from the main warmth. They moved over the fields, they hurried among the trees.

As I began to run for cover the brontomek turned its lasers on the people.

Streng was right about self-preservation. I don't know what was happening to anyone else and I didn't care. I like to think it would have been different if Susanna had been there but the thought affords me no comfort. We were at the peak of love and I would have put her safety before mine – Streng would say because I foresaw children from our Union and the Secondary Instinct temporarily outweighed the Primary. In a year's time, too, I would have given my life for her. In five year's time, ten ...? Thirty? How long do you have to know a woman before you can leave her to die? It's not a thing a man likes to think about.

Susanna was not with me. Thank God and leave it at that.

So I scrabbled up the slope, fighting my way through the brush and hearing the screaming from behind. And once – seeing a thread of golden light vaporize the night mist and crackle steaming among the branches nearby. Then I was over the ridge, scrambling down to the water's edge, convinced I could hear trees toppling behind me.

The tide was out. I waded through the mud, swam the narrow channel, sloughed through filth again and climbed to the wharf.

I made it to the visiphone in my living room, got through to Barker.

'Tell Susanna I'm OK,' I said.

Then I fell into a chair. Soon afterwards soft arms were about me, helping me out of my clothes, guiding me into a hot bath.

Twelve people died in the carnage at Blackstone's farm and we were lucky the number wasn't quadrupled. Piecing together the reports of that dreadful night it emerged that the brontomek had been uncharacteristically inefficient in its methods. Puzzled by the size of these running objects which its faulty sensors identified as field rats, it went into a frenzy of overkill, scorching each body into charcoal before moving on to the next...

During the following few days the colony was in chastened mood, and Mrs Earnshaw resumed control. Her first act was to redefine the status of Althea Gant and the other prisoners.

'You're free to move about the colony as you wish,' she told them at a public meeting one afternoon. 'But remember we still have your guns.'

Althea Gant answered for her troops. 'Thanks. There are certain persons I'll recommend for leniency when the Organization moves in.'

'That's enough of that!' roared Mrs Earnshaw. 'We want no favours from you!' She brought the meeting to a swift conclusion.

During those hot summer days, as the month of Vau passed and Zayin came, we often speculated as to the Organization's next move. There were many theories, the most popular being that they would, quite simply, starve us out.

'It's the cheapest way,' said Jane Swindon.

'I reckon they'll wait until we're off guard, then attack,' opined Tom Minty.

'Nonsense!' said Mortimore Barker loudly, glass in one hand, cigar in the other. 'They'd have attacked already, if they intended to. They can take us any time they like – but they won't. Not while the broadcast is still going out...'

'Couldn't they pick up the signals in Premier City and bypass Riverside?' somebody asked.

'No. It's too complex. There are three satellites involved – one overhead of us, the other two spaced at equal distances above Streng's route. They beam into our satellite which relays on to us. Any alteration would cost millions and mean shutting down for a period. The Sector would begin to wonder what was going on in Arcadia. No. The studio's a better hostage for us than a hundred prisoners.'

'Look at it this way,' Perce Walters – a reasonable man – told the assembled colony. 'You depend on our catch to stay alive. We have very little grain, few vegetables – when our stocks have gone, God only knows what we'll do. It's not safe to venture out on to the farmland, not with that goddamned machine on the loose. So we fishermen are keeping you, and it'll be that way for a long time, looks like. Meanwhile, our nets are falling apart, our boats are leaking, we have to pay full rate for repairs at Kevin Moncrieff's yard – but our return takes no account of this – or what we lose in depreciation.'

Chill Kaa broke in. 'Yeah, Perce is right, but there's no need to apologize about it, Perce. You people – either you pay our price or you get no goddamned fish!'

Mrs Earnshaw said, 'The rate was agreed by us all.'

'So now we'll agree another rate, huh?'

Mark Swindon spoke up. 'Be reasonable, Chill. We can't alter the rate here and now. All the rates are tied together. It'll have to be discussed in Committee.'

There was a murmur of relieved agreement. 'We'll give it priority,' said Tim Minty, another member of the Colony Committee.

But Chill Kaa was spluttering with rage, moon face pale. 'You think you can shelve it just like that? By Christ, since when did the Committee have any authority in this goddamned colony? Listen, you bastards, we vote on it right now. Do you want food or don't you? Yes or no! Put up your goddamned hands!'

As the uproar grew, Perce Walters stepped in front of Kaa. 'Cool it, man. This is no way. You're not the only fisherman, and I reckon the rest of us will agree to go along with the Committee, huh?'

He glanced around. There were nods of agreement.

'The Lovers will have something to say about this,' shouted Kaa.

'Hold it right there, Kaa!' snapped Perce, flushing. 'Just who are you goddamned Lovers supposed to be fighting? Are you saying you'll turn on your own people?'

'Yeah, and you'll be the first to go, you lousy scab!'

There is only one satisfactory way to settle such an argument, and I was glad to see that Perce Walters found it. He smashed Kaa in the face with his huge fist. As the man fell to the ground, blood welling from a split lip, Perce kicked him bodily from the improvised platform.

The incident appeared to finish at that point, but the repercussions were felt for weeks afterwards. The whole matter of the barter system came under scrutiny with the predictable result that *nobody* felt they were receiving value for their particular services. The system would have collapsed there and then were it not for the fact that we had nothing to put in its place.

The damage had been done. Since the Organization had

apparently withdrawn from the scene, the colony had lost a tangible scapegoat for its problems. So it had turned on itself. We entered a troubled period of discontent and internal wrangling, with a wealth of sub-groups and cliques forming and re-forming, challenging the Colony Committee, the Kindred, and the Lovers on every issue.

Meanwhile Ralph Streng was sailing round the world. Reaction from the Sector was coming in now, no doubt edited by Newspocket but nevertheless showing a mounting enthusiasm in the other planets. We saw shots of kids wearing Streng buttons, sailing model *Arcadians*. Every planet in the Sector suffered hours-long coverage. Since Hetherington owned the networks, he was able to make the news.

Mortimore Barker, however, was becoming increasingly unhappy. 'The guy's in trouble,' he told us one day, as we watched the yachtsman trolling over the stern, pulling in small silver fish which he tossed into a bucket. 'He's holding something back ... He doesn't even shout the way he used to.'

Streng sat winding in his line, looking lean and tanned. The sun had bleached his grey mane almost white, and he had lost a lot of meat from around his shoulders. He smiled at the stern camera.

'So I'm trailing a net,' he said as though continuing a monologue, although he hadn't spoken for almost twenty minutes. 'In case of accidents. A lone yachtsman can't be too careful ...' From the camera at the mast-head we could see the net, strung between the after ends of the two sponsons, dragging in the water. 'So far I've only caught fish,' he said. 'But one day, do you know what? I'm going to pull in that goddamned net, and you know what will be in there ...? *Me.*'

I shivered; there was something not quite right about his expression. 'Careful, son ...' murmured Barker. He glanced at me. 'It just might happen,' he said cryptically.

'I have company, though. A man alone has to make what company he can, and I've been lucky with my friends. There was William, a creature like a dolphin – I'll swear he was intelligent. The blackfish got him in the end. And there was a little bird, a mewler, he stayed with me for days. And Melissa ... Ah, poor Melissa ...

Streng seemed suddenly to pull himself together, shaking off the maudlin mood. 'Here, take a look at this,' he said. 'Here's something remarkable.' He moved over to the sonar screen and switched the instrument on. A shoal of little blips showed on the screen. 'See those? That's fish – how's that for an instrument? Sensitive enough to pick up the smallest sprat – hell, I have no fear of running aground with an instrument like this!'

It was becoming a recurrent theme with him, the public attempts to make light of his difficulties by elaborate overpraise of something inconsequential. He wouldn't need that sonar until he was on the approaches to Riverside.

I suppose a man runs out of things to say after a while – even a man like Streng. He hadn't reached the half-way mark yet, but already he was repeating his stock themes ad nauseam. At least he'd spared us the worst of his psychology to date, but I had the feeling that the reprieve was not permanent. As the days went by and the loneliness grew in him he likened his voyage to some of the epic space explorations of the past: Hartsborne and the Endeavour, D'Asbel Bu and the Tigram Hound.

Another theme was the evocation of the Relay Effect. '... this mighty ocean, so calm now, so devoid of menace – yet let us never forget the terrible havoc wrought by the Minds in their blind hatred of all living creatures...'

Barker used to wince when Streng started on that track. The terrible havoc wrought by the Minds was exactly what he *did* want people to forget, but there was no way he could get the message to Streng to lay off. 'I had to fake another breakdown in transmission today,' he would say. 'But I can't do it many more times. That goddamned independent observer is getting suspicious.'

The vacationing lawyer was based in Premier City but occasionally visited the studio, watching the 3-V images absorbedly, never mixing with the rest of us, hardly ever speaking.

For a time I avoided the studio. I couldn't stand his uncensored criticism of the boat. From the way Barker avoided me, I gathered that matters were not improving.

Finally, one day, curiosity got the better of me ... it was around Riverside noon but night was closing around Streng; he glanced at the stars, shrugged, blundered down into the glow of the cabin and unfastened the forecabin door. He returned towards us, climbing up into the cockpit leading a huge form. The thing sat down, and I saw the face in profile against the light from the cabin . . .

It was himself. It was Streng. There were two Ralph Strengs sitting in the cockpit.

Afterwards, Althea Gant said, 'It's the classic egotist syndrome. The amorph's defence mechanism is frustrated by the fact that Streng has no apparent Te – no ideal, no love object, nothing into which it can change in order to please him. Often, during this period, the amorph will undergo several tentative changes, discarding each one. Until it realizes in the end that the person Streng loves most is himself . . . I must admit, I'd thought better of the man. It was obviously a mistake to give him the creature.'

'Maybe it's the only thing keeping him sane, right now,' said Barker. 'At least he has his own company, if nobody else's.'

'His own company is exactly what he has,' said Althea Gant. 'The amorph of an egotist is different from any other amorph. The ordinary amorph is an *ideal* – it embodies all the good things a person knows about his Te, and probably none of the qualities he dislikes. It is based on a person's *knowledge* of his Te, and since nobody knows everything about another person, it is an imperfect image.

'But the amorph on an egotist is a different matter. Streng's amorph can duplicate Streng *exactly* – since it has mental access to everything which comprises the original.'

She smiled her thin smile. 'So if Streng is feeling the strain, the best thing he can do is retire to the cabin and get drunk for a few days, and let the amorph take over for him. Nobody would know the difference. There *is* no difference.'

But Streng continued to appear in person, so far as we could tell. He suffered lengthening periods of depression, he began to respond even more irrationally to trivial defects in the boat, he began openly to dose himself with medicaments for imagined symptoms. He was unable to sustain any sort of public cheerfulness for more than the first couple of hours of each new day. He even began to admit his own inadequacies.

'A long solo voyage will unearth unexpected flaws in the fabric of a man's character,' he mused on one occasion, in broad daylight. 'I wish, more than anything else, that I'd had the sense to bring some Immunol with me. A little harmless relief would be a pleasant thing, right now . . .'

But he had no Immunol, only alcohol, which wasn't the same thing. And two hours later the pump began to falter, and he had to strip it down, and replace a gasket, burning his hand on hot metal in the process...

That time, I felt sorry for him.

Later, when darkness came, he sat in the cockpit with the amorph and they argued interminable philosophies, and I felt sorry for the amorph, too. I don't suppose it knew whether Streng wanted it to agree or disagree.

That was the time when Susanna and I stepped out of the studio into the surprise of sudden daylight, and Susanna said, 'Did you see it, Kev?'

'See what?'

She watched my face as she said, 'I *thought* I saw it, just once. While Streng and his double were talking, something showed on the sonar screen. Something big.'

'A blackfish?'

'No ... It was a different shape ...' She gazed down the street at the lazy brown of the estuary. 'I only hope Ralph doesn't see it. It was... sort of scary, Kev.'

# fourteen

But it was not a sea creature which destroyed Mark Swindon's fish pens a few days later. The shortage of fuel for the trawlers was making itself felt seriously now, and the colony was coming to depend on the large corralled shoals at the mouth of the estuary, where Mark bred and raised the Arcadian fatty.

'God knows how long those fish will last,' he confided in me one day, as Perce Walters' trawler *Arcturus* unloaded a glittering haul at the wharf. 'The pens are still experimental. There's less than six months' supply for the whole colony there. We're going to have to start rigging sailing vessels, Kev.'

'The first step down the road to the primitive existence,' said Jane Swindon thoughtfully. 'I can't see us taking it. A lot of people still believe it's only a matter of time before we settle our differences with the Organization and things get back to normal. With civilization so near at hand, even the Lovers won't believe that we may *have* to go primitive.'

Then, one morning, Perce Walters reported that the fish pens were destroyed and the fatties gone...

'There's nothing left,' he told the incredulous group on the wharf. 'No posts, no nets, no fish – just a few broken sticks and bits of rope on the beach. Blackfish couldn't have done it, nor men in small boats. You want to know what I think? I reckon they deliberately drove that seavester through there, back and forth until everything was ripped away. The bastards. The dirty stinking bastards...'

The immediate result of this incident was the formation of three small armed groups who set off the following day to raid the Organization's crops in the north valley. They took barrows to bring back the spoils, and the colony cheered them on their way.

'This will show the goddamned Organization we don't intend to sit on our butts and starve,' was the general opinion.

During late morning puffs of smoke on the hillside signified a laser battle in progress, and later in the day the raiders returned emptyhanded.

Nobody had been hurt; the enemy had commanded the high ground and aimed low. But the colonists had been unable to make any progress against superior firepower. If things had got any hotter, there would have been nothing to prevent the Organization's defenders in raising their sights, and burning up the colony which lay exposed on the opposite hillside...

Among all the internal wrangling, the controversy of Streng's voyage, the growing food shortage, the amorphs seemed to have been forgotten. But they were still with us, that small group of aliens whom we had absorbed into the colony. During those difficult days I often encountered them in the most unexpected places and guises.

'I don't know where the hell they all are,' said Mrs Earnshaw one day, when I asked her what had happened to the private army with which she had defeated the Organization. 'I kept them around for a while. Then they drifted off. I don't have time to worry about them.' Indeed, as the last of the flour was used and the colony's staple diet became fish and wild rice, all the old woman's energies were occupied in defending her position as colony leader. The possibility of a coup was always in the air.

'Maybe you should round them up,' I suggested. 'They could be useful, you know.'

'The hell with them.' She gazed out of the window of her unit. In the diffused sunlight her face looked older, the planes less resolute. I said nothing for a while and we sat in silence, watching people moving to and fro outside. Chill Kaa walked by with busy stride, looking more purposeful than most.

'Where's Miss Cotter?' I asked at last. I hadn't seen Mrs Earnshaw's hired companion for several days.

'She's moved into a vacant unit, and good riddance. I couldn't stand her around the place any more, always agreeing with me. Yes, Bernadine, no Bernadine,' mimicked the old woman. 'And all the time she was waiting for me to die, in the hope that I'd leave her something in my will.' She cackled unpleasantly. 'Well, the Organization fixed her good. Everything I own is all tied up, so Elsie was wasting her time. I told her to get the hell out.'

I remained silent. Elsie Cotter had been with Mrs Earnshaw for many years, and it seemed a pity that the present misfortunes should have caused their relationship to fall apart. Yet it is a fact that hard times do cause such break-ups, despite all the crap the sentimentalists speak about pulling together in adversity. I felt sorry for Miss Cotter. I felt her motives had been misjudged.

I visited her later that day. She produced some sort of sweet tea brewed from a local root. It was barely palatable, but no worse than any of the strange artsy-craftsy drinks she'd pressed on me before the Organization cut off liquor supplies. We talked for a while, but she was not willing to discuss Mrs Earnshaw.

I was getting restless and wondering how Susanna and Barker were getting on at the Studio, when a door opened and, surprisingly, Mrs Earnshaw came in. She set some oatcakes on the table and nodded to me pleasantly. 'Thank you, Bernadine,' said Miss Cotter.

Mrs Earnshaw sat down. 'It's nice to see you, Mr Moncrieff,' she said as though I were a comparative stranger. 'You must come more often. Why don't you bring that nice girl of yours and we'll make up a four of bridge some evening?'

There was a sick feeling inside me. I said carefully, 'I'm glad to see that you two are on good terms.'

'Oh, but we always have been. Honestly, I don't know what I'd do without Elsie . . .' She smiled fondly at Miss Cotter.

'These cookies are delicious, Bernadine,' observed Miss Cotter, smiling back.

'I'm an old woman – and an old woman needs a capable body around,' Mrs Earnshaw told me. Somehow her face was softer, the harsh mastiff-like appearance softened. 'I intend to make sure that Elsie is well provided for, when I go.'

'Thank you, Bernadine,' said Miss Cotter . . .

I rose to go, and Miss Cotter rose too. 'I'll see myself out,' I said thickly.

Mrs Earnshaw sat there, smiling gently. 'Goodbye, Mr Moncrieff.'

Miss Cotter followed me outside. 'Please understand.'

'Go back to the real Mrs Earnshaw, Miss Cotter,' I said gently.

She stared at me. 'Whyever should I want to do that?' she asked . . .

Susanna and I pulled a kid out of the river one day. We were doing a few odd jobs around the boatyard when we heard the screaming and saw someone floundering in the water, several metres from the wharf and obviously unable to reach safety. I jumped into a nearby dinghy and pushed off; there was no time to look for paddles and Susanna paid out the rope from the wharf. I managed to get a grip and dragged the child halfway over the gunwale. Susanna pulled us in and we took the shivering kid up to my place.

She looked around thirteen years old; we'd never seen her before. I regarded her helplessly as she stood dripping on my carpet. She wouldn't speak. I assumed she'd run away from some sub-colony; she now represented a responsibility I was unwilling to accept. Fortunately Susanna the super-efficient was there.

'Put her in a hot bath while I go and borrow some clothes, Kev,' she said.

She left. I organized the kid and sat down with a drink to consider the matter.

We'd had no news from the other sub-colonies: Riverside was effectively isolated except for Barker's contact with the media in Premier City. For all we knew, a revolution might have taken place. This kid might be the vanguard of an army of refugees at this moment descending on us like locusts. I took another drink. I wondered which direction she'd come from. Probably from the south, over the forested hills. Then she'd crept into the colony along the water's edge, unsure whether she'd find the Organization running things or not . . .

'Hello.'

I turned around. She was emerging from the steaming background of the bathroom, a towel wrapped round her. She looked healthy enough, with round cheeks and rather plump pouting lips; and she had spoken, which was a good sign. I'd been afraid of one of these dreadful traumas which I'm told children are subject to. She sat on the arm of my chair and I noticed that her legs were free from the scratch marks which I'd have expected from someone who'd been ploughing through the bush.

'What's your name?' I asked.

She smiled, slowly. I was so goddamned naïve that I didn't recognize the expression on her face. 'Whatever do you want to know for?' she asked. 'I'm here, aren't I? You can call me Mariette . . . *He* does.'

With this cryptic remark she shifted her position and the towel slipped down a fraction from her shoulders, revealing the warm curve of a young breast. I moved too, embarrassed as my body began to respond to her closeness, to the just-bathed hotness of her radiating at me, to the expression on her face which I now couldn't mistake.

'Who's *he*?' I asked stupidly, trying to look everywhere except at the pointed little nipple which was rising from under the towel.

'Oh, forget him, silly. Think about *me*.'

She stood with sudden, childish impatience and the towel fell to the floor. There was a helpless scooping sensation in my stomach as I saw the perfection of her small breasts, the faint soft down between her legs. I found myself standing, reaching for her; she was still smiling, a secretive smile on those full lips, the tip of her tongue showing mischievously. My whole being was possessed by her, by the hypnotic attraction of that body which had none of the angular lines of a child, but was more the form of a miniature adult, of an impossible doll . . .

It clicked in my brain then, that same, sobering click of recognition, of realization.

I sat down, shivering.

When Susanna arrived back with an armful of clothes Mariette was sitting on the chesterfield, chastely wrapped in an abundance of towelling. Susanna took her into the bedroom, then returned to me.

'Something tells me you fancy that child, Moncrieff, you cradle-snatcher,' she remarked, gazing out of the window casually.

'Huh,' I grunted non-committally.

'Speaking of cradle-snatchers, what the hell is Will Jackson doing down on the wharf?' she asked suddenly, staring. 'He seems to be poking about among the boats.'

'Probably looking for the thing he calls Mariette.' I said as casually as I could manage.

She stared at me.

'Oh, Christ ...' she murmured ...

So the amorphs had merged into the colony and become accepted because of what they had to offer humanity, because of their subservience – as distinct from Kli a' Po who was never subservient ... and never accepted. It had happened before on a planet called Marilyn, and now it was happening again on Arcadia.

I met Paul Blake on the wharf, bent over his boat, and working with him was a mirror image of himself. I paused and spoke to them for a while, reminding them of the dangers of tampering with the minipile, drawing a sheepish look from one Paul for my trouble.

The other Paul smiled. 'Thanks,' he said.

The second one was the amorph, of course. I wondered about that for a while. I could conceive that Paul was sufficient of an egotist for his Te to take his own form, just as had happened in the case of Ralph Streng. But it seemed strange that the amorph should be so transparently a good guy.

It was days later that I discovered the amorph was not Paul's Te at all. Paul had little contact with the creature, since he had recently left his father's farm. The amorph was Ezra Blake's Te. It was the ideal of what Ezra would have liked Paul to be ... It wasn't so different from Paul in actual fact ...

Two days after that, an event occurred which surprised us all – except Enrico Batelli, who smiled faintly when he heard the news. Paul Blake disappeared, along with – or simultaneously with – Alicia Desjardins. We never heard from either of them again. The amorph lived on with Ezra at the farm, and whenever I called there and saw the two of them working together, it was difficult to conceive that anything had ever changed.

And so the amorphs fitted in.

John Talbot was living with a creature who looked nothing like his wife.

I glanced in at Hazel Streng's window one night, on my way to the club. She was sitting talking to someone. She was smiling, laughing. The someone smiled and laughed back, and I could hear the sound of their happiness as I walked on.

The someone was Hetherington's gift to Hazel Streng; it had once looked like a cat.

It now looked like Ralph Streng.

Hazel Streng was very happy with her gift. She hadn't been so happy in years.

And the real Ralph Streng sailed on.

'An ocean as calm as a mirror, the boat urged on by the gentle tropic breezes which caress the full breasts of the sails like a warm hand...'

Barker switched off the mike, turned up the background music. The 3-V alcoves showed the unchanging view of *Arcadian* trailing a bubbling wake while Streng sat in the cockpit wearing a white sun hat and little else. 'I don't think I've ever been so goddamned bored in my life,' remarked the publicity agent in a more normal voice. 'I mean, the man's doing nothing. Nothing's happening. Why the hell are we wasting our time with this crap?'

Althea Gant sat nearby, watching Streng meditatively. She'd been spending most of her time at the studio recently. 'We don't want him to do anything,' she said. 'Boredom is the correct atmosphere to evoke. The whole thing must appear completely uneventful. Routine. A man doing a job, that's the image we're aiming for.'

'The entire Sector must have switched off weeks ago. Nobody could watch this junk for more than ten minutes.'

Miss Gant smiled. 'They'll keep switching back, Mr Barker. Just to see if he's still alive. You saw Newspocket yesterday. People are already signing up to emigrate here. Arcadia is news, Mr Barker. And we're helping to make it.'

'You know what I'd do now, if I had my way? I'd manufacture a crisis ...' muttered Barker.

Althea Gant watched him thoughtfully. Like her soldiers and the amorphs, she had become an accepted member of the community, and we frequently had to remind ourselves that she was being held here against her will. In fact, I sometimes doubted that this was the case. It was certainly convenient for the Organization to have an observer among us...

Barker got his crisis two days later.

A sudden squall blew up, catching Streng by surprise. He'd been dozing in the cockpit while Barker droned about his unquenchable spirit, when the wind shifted.

We heard the flogging of sails as the wind spilled out. Streng jerked into wakefulness. The sky had darkened, the sea was suddenly choppy, black and menacing. It made me dizzy to look at the right-hand alcove, where the water pivoted crazily about the mast-head camera. Streng uttered a bark of alarm and grabbed the tiller. The boat heeled, the sea tilted.

Miss Gant said, quite calmly, 'I hope that amorph stays down in the cabin.'

'What about Streng, for God's sake? He could do with some help right now.' I snapped nervously. The sails were a mess, the boat broaching to, temporarily out of control.

'He'll cope,' was the reply from the Organization woman.

Streng was shouting across five thousand miles, 'There's water in the starboard sponson! She won't answer to the tiller!' The boat was wallowing sluggishly as tiny needles of rain seemed to drive across the studio towards us.

'A moment of high drama...!' Barker was yelling excitedly into the mike. I visualized channels being switched in city after city, planet after planet throughout the Sector as news got around that the Arcadian broadcast was worth watching again, because a man might shortly drown. 'A recurrence of the old problem – a leaking boat – now presents Ralph Streng with his greatest challenge so far! How will he handle it? Will the raging elements prove too much for even this courageous man and his frail craft?'

I seized Barker's arm. He turned on me, his eyes still burning with that ersatz excitement which he could turn on at will. 'Cut out the crap about the frail craft, will you?' I snarled.

'A figure of speech, my boy, a figure of speech.' Barker had switched off; he allowed Streng to tell the story as the yachtsman wrestled with the mainsheet, screaming oaths at his sodden, intractable equipment.

The mainsail split with a report like a thunderclap, an instant before Streng freed the ropes. The boom swung viciously, lashing against the shrouds with such force that I feared the mast might fall. Flogging fabric descended into the cockpit, blanketing Streng as he struggled to bring the boat's head round. All was confusion as the boat swung further. The jib filled suddenly. The boat picked up speed, fleeing before the wind as Streng fought his way clear of the clinging canvas.

He flung himself at the tiller, forcing the boat around in a wide, wildly pitching arc. The wind got under the tattered sail and snatched it out of the cockpit, streaming it across the surface of the water and making control of the boat almost impossible.

Streng fought the tiller. He glanced back, once, towards the camera: his lips were bared in a fierce grin.

'He's enjoying it,' I heard Althea Gant murmur incredulously.

Streng got a rope around the tiller and lashed it temporarily while he crawled forward over the cabin roof to cut the shredded mainsail free. He hung to the bucking mast with one hand, hacking away with the other, and I could have sworn I heard him shouting with wild laughter. As he stood there, practically naked with legs astride and his white hair a great sodden mane flopping in the wind, he reminded me of some mythological figure, drunk with the power of his own immortality, yelling defiance at the elements.

The halyards parted and the mainsail, freed, fell away over the side and began to drift rapidly astern. The motion of the boat steadied. Streng returned to the cockpit and took over the tiller. The squall died away as suddenly as it had arisen and the sea abated to a slow, rolling swell. After checking his course Streng turned slowly around to the camera and stared directly at us all, at a billion viewers on a dozen planets. He laughed again.

'Fuck you all,' he said.

'And so our hero triumphs once more,' murmured Mark Swindon.

Dusk was falling at sea; we sat in the studio waiting for Streng's uncensored comments on the storm.

'Hero?' queried Mort Barker. 'You have it wrong, Mark. Everyone hates his guts – that's half the fun. They want to see him die – just like people always want to see a lion-tamer die. They resent his omnipotence, his arrogance. That storm's just what the ratings needed.'

Susanna said thoughtfully, 'I thought he was cracking up. Yesterday, I'd have said a storm like that would finish him.'

'Another week of inactivity would have finished him,' said Mark. 'He thrives on action. He's an imaginative man, and inactivity gives him too much time to think.'

Streng had tidied up the decks. A replacement mainsail was drawing nicely. The ropes were neatly coiled and the self-steering gear set for the night. Streng himself sat in the cockpit with a beer, talking pleasantly. As might be expected, his monologue consisted mainly of self-congratulation.

'Fear is a thing of the mind,' he was saying. 'It does not exist unless you make it exist. Anyone with a modicum of common sense can reason fear away. For a person like myself, this afternoon was a stimulating experience – I faced the possibility of death in an illfound craft, with no chance of help or rescue...'

'He's doing it again,' I muttered sickly to the studio at large. 'Why the hell does he keep criticizing the boat, eh, Mort?'

Barker looked uncomfortable.

Althea Gant said, 'Because he's been told to, that's why.'

'What the hell do you mean?'

'It was arranged before he left. Be sensible about this, Mr Moncrieff. We knew there might be some excitement during the voyage, we knew Ralph might find himself in danger. The danger would be attributable to one of three factors – the planet, Streng himself, or the boat. We can't blame the planet because that defeats the object of the voyage. Ralph Streng is hardly the man to shoulder any blame himself. Which leaves the boat. If anything goes wrong, the boat must be blamed.'

I stared at them. 'What sort of publicity is that? We made a deal, remember?'

Mort Barker said apologetically, 'Yes ... Well, we removed your name from the boat, Kev, so you're protected from that angle. And when Ralph comes home, we'll make sure you get plenty of publicity.'

Susanna exploded beside me. 'You're a lot of rotten bastards, you know that? You're a bunch of shitty rotten bastards!'

Around that time I was shouting something too. It was some time before order was restored; in fact, it was only the sight of Streng yelling at us from the 3-V alcove which brought us to our senses.

The public broadcast was over. He could now indulge in his private tantrums.

'... might have been killed!' he was shouting. There was no sign of the amorph. 'Goddamned boat's leaking like a sieve, the sails are falling to pieces, the self-steering gear keeps malfunctioning so I have to stay up half the night at the tiller! And there's no use pretending I'm going to be home on schedule. The pumps break down every day – the salt water's getting to the wiring. They should have been properly protected – but no, Moncrieff said they'd be fine. He even tried to tell me I didn't need two pumps. Hell, I'm making no better time than an ordinary sailboat!'

'Let's get out of here, Kev,' said Susanna. 'You don't have to listen to this.'

'And as if all that isn't enough,' Streng said more quietly, 'Charlie's back.'

There was a movement among the others; I saw Mort glance at Althea Gant significantly. I was already on my feet and Susanna was half-way to the door, but we paused, sensing something interesting.

Streng had approached the stern camera; we could see him from the overhead position, adjusting the mountings. The view in the left-hand alcove was changing, swinging away from the boat. An area of choppy sea slid into view. 'There ... See that?' said Streng.

The water was black, the visibility poor. I thought I saw something, but I couldn't be sure.

Streng said, still in that quiet, almost amused voice which contrasted so oddly with his outburst of a few minutes ago, 'So the oceans of Arcadia are safe? And did you see the claws on that thing? Some lobster, huh? I wonder what it's worth, for me to keep that baby off the screen during daylight hours? Think about it, you people. Think about it, and get a message to me, if you like. You know where to find me...'

'He's talking nonsense,' said Althea Gant uncertainly. 'There was nothing there.'

Mort Barker said, 'This could be pure poison, publicity-wise. Don't you see, Althea? He's talking about a giant version of those little plankton that formed the Minds. Hell, one look at that and the whole Sector will panic! Can't you hear the scaremongers right now? They'll suggest those brutes could get together just like the little ones did, form a Mind as big as a dwelling unit, and control the planet!'

The scene swung again, and we saw the familiar view of the cockpit. 'So that's Charlie,' said Streng in matter-of-fact tones. 'And I think he's hungry. Now ... if only I could persuade that goddamned amorph to go for a swim, maybe I could get rid of the both of them ...'

As we walked down the street Susanna said, 'The amorph kept agreeing with him, so he put it in the cabin, Mort says. Uh ... Kev, do you really think he'd kill it?'

'If it suited him,' I said shortly. I was sick of Streng; I was sick of the whole goddamned conniving lot of them. They'd played me for a sucker. There had never been any intention that my boat should get credit for the voyage. Instead, I was fall guy. 'Forget it,' I said. 'Let's talk about something else.'

We walked on through the colony and, by common consent, crossed the bridge over the river and began to climb up through the trees towards the north ridge, where I suppose we'd had happier times. It was a warm, quiet afternoon. After a while we paused and looked back down at the colony; there was not a soul in sight, apart from Chukalek limping towards the Social Club.

The studio was visible beside the Club, a thicket of antennae sprouting from its flat roof. 'The bastards,' I muttered.

By now Susanna had bounced back to her usual form. 'It is gracious to forgive,' she said in oracular tones. 'Particularly as we can't do anything about it. Besides, forgiving makes you feel good.'

'Not me. I'd always rather think badly of people. My theory is: the more bastards there are around me, the better, on average, am I. Right now I feel like a saint compared to those bums.'

'Maybe God will strike those antennae and burn them all up for you.'

It was an inspiring, sacred thought. I felt better. 'The hell with them,' I said. We walked on.

Susanna said thoughtfully, 'It seems to me that we have two alternative courses of action.'

'Alternatives A and B?'

'I prefer to think of them as alternatives One and Two. One: we lie down on that grass over there, and maybe make love. Alternative Two I'm not sure you'll like,' she said quickly as I tightened my arm around her.

'Tell me, all the same. I love to hear your voice.'

'We walk on to the end of the trail, at the headland. Then we lie down on some grass and make love.'

I thought about it. 'Alternative One,' I said definitely.

She snuggled up against me. 'And then maybe alternative Two?'

We never did make alternative Two. The sun was hot and the grass pleasantly primeval, and here on top of the ridge, surrounded by brush and trees, we were well out of sight of civilization. So we gambolled around like a couple of animals for a couple of hours or so, allowing our instincts full play. When eventually we got our clothes back on we were dizzy with love, and I was thinking once more how good it is to be human after all, to be able to keep loving after the act is through.

We walked on, awkwardly and stumblingly, our arms around each other. Soon, too soon, we were reminded of the world around us.

A gap in the trees afforded a view in the northerly direction, over the valley of the Blackstone farm and beyond. Below us, the blackened ruins of the buildings stood derelict; further on, the green crops extended to the distant hills. There were few birds, no Arcattle grazed where Kli a' Po had once worked the fields. The brontomeks had done their work well. They would soon be back to gather the crop.

'The cornucopia of the Sector,' I murmured.

'It looks terribly boring,' said Susanna. 'I somehow imagined there would be little ranches, barns and haystacks, and animals.'

'That's what they wanted you to imagine ... What the hell are they growing down there, anyway?'

From our vantage point, it looked like some sort of root crop. We began to descend through the brush, emerging into the valley beside the quarry at the back of the Blackstone farm. I trod warily, holding Susanna's hand firmly. I had the sudden image of the rogue brontomek surging towards us from among the ruins of the farmhouse, smashing blackened walls and spitting fire. And somewhere, there were armed guards.

I peered cautiously down the fringe of the forest, eastward. Nothing stirred.

'What are you thinking of doing?' asked Susanna.

'We could take some fresh vegetables back, at least. Now we've got this far.'

A few metres before us a sticker plant sensed our presence and its tentacles stirred, began to reach in our direction.

'Look.' Susanna uprooted a nearby plant similar to those spreading across the valley. 'They're little carrots.' She sniffed the root, wiped it clean and prepared to nibble.

'No. Wait.' There was something familiar about that plant; it was certainly no carrot. I began to crawl forward to where the main spread of the crop bordered the forest, keeping my head down.

There was a sudden rustle from among the herbage and a small animal came bounding out, paused and blinked, dazzled at the sunlight, then blundered on, towards us.

The sticker plant sprang to attention. A tentacle snaked forward, grasped the worral by the hind leg. It uttered a squeal of fright, tore itself free and bounded directly towards Susanna and me.

About two metres away it died...

It died in the same way my Susanna and I would have died if we'd gone out among the crop. It died horribly, in a blazing flash and a crackling, sizzling. It dropped to the ground motionless, smoking gently, and we caught a whiff of burned meat.

It saved our lives – unintentionally, because it had no intelligence. It was only a pathetic little animal, and little animals die all the time.

'The bastards have ringed the valley with laser fences,' whispered Susanna ... She poked a stick towards the worral's body, moved the tip up and down. It burst into bright flames. I looked away to the right, saw a squat structure about seven feet high, against the far cliff of the quarry. Far away to our left, I saw its twin beside a tree. There would be others, dozens of them, standing guard around the perimeter of the valley, protecting the growing crop with invisible bars of hot light...

'Why?' asked Susanna, looking at the root in her hand.

I said, 'Because that's not for eating.'

She looked at me. We were both silent for a moment, assessing the meaning of our discovery. At last Susanna said, 'So all that talk about Arcadia feeding the Sector was just so much garbage, huh? And we believed it, Kev. Everybody really thought the Organisation was on the level ... Why did they do this? They'd have been found out, in the end. Hell, they couldn't have kept a secret like this for ten minutes, once harvesting started.'

'It wouldn't have mattered. Things are improving, the flow of emigrants has been reversed, Arcadia is getting back on its feet. The economy is booming. Did it ever occur to you how well-timed the whole thing is? Ralph Streng's arrival will coincide with the harvest, and you can bet Newspocket will swamp the media with celebrations. The discovery of what we're really growing here on Arcadia will be pretty small news by comparison. And because everything seems to be going so well, people will live with it for the sake of prosperity.'

I looked at the vast area of growing crops, and I thought of all the other such plantations, throughout Arcadia. Millions of tons of a small, innocuous-looking root which had once saved my life, saved the lives of many Arcadians ... when processed to extract the drug Immunol, which counters the Relay Effect. Which also has the side benefit of making a person feel happy.

I tried to tell myself it didn't matter. I reminded myself that many colonists used the drug regularly without ill effects, without addiction. Tom Minty used it all the time and he was a smart guy, if a little wild. Hell, everybody used it from time to time. I'd used it.

So what was bugging me?

The Organization's methods were bugging me. Up to now, everyone had *known* when they were taking Immunol. They'd slipped a powder in a glass of water. It was under the control of the individual. It made him happy.

It was quite a different matter for a ruthless, profit-oriented intergalactic corporation to have sufficient supplies of a cheap tasteless drug to make entire planets happy.

The distinction between making a planet happy, and pacifying it, is one of semantics only.

# fifteen

So we hurried back to the colony. In the past few hours my attitude to the Organization had undergone a complete reversal. Before today, I'd been willing to go along with things for the sake of peace and quiet, the prosperity of the planet and, let's face it, the hope of future profit from my boatyard.

But now everything had changed. The Organization had hoodwinked us all, played on our idealism and our greed, and was about to turn Arcadia into the Galaxy's dope-pusher. I don't know quite what was in my mind as the colony came into view, but I sure as hell intended to stir things up. I had nothing to lose.

'What's that truck?' asked Susanna suddenly, as we began to descend the ridge towards the estuary.

The vehicle stood in the main street, its rear doors open. 'It's the Organization supply truck,' I said wonderingly, staring at the quiet scene across the water. The street was otherwise empty.

'Maybe it's all over. Maybe the Kindred have come to terms,' suggested Susanna. 'Mrs Earnshaw was saying this morning that the food situation was critical.'

'I guess I ought to feel good about this,' I said, 'but I sure as hell don't. Those bastards couldn't have timed it better. Everybody's going to be so goddamned pleased they have food again, they won't be interested in the crop. By Christ, I can just hear that bastard Kaa right now. He'll be chewing on a chicken leg and calling me a troublemaker!'

Susanna said thoughtfully, 'Don't you think it's more likely that he'd accept the Organization's food then tell them to get the hell out of Riverside? That truck holds enough for a month.'

We crossed the bridge and climbed the deserted main street. I glanced inside the hovertruck as we passed; it was empty. The Social Club stood ahead.

No music could be heard at first, just a dull rumbling as of distant thunder or chronic indigestion. The Kindred of the Pioneers were in action. As we approached, the sound resolved itself into the pounding of many feet upon a resilient timber floor. A rhythmic clapping could also be heard. Vernon Thrale opened the door for us and the din increased a hundredfold, accompanied by a gust of warm air redolent of hot sneakers and barbecued chicken – the traditional aroma of the folk dance.

'My God,' muttered Susanna.

I'd been avoiding the Kindred's performances recently due to their tendency to develop into political meetings, and my memories had blurred with time. Now, seeing it all again, I was amazed anew. The entire colony was packed into the large dome, the Kindred occupying the centre. Wherever I looked, I saw jaws munching, greasy hands packing more goodies into eager mouths.

Overlaying everything was the music, strident and relentless and apparently hypnotic, since it was compelling the Kindred to behave in a manner alien to any human being in possession of his faculties. They wore curious white gowns gathered at the waist with a broad blue sash, billowing below into voluminous pantaloons, finally disappearing into stout leather boots. As if this were not enough to convince any sceptic of their authenticity, bright handkerchiefs were attached to their hands and ankles, streaming like vapour-trails as they performed their frenzied gyrations.

At first the eye could not perceive any pattern: the impression was of pink sweaty faces, randomly whirling arms, mass human activity with legs pumping like pistons, the floor trembling to the concerted hammerblows. Then, after a moment, an insane kind of order vouchsafed itself. The Kindred cavorted in groups of eight, like oxygen electrons. They formed circles and squares, broke up and reformed; and from time to time some exhibitionist would prance into the centre of each group and perform solo, with no apparent shame.

It was unreal. Maybe it was the contrast after the weeks of privation; maybe it was the usual reaction of a sober man entering a party which had progressed beyond the formalities: I don't know. In the space of a few hours the colony had become transformed. It was with some relief that I saw Jane Swindon standing nearby. I forced my way through a press of bodies and joined her, pulling Susanna after me.

'Is the war over?' I asked. I had to shout.

She grinned at me. 'Where have you two been, or needn't I ask? Here, have a drink.'

'Not right now. Listen, Jane, what terms did the colony settle on? Something's come up which might change things.'

She clutched her glass as a drunk barged by. 'I'm not sure; hell, I assume they'd be satisfactory.' She laughed at my expression. 'Come on, enjoy yourselves. You're too full of problems, Kev.'

Mark was nearby; I took his arm. He looked around in surprise, then smiled. 'Having a good time?' he asked.

'What deal have we made with the Organization?'

'Christ, I don't know. Does it matter right now?'

'You're on the Colony Committee, for God's sake. You must have given something in return for all this stuff.' There was food everywhere; a table at my elbow was loaded with cold meat and salads. A punchbowl stood nearby; judging by the effect the pink liquid was having on the crowd, it was considerably more potent than the slop usually available at the Kindred's functions.

'The Committee doesn't have much power these days,' said Mark.

A mass of balloons was descending from the ceiling. Nothing made sense, and I found I was clutching Susanna's hand for moral support. Mark was smiling at some girl on the other side of the hall, waving. Nearby, people jumped up and down, frantically popping the balloons as they fell, trying to destroy their beauty before someone else beat them to it. 'Listen, I think we all ought to have a talk about this,' I said, trying to penetrate the indifference which seemed to have gripped even Mark.

'Right now, you mean?' he asked.

Somehow we got him and Jane out of there – and, for good measure, Mrs Earnshaw. The old lady was breathless from dancing. It was a relief to get away from the insane scene in the Club, to have the door close behind us and extinguish the screams of laughter and fusillade of exploding balloons. In due course we seated ourselves in Mark's living-room and Jane poured drinks. Her face was flushed and she still smiled faintly, as though half of her mind remained up at the Social Club.

On the table was the Swindons' share of the loot: liquor, canned food, bags of basic provisions; flour, salt, sugar.

'I'm not drinking,' I said firmly, as Jane glanced enquiringly at me. Only God and Susanna know how much that simple remark cost me.

'Just what the hell is the matter with you?' asked Mark equably, taking a scotch.

'I want to know why we've caved in, and I want to know right now.'

Mark frowned slightly. 'Kev, I don't get it. We've opposed this independence crap all along the line – you, me, Susanna, Jane, Mort Barker and one or two others. We know Riverside can't go it alone, and we admit we have vested interests in not upsetting the Organization. So what are you bitching about?'

'Listen, Mark, will you answer my question, for Christ's sake?'

'You're not still sore about the bad publicity your boat's getting, are you?'

Mrs Earnshaw spoke as I was wondering whether a punch on the nose might clear Mark Swindon's brain. 'There's been no deal made so far as I know,' she stated. 'The food arrived, and we shared it out. It's as simple as that. Nobody's sold us out, Mr Moncrieff.'

A movement outside caught my eye; I walked over to the window. 'Then why are our prisoners getting into the truck?' I asked furiously. 'Are they thinking of leaving?'

Mark joined me. 'It's better this way,' he said, as we watched the members of Althea Gant's task force pull the truck doors closed. Air hissed, the truck rose ponderously from the road in a cloud of brown dust, and slid down the hill towards the wharf, towards Premier City...

'What hold do we have over the Organization now?' I asked.

'What hold did we ever have?' Mark replied in reasonable tones. 'Those prisoners were more trouble than they were worth, eating our food. Hell, the Organization never showed any inclination to come to terms over them. Forget it, Kev.'

'I have a great idea,' said Jane suddenly. 'Let's go back to the party.'

The dust subsided and the truck was gone.

A lone figure appeared, a tall, angular woman walking steadily up the hill from the wharf. It was Althea Gant. She had not left with the others. I watched her in surprise for a moment, then turned to face the room.

They were regarding me tolerantly. There was no hostility, just maybe a touch of impatience in Jane's face. After all, these people were my friends: they knew me and they knew my reasoning was not always sound. Right now, they thought they were humouring me. Kev's in one of his bad moods, but he's basically a good guy. Let's kid him along for a while, then we'll all get back to the dance.

I had an urge to shake them up.

'Susanna and I have just been over to the Blackstone farm,' I said carefully. 'The place is guarded with laser fences. Do you know why?'

'I understand they've been having trouble with worrals and wild Arcattle getting in and eating the crops,' said Mark.

His tone of quiet reasonableness enraged me. 'It's not that at all, you stupid bastard!' I yelled. 'It's because they're growing the Immunol root, and they don't want anyone to find out!'

Mrs Earnshaw smiled. 'They wouldn't want to keep a thing like that secret. After all the trouble over the Relay Effect, people will be glad to hear it's being stockpiled for the next time. The Organization is doing what the Government should have done.'

I looked helplessly at Susanna. She stood and joined me at the window. The others immediately began to talk about Vernon Thrale, and his plans for a cultural revival.

Susanna stood close against me so that her breasts touched my arm and immediately, in the midst of this incredible situation, I desired her. She stood on her toes and I felt her warm breath against my face.

'Darling, they're all drugged,' she whispered...

It hit me then, and I wondered why I hadn't realized before. The festivities at the Club, the mass euphoria, the indifference of these normally sensible people to what was happening around them – the classic symptoms of a heavy dose of Immunol.

'Did you drink anything?' I asked quietly.

She shook her head. The lively conversation at the table continued; Jane was mixing some more drinks.

I said loudly, 'Listen to me.'

'So long as it doesn't sound paranoid in any way,' said Mark with a grin.

I continued, 'If the Organization wanted to subdue the colony and release its prisoners without bloodshed, at the same time making sure Streng's broadcasts weren't interfered with, the simplest way would be to drug us all with Immunol. The current crop isn't ready yet, but I expect there's enough in the warehouses to take care of one small sub-colony. If I were the Organization, I'd spike the water supply, at the same time making a large delivery of doctored food.' I watched their faces.

'It makes sense,' observed Jane thoughtfully. 'Are you saying that's what's happened?' She indicated the supplies on the table.

'I think so. Don't you all feel . . . different? Think about it.'

They thought, reluctantly.

'I feel pretty good,' admitted Mark. 'I put it down to getting some proper food at last.'

The others agreed to feeling a pleasant euphoria.

I thought I was winning. 'So all we have to do is make sure we drink pure water – hell, there's a perfectly good river just down the hill – and eat fish and anything else the Organization haven't got their hands on.'

'Why?' asked Mrs Earnshaw.

I stared at her. 'Christ, to keep this goddamned drug out of our systems, of course.'

'Just wait a moment,' said Mark. 'Just wait a goddamned moment. Immunol is harmless and non-addictive. If I have to choose between feeling good and eating well, or feeling frustrated and eating fish, I'll choose Immunol every time. Forget it, Kev.'

'It's only the Immunol making you talk like that! Can't you understand, you goddamned fool?'

'You're probably right, but so what? The prisoners are gone. The Organization is feeding us. Everything's fine. There's nothing anyone can do – nothing anyone needs to do. We might as well use up the food; we're drugged already, so what does it matter? The next delivery will probably be clean.'

'How do you know? Have you seen the size of the crops they're growing? How will anyone in the Galaxy know if *their* next delivery is clean?'

He merely smiled. I felt sick, I took Susanna's arm and got her out of there. We left them discussing dance steps.

As we paused outside, hearing again the din from the Social Club, Althea Gant appeared suddenly, with Sinclair Singleton.

'Hello there, Mr Moncrieff . . . Miss Lincoln,' she greeted us pleasantly. 'On your way to the dance? What a beautiful evening this promises to be.'

Susanna gripped my wrist so hard it was almost painful.

'We thought we'd join the fun,' she replied gaily. 'Isn't it wonderful we've all settled our differences? Kev and I were just saying – we feel so good about everything, we could sing. We may do just that. In the privacy of our own homes, of course.'

Althea Gant laughed, Singleton murmured some pleasantry, then they entered the dwelling unit we'd just left.

Susanna looked at me thoughtfully. 'For a gorgeous guy you can sometimes be stupid, Kev. You were about to tell Althea Gant exactly what you thought of her, the Organization and the brand of liquor they serve. Now think about it carefully. Where would that have got us? My guess is, we'd have been fed to a brontomek, reduced to nutrients and distributed over the fields. So keep quiet for a while, huh? Make like you're happy, for the sake of both of us.'

Susanna moved in with me the next day.

I remember Ralph Streng once commenting on the meaning of culture in an uprooted society, and his contention that the old values have a very real worth in protecting people from the strangeness around them. I've often wondered if the Arcadian sub-colonies' quaint, almost Puritanical social set-up is another facet of this phenomenon.

Mark Swindon and Jane had been married two years ago by the Reverend Enrico Batelli in a church ceremony which had hardly changed over the centuries. In Riverside, marriage was the norm. Extra-marital relations were not exactly frowned upon, but it was always tacitly assumed that people who slept together would, before long, be taking their vows before our unusual priest.

Batelli himself had little difficulty in reconciling these quaint customs with his own views. 'A man's images are fortunately private,' he once told me. 'When I use the word "God", Riverside is happy with its image of that word – a wraithlike non-being which permeates the very walls of the church and observes their every act like an all-embracing bugging device. They don't need to know *my* image of God – neither do I tell them.'

'Your secret is safe with me.'

He was serious now. 'God is future happening,' he said quietly. 'He is an alien – a race of aliens infinitely more intelligent than us – whom we have yet to meet. Our purpose is to prepare for the meeting by learning humility and goodness and compassion, which is harder to learn than nuclear physics. We're going to need all the goodness we can muster, when we come face to face with Something that scares the shit out of us.'

So while Enrico Batelli tried by subtle means to prepare his flock for the Meeting, the members of that flock sang the old hymns and vowed the old vows.

Marriage was, I think, the psychological result of the environment: that outside unadmitted peril which caused the strengthening of family ties, drawing people together, so that united they could face whatever the hell the planet intended to hit them with. There was no overpopulation problem; kids were precious and had to be protected, for the sake of the social organism as a whole.

'So when might we expect to hear the ringing of the bells?' asked Jane Swindon with an archness surprising in that earthy personality.

'When we've accumulated enough sin to make it imperative,' answered Susanna.

Susanna and I were both from Earth, of course, where people did whatever they liked in such matters. Since the collapse of the World Emigration Commission the over-population problem had worsened again, and the permanent family unit had become a thing of the past. It seems natural to regard love as a transient thing; if it lasts so much the better – but there's no sense in tying yourself to an opponent for a lifetime.

The immediate result of our cohabitation (as Susanna called it in some glee) was that we both became deliriously happy, and thus indistinguishable from the Immunolized colonists.

'Was there ever a better disguise?' Susanna whispered one day, as we walked unsteadily up the hill to the studio, arms around each other, kissing frequently while people smiled at us in passing. Chill Kaa saw us go by and tapped the window of his unit, holding up a bottle in unaccustomed invitation, but we climbed on, merely waving to him. The Social Club door was open; we could hear the jiggling squeal of a fiddle and the pounding hooves as the Kindred practised a new step for the Regatta which was to coincide with Streng's return. Tom Minty stopped us, complimented Susanna on her appearance with no trace of his usual juvenile leer and invited us to a singalong the following night.

Riverside, under the influence of Immunol and the Organization, had never been a happier place ...

I repressed a shiver at the unsettling thought, kissed Susanna again, and together we entered the studio.

Mort Barker lounged back in his chair, drink in hand, smiling expansively. Nearby sat Althea Gant, watching the screen intently. Presumably she was the only undrugged person in the colony – apart from Susanna and I – and she intended to make sure that the circumnavigation was not wrecked by an outburst of irresponsibility on our part.

Streng was in a subdued mood. He peered at us from the 3-V alcove with an expression of controlled gloom. Behind him, as though to suit his mood, the leaden skies seemed almost to touch the sea.

'... cannot recompense me for the loss of my dear, faithful companion of so many weeks, so many hundreds of kilometres,' he was saying. 'I am a logical man. I have no artificial, hypocritical love for what we call humanity – that much I've made clear over these weeks. I like to think I have my friends, whom I value as a source of intellectual stimulation and, let's face it, flattery. But I can do without them. How strange it is, then, to find that the loss of one small animal, a mere cat, should affect me so deeply ...'

Barker was chuckling appreciatively. 'That's the way, my boy. I don't want to see a dry eye in the Sector ...'

Althea Gant said tonelessly, 'It's the contrast. The cold fish crying over a pussycat. And the pussycat doesn't even exist. Hell, he has a full-size replica of himself locked up in the forecabin.'

Susanna said, 'Oh. I thought maybe he'd pushed it over the side. Or maybe it had pushed him over. We wouldn't know the difference.'

'That's Streng all right,' laughed Barker. 'I'd recognize his style anywhere.' He swung round in his chair suddenly and regarded me owlishly: I realized that he was not only high on Immunol, but drunk as well. 'Our boy is winning through. He remembered his audience would miss the cat. For a guy like Streng, that's pretty sharp ...'

So the voyage continued, and the atmosphere in the studio was now one of optimism – an atmosphere which was prevalent in the colony these days. People even thought that Riverside's brief period of independence had been in itself a victory.

'We certainly made our point,' said Chill Kaa one day in the Club.

And this was the general feeling. People ate their doped food and drank their spiked drinks and although they must have been aware of the contamination they never made any comment about it. More particularly, they never speculated about the future – about what would become of them after Streng arrived home in a blaze of publicity and joyous festivities, and Riverside's part in the carefully staged drama was over...

Meanwhile Susanna and I played it carefully. We appeared in public as little as possible and when we did we tried to avoid Althea Gant. We let it be known that we were totally immersed in each other's company, which was not hard to do.

I expect Vernon Thrale wondered why we were such frequent visitors at the warehouse on the east end of the wharf. The fishing fleet had ceased operating now, and the trawlers rode at anchor in a long trot down the middle of the estuary. The warehouse held a good supply of frozen fish, however, and large quantities of ice which we melted down for fresh water. Our reputations as drinkers came in useful here: I'm quite sure Vernon imagined we spent the evenings drinking an endless succession of heavily iced whiskies before indulging in the nightly passion which a man of his ambiguous sexuality could only guess at.

A diet of fish and root crops can become remarkably distasteful after a while, however, and I decided before long to add some variety. I borrowed a laser rifle from Mark and took the ridge trail towards the point one afternoon, hoping to bag a worral or two. The rifle was a powerful one, unaccountably left behind by the Organization troops on their departure. I spent many enjoyable minutes lopping off high overhanging branches and watching them splash sizzling into the estuary.

I saw no worrals, but further towards the point the trees bore considerable evidence of laser fire; the undergrowth too was smashed flat in crisscrossing trails. The rogue brontomek had been combing the area for life-forms. With the help of its heat-sensitive detectors it had probably cleaned the area of animals by now and would find a human being acceptable prey. I trod carefully, listening for mechanical sounds.

When I reached a point overlooking the new deep-water wharf I was surprised to see the seavester was docked; I'd assumed that it would be spending most of its catching season at sea, rendezvousing with cargo ships which would transport the frozen protein mash to Oldhaven. I climbed down the path to investigate closer. An antigrav flipper sat on the wharf; men were loading flat rectangular objects into it.

'Hi there, you!' One of the men was beckoning. I hurried towards him; those rectangular objects were stretchers, and there were men on them...

'You're Moncrieff, huh? I've seen you on Newspocket.' He was dressed in the plain, dark-blue overalls used by the Organization seamen. The cloth was torn; I saw dark stains. 'Do you have a doctor in the colony right now?'

'Sorry. We have a medical orderly, but he can't tackle anything big. You must have heard Ralph Streng's away on the round-the-world stunt.'

'Hell ...' The man looked around distractedly. The flipper was lifting off with a whine. Two stretchers had been left behind. 'There's six more inside,' he said.

'What happened?'

Suddenly he seemed hardly to be listening; his eyes were inward-looking, as though some private nightmare had captured his attention. 'An accident,' he said absently. 'Just one of those things.'

I said casually, 'When do you reckon you'll be putting to sea again?'

'Shut up,' he said without rancour.

'The sea creatures on Arcadia have a way of defending themselves.'

'A malfunction in the pulverizing plant.'

'Of course ... Streng must be three-quarters of the way around the world by now.'

He met my eyes. 'He's lucky. He's goddamned lucky.'

The moment was timeless. I didn't know this man, and he'd remembered me only from a chance sight of some broadcast. But we each knew what the other was thinking as we stood in the afternoon sun with the injured men at our feet. I remember watching a junker dive untidily and come up with a small silver fish and I thought: Arcadia allows its own kind to eat.

I said, 'I don't think Streng poses any threat to the sea creatures.' There was nothing else to say. I turned away.

'Be seeing you,' he said automatically.

He never did.

Two days later Newspocket announced the loss of a seavester. They had to say something, otherwise people would have asked questions. They said the craft had suffered a malfunction of the directional gear and struck a submerged reef. She had been lost with all hands. The next of kin had been informed.

I walked along the trail to the deep-water wharf the following day, but the seavester was gone.

# sixteen

There were times when we were tempted to join the fun. Maybe we'd be sitting on the ridge above the colony with the summer evening growing cool around us and the warmth of recent love fading from our bodies; and Susanna would stand, pull me to my feet, and say, 'Time to face reality again, Moncrieff.'

I'd kiss her and, arms around each other, we'd start to walk back. Down among the domes people would be moving about, nodding to each other with good humour; and soon we'd join them, and nod and smile with the best. Years ago I remember a series on the 3-V: it was called Strangers Among Us, I think. The strangers were usually aliens with imitative capabilities rather like the amorphs – except they were invariably evil. They were unmasked in the last reel when, writhing and smoking from laser wounds, they resumed their natural – and unpleasant – form before a horrified audience.

Then the Galactic Rights Act was passed and put an end to such unsympathetic depiction of our tentacled brothers.

The point I am getting at, is that the situation was never shown from the aliens' viewpoint. No attempt was made to portray the feelings of an alien surrounded by hostile humans. Maybe the sponsors thought the audience wouldn't be able to identify.

Now Susanna and I were finding out what it was like. We were fundamentally different from everyone around us, and our job was to conceal that difference. It wasn't easy, but we kept hold of the idea that someday, somehow we'd find a way to let the Galaxy know what was happening in Riverside – then we'd be goddamned heroes.

Our best chance would come during the coverage of Streng's homecoming. Until then, we had to merge with the crowd and act happy.

Althea Gant was becoming increasingly concerned with Streng's schedule, since it was now apparent that his estimated positions were way out, and his ETA probably three weeks later than we'd hoped.

'It's very unfortunate,' she remarked one day, as we watched Streng cooking in the cabin. 'I've already made arrangements for postponement of the reception.'

Streng had emerged from the cabin with a plateful of some glop or other and was holding forth on the joys of the simple life. He spooned down a mouthful with every appearance of enjoyment. 'Rich in protein,' he said like a breakfast cereal commercial. 'Straight from the ocean to the pot. This beats any of that processed crap you people eat. And delicious, too . . .'

He extolled the virtues of his meal for a while, then proceeded to describe how he had come by it. 'A variation of my safety net over the stern. I used a finer mesh in small pockets and now I'm trawling for plankton. You wouldn't believe how plentiful it is . . .' He ate some more. 'I tell you, Arcadia has a great future.'

He was smiling, relaxed as he elaborated on his ingenuity, pulling in ropes and demonstrating his fishing rig. He dipped a hand into one of the fine-mesh pockets and scooped out shiny opalescent stuff. He spread it out on his palm. 'There's hundreds of them here, little things like tiny shrimps with vestigial claws. I've had a few under the microscope and I'm inclined to agree with the findings of Professor Mark Swindon of the Riverside Marine Research Station. For their size, they have an unusually slow metabolism . . .'

Mortimore Barker was shifting about in his chair unhappily. 'Careful, boy,' he murmured.

'There seem to be two distinct types,' Streng continued. 'One has shown a steady but slow growth, whereas the other remains almost dormant. They're not different species so far as I can see – and they're not different sexes either . . .'

'Fascinating,' Althea Gant said. 'This is interesting stuff, Mort . . .'

Streng faced the camera confidently. 'My theory is this. The dormant type lives long – lives maybe for fifty years, if it can escape the predators. I would liken it, perhaps, to the queen bee in a hive. This is the little creature which joins with its fellows to form the infamous Minds, which caused a certain amount of trouble a couple of years back, you may remember...'

*'Get off that subject, Streng!'* hissed Barker tensely, as though trying to project his frantic thoughts over four thousand kilometres.

'...whereas the active type behaves as a guardian, growing steadily. It will never attack the dormant type of its own species, even when starving. It eats and grows ...' Streng stared into the camera without expression, '... until it eventually reaches the great size of that monster which—'

'Cut!' yelled Barker.

The technician threw a switch.

I regarded Barker closely. His reactions had not been those of a man euphoric on Immunol. The same applied to the technician. It seemed that there were others in the colony, besides Althea Gant, who were permitted to lead a normal life...

After that episode, I felt safe in drinking whatever Mort Barker drank, which made life a little easier.

That was Streng's first real slip-up in public and it was covered up so quickly that I don't suppose anyone out there in the Sector spotted it. Others followed, however. Little references to the Relay Effect slipped out, and once the camera swung inexplicably to an empty section of sea, as though it had been loosened on its bracket and needed only the roll of a wave to shift it.

There was a concerted gasp and the now-familiar yell of 'Cut!' from Barker – but the sea was innocent of monsters.

Streng had been cooking in the cabin. Through the masthead camera we saw him emerge after a while, glance quickly at the sea, then straighten the errant camera up. His face appeared in close-up. 'Sorry about that,' he said casually. That night he made no reference to the accident. In fact he was saying very little during his off-the-air hours, which was causing Gant and Barker some concern.

Susanna had a theory. 'He knows he's going to be late home,' she confided to me one night, 'and he suspects the

Organization will welsh on the contract. He's also just a little bit unbalanced. There's something weird about how calm he is these days. My guess is, he intends to foul the whole project up in some spectacular way. And at the same time, hedging his bets, he'll make it look like an accident. As a matter of interest, do you know what his instructions are about the amorph? He'll have to dispose of it somehow before the homecoming...'

The next time we visited the studio, Mrs Streng was there. She sat in a chair facing the left-hand alcove, where her husband could be seen doing some repair work on the cabin roof. She was smiling vaguely.

'Listen to him. Watch him, Hazel,' Barker was whispering. 'Does he seem OK to you? I mean, you know him better than anyone.' Obviously Mrs Streng had been brought in to give a second opinion.

The smile remained fixed on her face. '*Nobody* knows Ralph...'

On the Wednesday of the following week came the tragedy...

There were just three of us in the studio that morning: Mort Barker, Susanna and I. The technician was away; Mort was filling in for him. Althea Gant was in Premier City for a couple of days leaving Sinclair Singleton once more in charge. The amorph's position of authority was nominal only. He had lived in the colony for too long to be any use to the Organization. Not only were his sympathies entirely with the colonists but his very appearance had changed. As a result of his constant exposure to the fishermen, Mark Swindon, Tom Minty and other male members of the colony, he was changing sex. He was, in fact, well on the way to becoming a very attractive woman.

So Susanna, Mort and I sat in the studio, drinking and watching Streng stitching a split sail. It was a strained atmosphere. Susanna and I were not drugged but were supposed to think that Mort was. Mort, conversely, was not drugged but thought we were, or so we hoped. No member of the Organization was present – so if only we'd trusted one another, we could have spoken freely.

I have since regretted that we spoke only of neutral topics.

'Of course, I shall be home before the hurricane season,'

Streng informed the camera in flat tones, stitching away. 'And I'm not sorry about that. I doubt the ability of this craft – or any catamaran, for that matter – to withstand the extreme twisting forces imposed on the cross-members by heavy seas.'

Mort glanced at me. 'Sorry, Kev,' he said. 'There's no way I can fake any more breakdowns except in a real emergency. The independent observer in Premier City is suspicious.'

'Don't give it a thought,' I said airily, fuming within.

'It will be good to see Hazel again,' said Streng, laying down the sail and looking thoughtfully across the ocean. He was in a strange mood. 'If you're listening, my dear, I'd like you to know that I've been doing a lot of thinking, out here alone. Away from the constant pressures of civilization, a man gets to see things in perspective ...' He sighed and stood. He rested his elbow on the cabin roof and regarded the camera sombrely.

'I'm going to be late home,' he said. 'There's no use pretending any longer. The voyage was more arduous than anyone expected, and the boat did not perform ...'

'I don't like his tone,' muttered Barker apprehensively.

Streng continued, 'I have not lived up to the terms of my contract with the Hetherington Organization – which is to say that the voyage has been a failure financially, so far as I am concerned. But more important to me is the personal failure. Those of you who know me, know that I am a man who likes to succeed. This time I've failed.' His voice rose, 'But by Christ, if I'm going to fail I'll do it honestly! I intend the whole Sector to know ...'

'This is it. This is it.' Barker was on his feet with incredible speed for one of his bulk. 'I could see it coming.' He flung himself at the control console and threw switches.

Streng had descended to the cabin. We could see his broad back, his strong hands prising away the temporary battens which held the forecabin door shut. Working fast, he picked up a crowbar and we heard the squeak of extracted nails, the splintering of wood.

'Come on out and show yourself,' he shouted, twisting the knob, jerking the door open and stepping aside so that the camera got an unobstructed view ...

Weeks later Mark Swindon gave me an explanation which made some kind of sense.

'The amorph had tried its utmost to accommodate Streng's whims,' he said one night, as we sat in his semi-darkened living-room drinking beer, watching the lights of a trawler ploughing steadily up the estuary. 'It had to duplicate him, because he represented his own ideal – he was a complete egotist. That much was instinctive.

'Then, it set about pleasing him. It tried agreeing with him; it tried injecting a little conflict into their relationship – I've no doubt it tried everything. That's the way the amorphs work. The only reason this amorph failed is because Ralph Streng is an impossible man to please – as Hazel Streng found out, long ago. He wants perfection in everything. And when his own Te proved less than perfect by his own standards, he locked it away.

'He removed it from his sphere of influence. As a human, it needed food – so, in self-defence, I imagine that it began to lose its human form. I visualize it as becoming a lump of brainless protoplasm waiting for an identity to latch on to.

'And swimming close beside the boat, was Ralph Streng's monster, Charlie...'

Mark Swindon smiled grimly. 'There is no doubt that Charlie existed. As Ralph had theorized earlier, he and others like him are the adult form of the worker-protector plankton type. So outside that thin hull was Charlie, and inside was the amorph.

'And the amorph instinctively selects its form based on the proximity of another life-form. It doesn't have to *see* that creature – which is why it is able to reproduce the internal organs as well...'

So we sat there, that night, and after a while the wharf lights went on and the trawler began to unload a catch.

Streng had stepped aside, behind the open door, so he did not see what we saw, at first...

It came out of the forecabin in a scuttling run which carried it across the cabin floor to the foot of the steps to the cockpit.

Now Streng saw it. He crouched there, eyes wide, while the thing picked at the steps with a dreadful scraping noise. It was about two and a half metres long and a metre high; it stood on a dozen slender chitinous legs and possessed two huge pincers with which it was plucking at the rungs of the cabin steps. Its resemblance to a huge lobster ended here, since the flukes of its tail were vertical and the tail itself moved in a sideways direction, lashing to and fro while Streng huddled back against the bulkhead.

The creature began to climb the steps, grasping at the rungs and hauling itself up, its claws scrabbling at the floor. We were looking straight into its jaws, which consisted of a mass of spiked and armoured plates in constant gnashing motion. Somewhere there were eyes, but the brute's head was so bristling with protuberances that these were impossible to detect.

I heard Barker groaning with horror. The thing seemed to be coming straight for us, clawing its way out of the 3-V alcove in terrifying fashion. I had to keep reminding myself that this was the studio; that it was Ralph Streng who might die, not me. All this was happening many kilometres away.

Then the creature slipped.

With a hiss of frustration, it lost its grip and fell clattering and scrabbling into the cabin. Streng, sensing his opportunity, came out from behind the door and plunged into the forecabin from which the creature had originally emerged. He dragged the door towards him. It jammed against the monster's tail.

'Get in there ... Get in there, for Christ's sake,' I heard Barker moaning. Susanna was silent.

The creature wheeled around with a muscular twitch, and saw Streng, who snatched at the door handle. He missed his grip. A huge pincer reached for him. He backed into the cabin, took up a broom and held it before him. His eyes were watchful; there was no panic there, now that he had recovered from the initial shock. It was incredible. I, personally, would have been screaming and crapping all over the place.

The creature took the broom from Streng with a jerk that almost precipitated the man straight into its jaws. He recovered, flung a sleeping bag over the horny head and catapulted himself forward, sliding underneath the armoured belly, scrambling across the cabin floor and grabbing for the ladder. He went out of sight of the camera, then his face appeared level with the cockpit. He reached up to swing himself on deck. Behind him, I saw the monster whirling round.

It caught Streng by the ankle just as I thought he'd made it; just as Barker was squealing some relieved oath. His face disappeared abruptly as he was snatched back into the cabin.

There was a dreadful worrying noise, a hissing, and the first sound Streng had uttered: a yell of agony.

His face appeared again, twisted with pain. Again he reached out, grabbed the cockpit coaming and pulled himself up. This time he made it, and collapsed face down on the cockpit floor. His left leg hung in bloody tatters, almost severed at the knee. A huge, blood-spattered pincer reached out of the cabin and felt around searchingly, knocking against the fibreglass, snapping its jaws.

Streng dragged himself to the cockpit seat, began to inch his way out of the well on to the deck. Behind him, the nightmare head of the creature appeared again. Festoons of viscid digestive fluids trailed from its jaws.

Streng was crawling away from us now, away across the cabin roof towards the mast, and we could see the blood pumping from a severed artery just below the knee. The creature heaved up, hissing and salivating, and reached the cockpit with a clashing of chitin and a scraping of sharp claws. It raised its head and looked around – and now I saw the eyes, set on stubby stalks just above the jaws. It sighted Streng.

Somewhere around us, somewhere nearby, somebody said, 'I'm not going to watch any more.' It must have been Susanna. I admired her will-power, afterwards. Myself, I stayed to the end. I couldn't leave. I can't explain why I didn't leave, because I surely didn't want to see Streng taken to pieces.

He reached the mast. He clawed himself upright, embraced the glittering aluminium. He stood opposite the sail – which bellied out to starboard, with the wind behind – and began to climb, slowly, agonizingly, left leg dangling uselessly.

The lobster-thing picked its way out of the cockpit and started across the decking. It ignored the ropes which became tangled loosely around its legs.

Streng lost his grip, slipped half a metre, began to fight his way up again, jamming his fingers in beside the sail. His biceps knotted and trembled. He couldn't use his legs. He wasn't going to make it. His face stared up into the mast-head camera. I can see it now, those nights when sleep won't come and the memories crowd in – I can see that face, streaming with the sweat of effort, the sweat of fear. Staring directly into that camera, staring at us all, out of the 3-V alcove. One man about to die, before an audience of millions. While down there in the background the sea creature watched, calculated, reared up. Extended a pincer.

Streng kicked back with his good leg.

The creature took him by the ankle. It reminded me of a fruit-picking machine. It took him delicately by the ankle and plucked him from the mast.

Then it laid him on the deck and devoured him.

Later, Althea Gant flew in from Premier City, arriving around five o'clock. I saw the antigrav set down with a quiet hum in Bridge Meadow, near Ezra Blake's place, and guessed who it was. An hour later, the Organization woman was on our doorstep.

I offered her a drink but she refused. Stupidly, I said, 'It's not drugged.'

Althea Gant said flatly, 'I never thought it was.'

So we'd been wasting our time trying to keep *that* a secret.

I said, 'What can we do for you?'

Her face was old-looking: the unnatural old look which comes with strain and maybe sorrow, and in some people never goes. It was easy to guess that the Organization had quickly placed the blame for Streng's death on her angular shoulders. I'd have done the same, if I'd been the Organization.

She said, 'I was in Premier City when the news came through. I came right back. I . . . Did he . . . ?'

Susanna said gently, 'You know Ralph. He put up a fight. But it was quick, when the end came.'

Miss Gant nodded, biting her lip, while I tried not to stare. I'd naturally assumed that her main concern would be whether anything could be retrieved from the wreckage of the project, or whether Streng had in any case talked too much before the escape of the creature. I wondered what the Organization would do now. Probably announce that Streng had been killed when his gas tank fractured and exploded – another reflection on my boat . . .

'You've seen Mort?' I asked.

'Yes.'

'I'm surprised he didn't come here with you. I imagine he'll have told Hazel Streng by now.'

Her eyes were haunted. 'I suggested he took a holiday. I expect he's packing. This business has been a strain on all of us; there's nothing Mort can do right now.' She glanced from me to Susanna. 'Nor you two. Why don't you get away for a while?'

'We may do. When we get paid. Uh . . . What sort of

announcement are you going to make to the Sector?'

'We're not.'

'You have to say something. Hell, the thing was working up to a climax. The ratings were good.'

She snapped, 'Do you think I don't know that?' Her lips were trembling. 'Shall I tell you why the Organization has decided not to make any announcement, Mr Moncrieff? It's because so far as the Sector is concerned, Ralph Streng isn't dead. The voyage goes on.'

'Nobody will swallow that. They'll want to see for themselves.'

She smiled brightly, artificially. 'And so they shall. So they shall.'

'I don't get it.' Nervously, I began to wonder if the death of Streng had unhinged her.

'Then get this, Mr Moncrieff. The Organization is powerful and it controls the media. If we say the voyage is continuing uneventfully and that Ralph Streng lives, and we back it up with some fancy camera-work – then in the minds of the human race he *does* live. The human race, that is, all excepting two or three people who thought they saw him die...'

Soon after that she left.

It's surprising how stupid we can be. I couldn't at that time, understand the purpose of her visit.

It was much later when another knock came at the door.

Susanna and I were still up. We weren't saying much and we didn't feel like making love. We were inhibited by that stupid human dictum which states that people must remain sad when an acquaintance dies, until a decent time has elapsed. As I sat there drinking the last of the scotch – mixed with water because we'd run out of ginger ale and I didn't trust the recent shipment – I found I was wondering how long a decent time was. An hour? A day? A week?

'Who the hell is that?' I grumbled, making for the door.

Two men stood there, strangers. They walked in uninvited, pushing me aside. They stood in the centre of the living-room and Susanna got slowly to her feet, eyes widening.

'You two. Face against the wall. Over there.'

There was a blunt laser pistol in the hand of the larger man.

And there was something rotten in his eyes which told me he would be happy to use it.

# seventeen

They took us outside. It was dark, and it had just begun to rain. I don't think I've ever seen anything quite so desolate, quite so hopeless as my boatyard looked at that moment. The lamp on the slipway afforded a feeble yellow glimmer, enough to see the carcasses of three skitterbugs lying among the offcuts of timber and pots of crusted paint. Work had ceased recently: partly due to my disappointment at the way the publicity had backfired, partly due to the need to keep up a pretence of Immunolized euphoria, but mostly due to a huge ennui with the whole goddamned business. I'd had enough of boats for a while.

I wondered where they would kill us. I imagined they would make us stand on the wharf, facing the water. Then they'd gun us down; when our bodies were later recovered from the estuary, our deaths would be blamed on the runaway brontomek.

'Over there,' said the hood in his flat voice. 'Over on that float.'

I was far enough gone in despair to hope he was good with that laser. A straight shot through the back of the head, and the same for Susanna. I wouldn't like either of us to be inexpertly cut in half...

'Right, now sit down, both of you. Beside the boat.'

We sat on the wet planks of the wharf, feeling the floating structure sway as our captors approached from behind. I watched the small, rounded shape of Paul Blake's skitterbug bobbing beside us. I had a stupid thought, then. I thought: I may be about to die – but I gave the world the skitterbug. As though it was something to be proud of.

I hardly noticed that my wrists were being bound. Then I saw the smaller man bend over Susanna and tie her wrists too, with yellow rope from my yard. Satisfied, he straightened up and we sat there, wondering what would happen next.

There was a muttered conversation, then the gunman jerked Susanna to her feet and thrust her forward. 'In there,' he said. She stumbled; he pushed again and she half-fell into the small cockpit of Paul Blake's boat. I followed, wondering what the hell these two were playing at. Susanna and I sat squashed side by side, hands awkwardly bound behind our backs, while the seat belt was securely tightened across our laps, and the shoulder harness buckled on. Then one man cast off fore and aft, holding the tiny craft against the wharf while the other fooled around under the hood.

'Right,' he said, standing.

His companion pushed. The skitterbug lurched, then drifted slowly away.

He said, 'You can shout if you like, but everyone's up at the Social Centre. There's a big dance tonight. They won't hear you. Not for a while, that is...'

We watched them walk away along the wharf, their footsteps loud and hollow in the still night. Rain was seeping down my neck.

Susanna's voice was shaky. 'Did he do what I think he did to the boat?'

'Uh, huh.'

'Darling Kev, how long do we have?'

'Ten minutes, maybe more. There's a built-in safety margin. They think we'll drift downstream, and blow up like a tiny atomic bomb. But that won't happen.' I let it lie there.

'Please tell me what will happen, Kev. I'm a big girl, hadn't you noticed?'

I swallowed. Thinking about it was bad enough. Saying it was nearly impossible. 'The heat will rise, and the casing will crack. There'll be a lot of molten metal flying about ... It comes to the same thing. When they find what's left of us, they'll think it's an accident. If they're not too high on Immunol to think at all.'

We wasted a moment or two in silence, then Susanna made a big effort. 'We have a little while yet. Hey, lean over and try to kiss me, you bastard. Make the most of what's left, huh?'

We were moving beyond the range of the wharf light, but two moons were casting a diffused glow through the clouds. I looked at Susanna.

Her eyes were bright and she was smiling. With her wrists tied behind, her shoulders were forced back. This, combined with the wet dress and the bondage effect of the harness, caused her appearance to be little short of spectacular. 'God, I love you so much,' I muttered.

'We must try this position again sometime ... Kev, why are we drifting towards the bridge?'

I glanced at the shore; she was right. We were moving upstream. 'The tide's coming in,' I said. 'It doesn't make any difference. Like the man said, everyone will be at the Club.'

We shouted for a while.

We heard the echo from the high banks, and faint sounds of music from up the hill. The colony lights were fitful in the increasingly heavy rain.

Susanna said, 'The water's quite shallow here. If we rocked the boat we might be able to overturn it. Then the water would get in under the hood and cool the pile. Meanwhile, the boat would have righted itself before we drowned ...' she tried to smile, 'because we're g-good guys...'

We swayed to and fro in unison. Hampered by the shoulder harness, our slight movement had little effect on the boat. After a while we gave up and tried shouting again. Later, we abandoned that project too.

Eventually Susanna said. 'My legs are beginning to get warm. I hope it's not disgusting rays from that minipile sterilizing me before I've even had a chance to bear fruit. I was so hoping you and I might—'

'Quiet,' I whispered. 'I thought I heard something.'

'Like what?'

'A voice I think. Shouting, a long way off.'

We listened. We struggled against the ropes and the harness. We yelled.

We listened...

Large drops of water fell from the bridge, rattling on the hood of the skitterbug, soaking into our clothes. Far away I heard a worral chattering. Nearer, a junker swooped, hitting the water with a startling splash, climbing away with a noisy flapping of wet wings. I couldn't stop my legs trembling so I shoved them hard against Susanna's; but hers were shaking too.

A voice came back, 'Is that you, Sweetheart?' It was closer.

'My God, we're saved,' announced Susanna calmly.

'It's Will Jackson,' I said.

The boat bumped against the pilings of the bridge. 'Is Will Jackson a suitable saviour?' asked Susanna doubtfully. 'I have this awful feeling the bum might just walk on by.'

And I was remembering a thought I'd had, weeks ago. A practical, logical thought under the circumstances, when Will Jackson and I had been alone in the dark and the confusion...

I'd thought: *I could kill you now, Will Jackson, and nobody would ever know, and Riverside would be a better place ...*

But instead I'd said, 'Fuck you.'

And he'd replied, 'And fuck *you,* too.'

In this manner we acknowledge our dependence on each other and on the laws of society.

'Who's that?' came the familiar voice.

'Uh, Will, it's Susanna Lincoln and I. Just climb down the bank and lend a hand, will you? We have a problem.'

'Have you ... Uh, have you seen Mariette anywhere?'

'Yes ... I think so. Just a while back. Come on down, and I'll tell you.'

I hadn't meant it to sound like a deal. He scrambled down to the water's edge a few seconds later, wearing an ancient hat and a seedy raincoat of the type worn by indecent exhibitionists. He stood, balancing uncertainly on a tangle of roots regarding us in some puzzlement. 'What you doing there, huh?'

'It's a long story, Will, but right now we're stuck.' I could feel the heat burning against my legs as the reactor shield warmed up. 'Just pull us in and undo this seat belt, will you?' I tried to sound casual, I didn't trust the man. If he knew the minipile was critical, he might just take it into his head to leave us there.

As I might have done, if the positions were reversed ...

He hooked a twisted stick over the cockpit coaming and drew the skitterbug to the bank. Still with that puzzled look, he began to unbuckle the seat belt, fumbling slowly, fumbling and muttering about the weather ...

Susanna was tense beside me. I wanted to yell at the old fool, command him to hurry, hurry before we all fried.

The seat belt was undone. He examined the shoulder harness, peering in the dim light. I smelled the sweat of him. 'The buckles are on this side,' I said.

'Can't understand why you can't do it yourself,' he grumbled.

'We've got ourselves wedged in here,' said Susanna breathlessly, and I wanted to laugh, but was afraid it might turn hysterical. 'We've tried and tried, but we just can't seem to get our hands free. This bug wasn't designed for two.'

He scowled at her suspiciously. 'Listen, this isn't some sort of gag, is it? By God, if you two—'

But the steel clicked and we were free. Susanna and I rose

together, the bug lurched violently as we hurled ourselves at the bank, Jackson went over backwards and the three of us floundered in the shallows.

'Run like buggery, Will!' I yelled. 'The boat's about to blow!'

The urgency communicated itself to him. We scrambled up the bank and set off up the road, Jackson in front, ancient legs trotting stiffly under the flopping raincoat, while Susanna and I loped behind awkwardly, unbalanced by our tied hands. My back was prickling as I ran, expecting at any second the searing agony of a shower of molten metal burning into my flesh. We reached the first dome at the foot of the hill. 'Get down behind here!' I shouted.

As we flung ourselves around the corner the sky lit up, the domes became bright crescents of light and, a second later the strangely hollow boom of an explosion reached us. We lay there, pressed against the dirt. No molten drops spattered us, no gust of hot wind swept through the street. The explosion had been blanketed by the bridge arch. The damage would be minimal. There would be a high level of radioactivity around the area, but the Organization would send in a decontamination team immediately. They would have to clean the place up before the fake homecoming otherwise the welcoming crowds would be reluctant to gather.

Jackson said sourly, 'You should have told me about the boat in the first place. I might have been killed.' He stood, brushing ineffectually at his coat with dirty hands. He didn't seem to be unduly concerned. He didn't have the imagination. We stood also, and he shuffled about impatiently. 'Okay, where did you see Mariette, then?' he asked gruffly.

Susanna said, 'Down by the wharf, Will. Near the warehouse. I *think* it was her.'

He untied our wrists, then set off with eager steps, a shabby old man in a grubby raincoat. I said, 'He gives me the creeps.'

'I feel sorry for him. Kev, he can't help the way he is. Mariette was created out of his mind, the way he wanted her. What he didn't know is that his Te, his ideal little girl, would naturally be the type to, uh, shop around. He lost her at the same time as he got her. It's sad, in a way.'

'He's a dirty old man,' I said hypocritically.

From up the hill came voices, shouts. The music had stopped.

The colonists were coming to find out what the hell the explosion had been, and among them would be the two hoods.

'Let's get out of here,' I said.

The reaction hit us half-way up the far hillside. We lay down in the rain and shuddered, clutching each other, trying not to vomit.

We found the body of Mortimore Barker the next day, floating face-down in the eddying water of Anchor Pool.

After a wet, uncomfortable night in the burned-out wreckage of Kli a' Po's farm, we were making a cautious reconnaissance along the ridge, hoping to contact a friendly colonist who might be prepared to hide us for a while.

'I never expected to find that sleeping with you is hell,' yawned Susanna, peering blearily down at the estuary. 'What's that?' she asked suddenly.

Something in her voice caused a frisson of apprehension to run up my spine. There was a dark shape floating there, turning slowly with the current, nudging the film of flotsam in the backwater of Anchor Pool...

'So he knew too much as well,' remarked Susanna tensely, as we regarded the slack, fat features of Mort Barker. 'Christ, I can't believe this is happening, Kev. I really can't. Listen – did those men really intend to kill us, last night?'

'We've got to get out of here,' I muttered. 'We've got to get away from Riverside. Maybe we stand a chance in one of the other cities. Oldhaven, maybe. If we could get hold of a car...'

'The Organization's in charge of the whole planet. They'll have passed our descriptions round. They'll have our pictures on Newspocket, wanted for some crime or other.'

'I realize that, for Christ's sake.'

'Darling Kev, don't get crabby.' She took my hands, looked into my face, with her wide blue eyes. Her hair was thick and tangled, her dress filthy, yet she was very beautiful and my despair abated somewhat. She went on, 'Our best chance is in Riverside. If we can contact the Swindons they'll look after us, doped or not.'

The gross body of Barker lay before us, water streaming away from the clothes. There was a dark burn on the chest; that gunman could aim straight. I'd closed Mort's eyes; somehow I felt less guilty now he wasn't staring at the sky.

'I wonder if he told Hazel about Streng,' I said suddenly.

Susanna said slowly, 'I ... I hope they got him first. It means one less person for them to kill.'

'Hell, she'll have to know in the end.' I regarded the body. 'What shall we do with him?' I asked helplessly.

'We can't leave him here. It's going to get hot, today. Listen, Kev, that's not the Mort Barker we knew. It's just a lump of meat that Mort left behind. So let's be practical, huh?'

I just wanted to hear her say it, that was all. I nodded, and we rolled Mort back into Anchor Pool. It was hard work and his entry into the water caused a miniature tsunami to wash across the little bay. I took up a long stick and prodded him and tried not to think of barbecued whole pig. The body floated away, out into the main stream where it revolved once, then moved smoothly towards the sea.

Susanna said, 'All that hard-bitten adman stuff – it was mostly an act, you know.'

'I know. I saw his face when Streng died.'

We climbed back to the trail. The sun was warm and it would be warmer. We could see the pale faintness of a moon against the blue sky in the east; the clouds were all gone and it ought to have been a great day. A sticker stroked my leg thoughtfully as I walked past, but decided I was too much for it to handle. Worrals dozed in the branches, clutching their young. Somewhere an Arcow groaned. We sat down on a rock beside the trail, holding hands. Opposite us was a metal plate.

IN MEMORY OF
The Reverend Emmanuel Lionel Blood
Police Officer William Clarke
Eric Phipps
Alan Phipps
Alfred Blackstone
'They died that we might be saved'

'Well, they were wasting their fucking time, weren't they?' exploded Susanna suddenly. Then she began to cry, and maybe I did too.

'Easy, darling. We'll work it out,' I said feebly, after a while.

She looked at me, tear-streaked. 'How? Listen, Kev. Mort wasn't a bad guy, but he's dead. I'm sure you and I are average sort of guys, but we nearly died last night. Two men tried to kill us. They were only doing what they were told. They're stupid and animalish, and I expect they have wives and kids to feed.'

'What are you trying to say?'

'I'm asking you where the villains are, Kev. All these terrible things are happening, and Ralph's dead and thirteen people were killed by the brontomek, and *somebody* must be responsible. Who is it?'

'Hetherington,' I had a sudden vision of that toadlike form in its wheelchair, issuing instructions: kill, *kill* . . .

'Not Hetherington. He's just an old man kept alive with electrodes and tubes. You can't blame the Organization either, because they're just average guys again, doing their jobs. They're all responsible to the shareholders – and there must be millions of them. I'm a shareholder myself, as a matter of fact. So where's the villain, Kev? In all that long chain, from myself right back to myself, who can I blame?'

'God only knows.'

'Ralph Streng knew.' She had stopped crying; she stared at the metal plaque as though willing it to give an opinion. 'It's our instinct of self-preservation. Each of us is looking after himself just a little bit more carefully than he looks after the next guy. There's nothing wrong in that: that's basic. It's natural. But Kev – when it's nobody's fault, and yet I want to blame somebody, it makes me cry. This whole awful business makes me feel so sad. I wish I could reason it away, like Ralph could have done.'

'I think I'm glad you can't,' I said.

In the end we contacted Mrs Earnshaw, and she took us in. Her dome was on the outskirts of the colony and possibly safer than most – search parties of armed men were leaving the colony every day, returning at nightfall. The old woman was unconcerned at the possible danger to herself, and not entirely because of her Immunol intake.

'I did the same thing for Professor Swindon, once,' she said, peering through a gap in the drapes in conspiratorial fashion. 'You're quite welcome to stay with me as long as you like.' I guessed she was feeling lonely. She never mentioned Elsie Cotter, who was still living along the street with the amorph.

'It's dangerous for you, Mrs E.,' I said. 'Maybe just for the night, huh? Can you get Mark Swindon here, do you think?'

'Of course.' The old woman grinned suddenly, an unusual

softening of her normally stern face. 'This is quite like old times.'

In due course Mark and Jane arrived and we discussed the situation sitting among the incredible collection of imported bric-à-brac with which Mrs Earnshaw's living-room was cluttered. I drank scotch, and so did Susanna. We needed it, and to hell with the Immunol content.

I asked Mark about that.

'We're still drugged,' he admitted cheerfully. 'Although the effect doesn't seem quite so satisfactory these days. Maybe we're building up resistance; whatever it is, there are occasional outbreaks of responsibility in Riverside. Hell, the Colony Committee met yesterday, and discussed matters quite lucidly.'

'What did you find to discuss? I thought everything was being done for you.'

'We have to make certain arrangements for Dr Ralph Streng's homecoming,' he said, in an official voice. I glanced a warning at Susanna. There was no point in anyone else knowing the truth.

'Listen, you two,' said Jane suddenly. 'Did you really try to kill Mort Barker and foul up the broadcast?'

'Is that what they're saying?'

'Yes ... That's why the transmission's stopped for the time being, isn't it? They said you burst into the place, attacked Mort and the technician so severely that they had to be taken to Premier City Hospital, then set about the equipment with a fire axe.'

'It's not true,' said Susanna. 'Don't ask us to explain.'

Jane looked relieved. 'I didn't really think so,' she said. 'But with Organization posses out looking for you, it seemed to clinch things, you know what I mean?' She regarded us quizzically, waiting.

'They're not going to tell you, Jane,' said Mark ...

Later I broached the subject which had been the reason for bringing Mark there. He agreed to take his sloop *Carousel* down the estuary and around the north headland where he would moor her, on the pretext of using her as a base to repair the damage to the fish pens.

Susanna and I would then live on board.

One day the brontomeks came back.

We were sitting on the short salt grass of the clifftop, near the hoist. The sea was calm and blue with a million tiny flecks of silver where the sun touched the wavetops. Nearby, fairly close under us, *Carousel* rode at anchor. A flock of mewlers hovered near the stern like drifting confetti, snatching plankton from the surface in their tiny bills. From the ledges of the cliff below us we could hear the junkers disputing nesting ground.

Then we heard a different sound.

It came from the west, from behind the obscuring sweep of trees. It was a dull, continuous grumbling which had probably been going on for some time but had suddenly come to our senses.

'It sounds like trucks,' said Susanna, standing up and staring inland. 'You don't suppose they've sent an army in to look for us, darling?'

'I doubt it. We're not that important. They know we can't do anything without the support of the village ... Look. There.'

A distant object was moving across the green flatness of the root crop. A paler line marked its wake. Then another black rectangle came into view, and another. Soon twenty of them crawled over the plain on parallel courses like well-drilled snails, each leaving a thin trail in the verdure.

'They're harvesting,' said Susanna flatly.

I knew what she was thinking. This was the culmination of Stage One in the Organization's exploitation of Arcadia. We were witnessing history. There was nothing we could do about it, as usual. The whole operation was too vast to be affected by mere individuals; we should have realized that long ago. So we sat down again, and watched enough dope being harvested to subjugate a planet.

The days went by, hot summer and occasional cool rain, and Susanna and I lay about the boat fishing and making love; sometimes climbing the cliff and viewing the progress of the harvest; and once taking the trail to the colony and visiting Mrs Earnshaw at night.

The old lady was pleased to see us again and passed on the colony news. There were signs that a physiological resistance to Immunol was building up in people: either that, or the Organization were decreasing the dosage.

'They're probably running out of the stuff,' Mrs Earnshaw opined. 'They've been using the Immunol the Government stockpiled over two years ago in a hurry, during the Relay Effect. If they've had to suppress any other colonies there can't be much left.'

We didn't mention the huge tank we'd seen yesterday, near the Blackstone farm. It was new, mounted on fresh concrete, with every appearance of a laser fence about it. There was also what looked like a guardhouse. The tank would have held enough to pacify a large colony for a year. Nearby was the Riverside reservoir...

Before we left, loaded with liquor of guaranteed purity, Mrs Earnshaw said a strange thing.

'You know,' she said, 'if the Organization did cut off the Immunol now, and the colony went back to ordinary food and drink, I don't think the people would be too pleased...'

It was an angle we hadn't thought of, a valid and alarming one.

On our way back to the boat, we caught sight of Hazel Streng. She was gazing out of the window of her unit, and she looked as though she'd been crying. I wondered what great sorrow she had, that Immunol couldn't erase.

It was on the following day that we got our big surprise.

We met Enrico Batelli on the ridge trail; the priest listened intently as we described what we'd told nobody else, not even the Swindons – the death of Ralph Streng.

'Newspocket are still apologizing for the breakdown,' he said thoughtfully, pulling the little machine from his pocket. 'They said they hoped to have it fixed by today.' He switched on. A newscaster was babbling enthusiastically.

It was much the same crap as usual, at first. Arcadia was booming: the harvest was looking very promising, following the prolonged fine weather. The actual crop was unspecified, but shots were shown of wheatfields and superrice paddies. Cynically I assumed that these were probably on Arcturus V, but then I realized that there could quite easily be considerable genuine agriculture on Arcadia. The Organization had the whole goddamned planet to play with.

Then the scene changed. A fat, heavily jowled face appeared on the screen, smiling.

I heard Susanna draw a sharp breath.

'It's not Mort,' I said quickly. 'It's some guy made up like him.' Yet the resemblance was uncanny.

'... working ceaselessly day and night,' the man was saying, 'to restore our link with the gallant lone yachtsman, Dr Ralph Streng. And now, just two days before his triumphal arrival in the little colony of Riverside from which he set forth so many months ago – here he is! Folks, Dr Ralph Streng!'

And the boat was there, the *Arcadian*, skimming over a choppy sea with a fair breeze; the sails were set, the ropes neatly coiled down . . .

And in the cockpit sat Streng.

# eighteen

Two days later Susanna and I sat at the window of Mrs Earnshaw's unit, overlooking the estuary and the wharf. It was a fine day. Reports stated that the homecoming yachtsman had passed the deep-water harbour and was heading up the river towards us. The Newspocket commentator was ecstatic; high-flown phrases rolled off his tongue and the scene incessantly cut from a head-on view of *Arcadian* to the assembled crowd on and around the wharf.

It seemed that half Arcadia had come to Riverside to witness the event. All day the hoverbuses and the antigrav transports had been coming in, and the hillside opposite the colony glittered with reflected light from a thousand binoculars, cameras, beer cans and other trappings of tourism. Skitterbugs dashed about the water, giving an impromptu display of skill and foolhardiness and, I hoped, a free advertisement for myself.

A barbecue pit smoked beside the warehouse, presided over by Chukalek. The colony cook had been out of favour for some time, ever since Mrs Earnshaw had found an aphrohale butt and a short length of green twine in a dinner roll. Enquiry had revealed that Chukalek had momentarily laid down his therapeutic handful of dough – which a near-sighted assistant had then mistakenly placed on the baking tray together with a fresh batch. Even the effect of Immunol could not dilute Mrs Earnshaw's rage and disgust, and Chukalek was suspended on a unanimous vote of the Colony Committee. Now, taking advantage of the confusion and celebrations, he had reinstated himself, and I noticed the group around his pit included two members of the Committee, eating soyburgers with every appearance of confidence. Apart from Mrs Earnshaw, only Kli a' Po was present in the unit. The alien had been dispossessed of his temporary accommodation by incoming Organization people, and Mrs Earnshaw was putting him up for a couple of days.

In deference to her hospitality, he had absorbed his duplicates. 'It's no problem,' he explained to us. 'Since they took the farm from me, I've hardly felt the need to multiply. And then there was the food shortage ...' His gaze flickered from Susanna to me, 'And what about you, Mr Moncrieff? Have you and Miss Lincoln been indulging in your reproductive rites?'

'Constantly,' laughed Susanna, saving me the trouble of muttering something. 'One hundred and ninety-three times, at the last count.'

'Quite,' said Kli, with the flicker of some unreadable expression – probably distaste – crossing his face. He eyed me for a while. 'What are your plans?' he asked.

'You mean right now?'

'Yes. I imagined you'd secreted yourself in the colony with the intention of carrying out some scheme. This is your chance, the day you've been waiting for. The eyes of the Sector are on Riverside. I'm interested to know how you intend to expose the Organization for what it is.'

Was he being sarcastic? There was no way I could tell. I said bitterly, 'What the hell can I do, Kli?'

He made his laughing noise. 'Life must be interesting for you people. So many emotions: anger, outrage, frustration, fear – I wonder what they feel like? I see only their outward manifestations, but in the end they all cancel down to the non-emotion of acceptance. It seems to me that you might more easily have accepted the situation in the first place – as I did – and saved a few lives. After all, I understand lives are precious to you.'

'Be quiet, Kli,' snapped Mrs Earnshaw. 'Otherwise you'll find yourself homeless for the third time.'

She poured us drinks and we drank; it didn't matter now whether the liquor was doctored. The commentator was still maintaining his hysteria. '... and just look at the man now! After all these thousands of miles, all these weeks of privation, and still he cares for the faithful boat which has borne him safely home again. What a tribute to the designer and builder this is. While Ralph Streng washes his deck and coils down the ropes, let us give thanks to another Designer and Builder, without whose special care our gallant yachtsman would never—'

This must be Mort Barker's script, the one in which he'd promised to give me full publicity – although right now God seemed to be getting a better press than the Moncrieff boat-yard. Mrs Earnshaw cackled as the platitudes rolled on.

'What a pity Mr Barker wasn't well enough to do it himself,' she said. 'He has a way with such words. Have you heard from him lately, Mr Moncrieff?'

'Not lately.'

'Look at the soldiers,' said Susanna hastily.

They came marching along the wharf in relentless formation and people moved aside to let them through. I've often wondered about a platoon of marching troops. If you didn't move aside, would they simply mow you down with their heavy boots, tramping over you and leaving you bleeding? I rather think they would.

Mrs Earnshaw gave a snort of disgust. 'They're not the Arcadian Armed Force,' she exclaimed. 'And heaven knows I've little enough time for them. But this is the Organization's private army. It's nothing less than gang rule!'

'Effective, though,' said Kli a' Po. The troops halted at the end of the wharf and formed two ranks, presumably for the triumphant pseudo-Streng to walk between. The soldiers wore bright scarlet uniforms and glittering buttons and swords – but I guessed the swords were not their principle means of defence. They would also be carrying laser pistols. They were not merely a guard of honour, they were a tough fighting force, here to see that Riverside behaved itself.

Even from where we were, we could hear isolated noises of derision from the crowd.

Then there was a great cheer, echoing between the hillsides. A flotilla of trawlers, decked in flags and spraying fountains of water from their hoses, came sweeping into sight around the bend. The skitterbugs raced down the estuary to meet them. A group of quaintly clad Kindred broke off their cavorting and rushed forward to get a better view. Sirens wailed and the church bell tolled.

Mrs Earnshaw said thoughtfully, 'It is a measure of human stupidity that I find this moment moving – knowing what I do.' She dabbed surreptitiously at her eyes with an antique lace handkerchief.

This was finally, irrevocably too much for me. 'For God's sake, Mrs E.,' I cried. 'You don't know half of it! The whole thing's a goddamned fake. Everything! Ralph Streng's dead! That's a fucking impostor! And the Organization murdered Mort Barker!'

She stared at me, her papery skin paling.

'It's true,' said Susanna.

Kli a' Po said, 'I have to agree. I thought it best not to say anything, however. Nothing can be done.' I think I detected a firm reproof in his tone, but I couldn't be sure.

We explained briefly.

'By God,' grunted Mrs Earnshaw, regaining her colour and more besides. 'By God. If I'd known about this before, I'd have organized some unpleasantness on the wharf this afternoon, troops or no troops. The Immunol's worn off. People are ready to fight again!'

'To what end?' murmured Kli. 'Let the Organization have its charade. It will succeed in its object. People will come to Arcadia. Isn't that what we all want?'

And now the *Arcadian* was in view. The crowd was dancing on the far hillside, waving banners, exploding firecrackers. The troops had drawn their ceremonial swords. Antigrav shuttles traced welcoming words across the blue of the sky.

We hardly noticed the door open.

Then a voice spoke. 'Sorry to interrupt,' it said harshly. 'But I'll have to ask you all to come with us.'

Four men stood there, laser pistols in hand.

Althea Gant was in the studio, together with a number of strangers: Organization officials. She regarded us expressionlessly as we were herded in. We were made to sit on the floor, against the wall.

'I've no time to deal with you now,' she said. 'There's too much happening. Just sit right there, huh?'

The studio had undergone a change since I'd last seen it. In addition to the two original 3-V alcoves – the views of *Arcadian* from masthead and stern – there were now three other scenes arrayed along the wall. The cameras transmitting these were obviously mobile. The room swarmed with technicians: T-shirted men and women with spectacles and harassed looks, indistinguishable were it not for the fact that most of the women had breasts.

At one point Althea Gant returned to us. 'Listen, Moncrieff,' she said, 'I now understand you were at the deep-water wharf when the damaged seavester arrived, huh?'

'Add it to that goddamned list of my crimes against the Organization.'

There was nothing I could do and I didn't intend to try. I'd had enough: enough of struggling, enough of running. The scene in the alcoves opposite changed; each one showed the fake Streng, from a different angle. He stood in the cockpit of *Arcadian* and, as I watched, flung a coiled rope to someone off camera. He was smiling, his flopping mass of grey hair glinting in the sunlight. He looked cocksure, unbeatable, unbeaten; he looked like Ralph Streng. The cameras zoomed in.

'Just who the hell is that man?' asked Mrs Earnshaw.

Althea Gant was watching, tense, even at this moment of triumph not quite sure of herself, not quite sure that everything was going well. I noticed that one of the cameras was panning across the crowd – a useful scene to cut to, if the pseudo-Streng suddenly decided to come clean.

The impostor leaped athletically to the wharf. The din from the crowd was deafening; in the background faint music could be heard and the monitor showed a rapid series of cuts from scene to scene, Streng to crowd to Streng from a different angle, to Mrs Streng...

Hazel Streng walked forward.

That camera must have been on the opposite side of the estuary, because it showed her walking forward endlessly, zoom lenses keeping her in focus, until for the last few steps she began to trot, then run...

Then she was enfolded in strong, sunburned arms, and we caught a glimpse of her face, tearful yet ecstatic as she clung to those broad shoulders, weeping and laughing...

'It's that goddamned amorph!' I said. 'It's that thing she had living with her. No wonder she was crying the last time we saw her – you'd taken it away. How the hell did you get it on to the boat?'

Miss Gant was still watching the repeaters. 'Took it there by antigrav. The observer had already swallowed the story about the breakdown. Why should he suspect anything when the normal picture came back with Streng at the tiller?'

Now the voices of the crowd merged into a hymn of thanksgiving. Something about Mine Eyes having seen The Glory of the Coming of the Lord. I imagined they must mean Streng.

I gained some small satisfaction from the sounds of a few noisy dissidents, probably Tom Minty and his friends, who shouted obscenities while Streng and his wife walked between the guard of honour, like a bride and groom at a military wedding.

Beyond the guard they paused before the Reverend Enrico Batelli.

Susanna said, 'Uh-huh,' in an expectant sort of voice.

This was it. I looked at Althea Gant and I think I smiled. She didn't see me, which cost me a little satisfaction. She was watching the screen, and her knuckles were clenched white. This was the big official welcome; it would look strange if a technical hitch had to be engineered at this juncture.

'In the name of Riverside, of Arcadia and indeed the whole Galaxy, I can only say, "Well done, Ralph,"' intoned Batelli...

And with those words he set the tone of his address.

'I don't believe it ...' whispered Susanna after a few minutes. 'How could they have bought Enrico?'

'The little bastard was happy enough to hold a service at the departure,' snapped Mrs Earnshaw. 'After that display of hypocrisy, I wouldn't put anything past him.'

'... once again proving,' continued the priest, 'if proof be needed, that the waters of our great oceans are innocent of malignant life forms. But not for one moment do I wish to detract from Ralph's feat. Despite the sceptics, the destroyers who sought to hinder the development of our planet with their tales of gloom and despondency, of terrible things lurking in those calm waters – despite all this, Ralph set sail unafraid, a latter-day Columbus.'

'Is he kidding?' I'd never seen Susanna so mad as she stared furiously at the image of Batelli with those blue eyes of hers. 'Is the bum serious? Or is that another amorph, Gant? Is that a fake Batelli as well?'

'That's Batelli,' replied Althea Gant quietly. 'I'd hoped he'd see sense. Otherwise we'd have got another man in. It would have been simple enough. But Batelli has a certain flair, don't you think?'

'I'll say he does.' Susanna glanced incredulously at me as the priest went on and on, praising Streng, condemning those who had urged caution following the Relay Effect.

'... there has been sabotage, there has been discontent. I pray to God that all this nonsense will be forgotten now, in the glory of Ralph Streng's homecoming which should prove to us all that our strength lies in positive united effort – while giving full rein to our precious human trait of individuality. Yet Ralph's triumph is in many senses the result of a team effort, and we should not forget those who have laboured unseen. If I may mention a few: Kevin Montcrieff, who built the sturdy craft; Mark and Jane Swindon, for their advice on matters marine; Susanna Lincoln, for her invaluable work in public relations; Mortimore Barker, who unfortunately cannot be with us ...'

'Well, thank you Enrico,' I said sarcastically.

Althea Gant was frowning at the image. 'That was a mistake.'

'Criminals don't usually get such a good press, huh?' asked Susanna.

But Batelli was back on the right track again. '... Arcadia marches forward, and eager pioneers are at this very moment arriving on this great planet of ours, bringing with them their skills, their enthusiasm, their undying determination to forge for themselves and for all of us a new fulfilment ...'

It was sickening, and it went on for quite a while, and if I hadn't been certain that I would be dying soon, I would have got burned up about it. Susanna was braver than I, and not so afraid of death, and she succeeded in becoming very unpleasant – but uselessly, of course. Life in the studio went on, and the wheels of the Organization turned unchecked.

Then a milk-white antigrav flipper touched down, and pseudo-Streng and Hazel Streng climbed into it, and waved to the crowd. The machine rose soundlessly and hovered about twenty feet from the ground. The noise from the spectators was overwhelming; a weird kind of hypnosis seemed to have gripped them. They chanted and roared and waved flags and banners, while their hero raised a calm hand from his seat in the flipper.

The cameras dipped, panned across the estuary. The skitter-bugs were coming again, streaking towards the wharf in line abreast, towing water-skiers, all in white.

The angels had returned to Riverside.

They rose from the water, banked and climbed rapidly towards the hovering flipper. The machine set off slowly eastwards, flanked by the nude, winged girls, and the crowd fell silent, hushed by the beauty and symbolism of the spectacle.

Before they passed out of sight behind the trees it was noticeable that the angels were losing height. Unlike real angels, they were subject to the tyranny of gravity, and were obliged to make a landing upstream, beyond the bridge.

'The hand of Mortimore Barker even from the grave,' intoned Kli a' Po.

'That's it. Wrap it up,' snapped Althea Gant decisively, as the cameras wandered uncertainly over the crowd, and normal life returned to the 3-V alcoves in the guise of a child screaming, a woman picking her nose, a man drinking beer. The technicians milled around in self-congratulation, slapping one another on the back, speculating as to the next assignment. People began to carry things out. One by one, the alcoves went blank.

In the end, the room looked like a small theatre again. I'd got so used to thinking of it as the studio that I'd forgotten its original use. The equipment was all gone, the festoons of wire rolled up, and technicians and the Organization officials departed and the place was quiet. Nine of us remained: Althea Gant and the four guards, and Susanna, myself, Mrs Earnshaw and Kli a' Po. Neither the technicians nor the officials had evinced the slightest interest in us. We were effectively dead – non-persons.

I noticed a tiny version of Kli sidling away under the stage. It couldn't help us much, but at least it would ensure the alien's overall survival. He'd probably exuded small spies all over the village this last few weeks.

'You people,' said Miss Gant, 'you come with me. There's an antigrav outside and I'd like you to board it without any trouble – otherwise my men will be obliged to shoot.'

So this was the end. We were to be killed and dumped in some uninhabited spot for the sticker plants to feed on. I felt tired, and the liquor I'd consumed at Mrs Earnshaw's had settled into a nagging ache behind my eyes. I was almost accustomed to the idea of death – but I would miss all the loving with Susanna.

We stood up, and made our way to the door. That's how far we got.

Then the visiphone rang.

Althea Gant regarded it; it hung on the wall at the far end of the theatre. She shrugged, told the guards to wait and walked towards it.

I saw a man's face on the screen; he talked earnestly and at some length but I couldn't hear the words. At one point, Miss Gant turned and glanced our way, as though discussing us. At last she hung up and returned.

She said to the guards, 'You can let them go, now.'

I said, 'What?'

'I mean you're free, Mr Moncrieff. You're free to go home, to drink scotch, to make love and build boats. You're free to do whatever you damned well like, you understand? Orders from above. We're all dependent on orders from above, aren't we?'

'Not me,' said Susanna flatly.

'Do you want to bet on that, Miss Lincoln?' Suddenly, incredibly, Althea Gant was crying. I didn't know if it was frustration, relief or what. But just for a moment her thin lips quivered and her eyes went bright as she looked at Susanna. Then she said, 'I'd like to meet the sub-colony representatives in Premier City on Friday at one o'clock. You'll find our temporary office at the spaceport.'

'What the hell for?' I asked.

'There are releases to be signed, and compensation to be assessed. You'll be wanting to make certain claims against the Organization, and we'll be wanting certain guarantees from you. There's the question of salaries, and damages to Mr Kli a' Po's farmhouse while it was under requisition. The Organization is fair in such matters. A successful business is not built on underhanded dealing.'

'But why Friday?' asked Mrs Earnshaw. 'You were talking about five years' time before.'

'Because the Organization is pulling out of Arcadia, with effect from next week,' said Miss Gant.

# nineteen

Outside people were dancing in the streets.

I saw the Kindred of the Pioneers, having formed an impromptu group, weaving an intricate measure near the Club entrance, while Vernon Thrale sawed furiously at his fiddle. I saw Will Jackson and Mariette arm-in-arm with Elsie Cotter, prancing about to a counter-blast of music from the Club windows, waving bottles. Behind this, all the way down to the wharf, the crowd jigged, shouted and drank – and across the estuary, on the far hillside, the huge mass of spectators were moving in a solid tide towards the bridge, intent on joining the festivities.

Just for one moment I was puzzled. How could they have heard the news so soon?

Then I remembered that they were celebrating Streng's homecoming. And the colonists, caught up in the mass enthusiasm, had forgotten Streng the man and were lauding the prowess of Streng the Image.

I said to Althea Gant, 'What are you going to do with Hazel Streng? She must represent an embarrassment to the Organization, huh?' I had to shout; the din from the crowd was overwhelming.

She looked flustered. 'She'll be taken care of.'

'Like Mort Barker?'

'Listen to me, Mr Moncrieff. There are some unpleasant things that must be done for the ultimate good. Mort Barker was a case in point, and so were you. In the case of Mrs Streng – well, she'll be quite happy in some peaceful neighbourhood on a quiet planet – with the companion of her choice . . .'

Sickened, I drew Susanna away in the direction of the Swindons' place. I needed a drink.

Suddenly, the Reverend Enrico Batelli was standing before us. I tried to walk past him. I didn't want to speak to him.

He laid a hand on my arm. 'I guess you think I sold you out,' he said. His eyes searched mine. It seemed to matter to him.

'You gave me some very good publicity, Batelli. Now get your goddamned slimy hand off me before I smash your face in.' I shook myself free and plunged away, dragging Susanna with me.

'Wait, Kev!' he called after me, pushing through the crowd which enveloped us. He bobbed up in front of us like a saturnine sheepdog, heading us off. 'Listen, I knew the Organization was quitting. There was no point in fouling up the publicity. Arcadia's going to need it in the next few years.'

I paused, regarding him closely. 'You couldn't have known. Althea Gant only just heard herself.'

'What reason did she give?'

'Look, do we have to talk here?' People were jostling us; I felt ten years older with the desire for drink. 'She said their economists had decided the planet wasn't a viable proposition after all. Various unforeseen factors had come to light.'

That was what Althea Gant had said, more or less word for word. She'd been unwilling to commit herself further.

Suddenly, all around us, Newspockets were whining loudly.

The noise of the crowd abated. People fumbled in their pockets, pulling out portovees, switching on. Little groups formed quickly, Newspocket subscribers in the centre of each. It is a familiar scene, repeated from time to time all over the Galaxy. One day, I promised myself, I'll just walk on, and ignore that impatient, impertinent buzzer. This day, however, I slipped out my Newspocket . . .

'. . . very important announcement of great interest to all Arcadians. It was announced in Council ten minutes ago that the Hetherington Organization has decided upon expert advice to relinquish all claims to land and other property on the planet of Arcadia. All employment contracts will be cancelled with the compensation scale to be negotiated with the Arcadian Council. The Organization . . .'

The rest was inaudible, as the crowd erupted around me.

The enthusiasm at Streng's homecoming was nothing compared to this. A myriad items rose into the air: hats, programmes, even Newspocket receivers as the Arcadians gave vent to their delight with a roar that echoed between the hillsides like thunder. Everywhere I looked I saw faces frozen into an instant of mindless, orgasmic ecstasy with open mouths and bright empty eyes, arms raised, clutching air, clutching their neighbours, voices yelling pure, wordless joy.

They were independent again. They were individuals again. They were free . . .

After a while the roar became a mere deafening babble and I became aware of Batelli's sad eyes still fixed on mine.

'With such delight Arcadia greets the prospect of poverty,' he said.

We sat in the Swindons' unit with the familiar furniture around us, the familiar drinks in our hands. The people were familiar too; the good guys who we liked to have around. Outside it was dark; just a couple of moons in the sky, low over the hilltop. The crowds had gone home, but the Riverside colonists were in the Social Club still celebrating, celebrating.

Jane arrived shortly after we sat down, with the news that Chukalek had had to be taken to the medical unit for emergency treatment following the rupture of a blood vessel in his thigh. 'He didn't even notice it,' she said. 'The poor guy was standing in a pool of blood – and it had to be Mrs Earnshaw who spotted it while he was doing her steak, medium rare.'

Susanna laughed immoderately while the rest of us made noises of sympathy.

Mark had meanwhile been in the process of describing to us the reasons behind the Organization's volte-face. After a searching glance at his wife, who had kept a straight face during her report, he resumed.

'Enrico knew, of course. I hope you weren't too hard on him, Kev. He'd been helping me with my research ... Not that there was much researching to do. The facts were becoming obvious to all of us. Yesterday, the final tests clinched it.'

'Go on.'

'Briefly, the plant from which Immunol is derived is losing its effectiveness. At first I thought the colonists were building up resistance to it, but then I investigated a little further and turned up some interesting facts. Meanwhile, the Organization scientists were proceeding along parallel lines. We both came to the same conclusion. Immunol simply doesn't work any more. The crop is a failure.

'I don't think we ever quite realized how much the Organization were depending on Immunol for their profit margin,' he continued thoughtfully. 'Sure, they intended to export grain and other crops, but there's very little percentage in that. The basic reason for their presence here is Immunol – and now that's failed, there's no point in them staying. They're businessmen. The profit lies where the minerals are – the uranium, the gold. There's no profit in a shipful of wheat.'

'Listen – how can they be sure that next year's crop won't be full strength again?' I asked.

'The Immunol root relies for its propagation on small shoots or tubers, like the potato – which could result in its quickly crowding itself out. So it has a flavour attractive to animals – while retaining a composition resistant to digestive breakdown. Arcattle, mainly, pluck the plant out of the ground, chew the juices out, and excrete the fibrous matter elsewhere, where it takes root and grows.'

'Disgusting,' said Susanna.

'It's very practical and natural,' said Jane, and Susanna gave me a secret grin, having discovered a chink in Jane's formidable armour.

'I'd even say it was beautiful in its simplicity,' said Mark, kidding his wife along. 'But millennia ago, it had a drawback. Once every fifty years, any Arcow within a few kilometres of the coast walked into the ocean and was eaten by blackfish. It took a long time for the Arcows to come back. So, to condense a few million years of evolution, the roots which survived were those which had developed a narcotic to blanket out the telepathic summons of the Minds – by inducing a general euphoria and lowering of mental faculties. The Arcattle didn't walk into the water if they'd eaten the root. Instead, they lived and shat.

'But it wouldn't have worked if the plant had produced the drug continuously. The Arcattle would have become immune. So production of Immunol became a cyclic thing, triggered by the approach of the syzygy of six moons. Like so many life-forms on Arcadia, the root had become subject to this fifty-year cycle of ours. This year's crop is low in Immunol. Next year the root will be no more effective than a carrot.'

'And so the Organization departs gnashing its teeth,' said Jane.

Mark said, 'And we have to pick up the pieces . . .'

Following the night of celebrations there was an air of almost stunned quietude in the colony the next morning. By noon, however, people were beginning to move about again and a Colony Committee meeting was called for the afternoon. The weather remained fine and Susanna and I decided, after a couple of noon-hour drinks, to repossess the *Arcadian* and clean her up.

The catamaran was tied up at the east end of the wharf, forgotten since the hero's welcome of yesterday. I wondered what plans the Organization had for her. I hoped – with some justification, I think – that they looked on her as a white elephant now her purpose was fulfilled. It seemed quite likely that I would be able to buy her back for a song.

'But what about all the money we owe, darling?' asked Susanna worriedly, running her eyes over the battered boat and calculating the expense involved putting her back in shape.

'I think I can swing a deal with the Organization,' I replied. 'It's a drop in the ocean to them. They had their fingers burned badly in Arcadia so it's to their advantage to hush things up.'

We cast off the catamaran and walked her along the wharf to the slipway. I climbed on board and entered the main cabin in some trepidation, expecting to find Streng's blood all over the place; but it had been cleaned up. The interior was in perfect shape, in fact, an interesting sidelight on Hazel Streng's concept of an ideal man's qualities.

It was difficult, even now, to believe that Streng was dead. In life he'd presented such an indestructible appearance. Susanna had once said, 'If Ralph Streng ever meets Death face to face, I swear he'll persuade him to take the old lady next door instead, for reasons of the utmost logic.' Yet we'd all liked the bastard. Or thought we had, now that he was gone.

Susanna followed me in and sat on the berth in the small forecabin. A shaft of sunlight slanted through the porthole and ignited her hair into a golden blaze as she sat there looking at me. I forgot Streng as the poky interior suddenly became alive with her beauty and sexuality. I groped my way towards her and we fell together on the berth, kissing wildly, fumbling at each other's clothes and uttering wordless sounds of love.

I don't know what the hell had got into us. Maybe it was reaction, relief after months of strain and worry, but within five minutes the ghost of Doctor Ralph Streng had been well and truly exorcized from the boat and my wonderful girl was gazing dreamily into my face in catlike satisfaction.

'I like this boat of ours,' she said at last. 'What are you going to call her?'

I'd been wondering about that myself. Now that the publicity stunt was over, the mundane *Arcadian* could be painted over. 'I'd thought of *Easy Lady II*?' I said. 'But it doesn't quite fit. I think I'll settle for *Golden Girl* . . .'

By all accounts the Committee meeting that afternoon was fruitful too. Most of the important matters were dealt with, and it was decided that priority would be given to rebuilding Kli a' Po's farm, after which the efforts of the community would be devoted to other joint projects. For the time being, a simple version of communism would prevail until the colony was judged to be on its feet.

'It was surprising,' Mark Swindon told us that evening. 'Mrs Earnshaw suggested we help Kli out, and everyone agreed without a murmur, even Tom Minty. It looks as though our alien's been accepted at last. Uh ... I was pretty pessimistic last night, I reckon – but now I can see some hope. I really think people are going to work together; for a while, anyway.'

'Who represents us at the Organization meeting on Friday?' asked Susanna.

'You and Kevin, for a start. Kev is a fairly crooked sort of businessman and should get us a good deal. And Jane here, and Mrs Earnshaw. A strong team, I reckon.'

'They said I sold them out, last time,' I objected.

'And they'll say it again. Don't let it worry you, Kev. Jane will shoulder the blame.' He gazed fondly at his pretty wife. 'Nobody in the colony will dare say a word against her.'

On the next day, work began on Kli a' Po's farm. Susanna and I took time off from discussing our strategy for the meeting, and joined in with the workers. I've rarely known such an atmosphere of enthusiasm on a building site, and I began to find myself in agreement with Mark. With this kind of community spirit, Riverside could go places. Very little machinery was used; in fact very little was available, but work proceeded with incredible speed. Trees were felled and bucked in the ridge forest, the logs were skidded to the site by another team, trimmed and placed in position by a third. By mid-morning the walls had almost reached eave level.

All the time, the huge, stark forms of two dozen brontomeks stood silent nearby. They seemed almost to absorb the sun and cast a cold shadow towards us and sometimes I would have the uncanny feeling that they were watching us, biding their time. Then the friendly chatter of the tractor would issue from the forest and the skidding team would come into view with another log, and the fanciful spell would be broken.

Finally, at around three in the afternoon, a hoverbus drew up and emitted a group of overalled Organization men. With hardly a glance in our direction they climbed into the cabs of the giant machines and soon the ground trembled to thundering wheels. The last we saw of the brontomeks was a distant haze of dust hanging over the Inchtown road . . .

And so the colony's first days of independence hurried past in hard work punctuated by nightly celebrations. The Kindred of the Pioneers enjoyed a further rise in popularity and there were few colonists who did not, at some time or other, prance inexpertly around the floor to strange old Earth tunes from Ireland, and Greece, and Russia.

I exclude myself from that nonsense; also Mark Swindon, who once grunted sourly – when Jane tried to drag him to his feet – that he was not terrified of the hostile environment, neither did he feel the need symbolically to display his sexual prowess. Whatever the subconscious explanation for the gyrations around him, he'd found, long ago, that scotch and ginger afforded greater satisfaction.

'And I've always found symbolic displays unsatisfying,' said Susanna. 'A poor substitute, at best.'

Jane glanced at me and I shook my head; shortly afterwards she left us in the company of Batelli and soon we saw them involved in an eightsome, clapping hands, caterwauling, stamping and prancing. They obviously enjoyed themselves hugely . . .

And the following day there was a long-distance call for me. Jake was on the screen, from Jake's Chandlery.

'Uh . . . Kevin,' he said. 'I'd like a talk with you – I understand you'll be in Premier City tomorrow.'

'Yes?' I said guardedly.

'It's not your bill,' he hurried on. 'I've been getting a few enquiries about your boats, from out in the Sector. I wondered . . . Maybe we could talk about an agency arrangement, huh?'

When at last I got rid of him and hung up, I turned round to find Susanna standing by my shoulder. I said, shakily, 'It looks as though we might have struck it rich, darling . . .'

# twenty

We'd spent the morning sightseeing round Premier City. Signs of the Organization's imminent departure were everywhere: displays were being taken from store windows, trucks being loaded at service entrances and – too infrequently – new signs were being fixed to the façades. Many stores stood empty, and would be standing empty for a long time . . .

This had cast an air of gloom over our little group; even Susanna and Jane were not their usual bubbling selves as the implications of the Organization's departure were brought home to us. We visited the spaceport and the story was the same: trucks bringing containers which were quickly swallowed by the giant maws of waiting space shuttles; huge items of agricultural machinery rumbling in endless lines from all points of the compass to parking areas so extensive that brontomeks seemed to cover the plain as far as the distant hills.

Then there were the people, hundreds of them, shuffling in orderly lines from featureless rectangular buildings across the concrete to passenger shuttles. There was something inhuman about their compliance and their lack of personal possessions.

'They're amorphs . . .' Susanna had said.

Occasionally a shuttle would take off, voiding fire into the exhaust pit and climbing away into the blue sky, leaving a throb of thunder in the air. Little columns of smoke would arise from the perimeter vents and occasionally there would be a fat, incongruous smoke ring. Several times we saw shuttles touch down. Mostly these were empty Hetherington vehicles come for more cargo, but one was an independent. A stream of gaily dressed humans and humanoids crossed the concrete towards the nearby terminal building. They were immigrants, fruits of the Organization's publicity.

'And we must make goddamned sure they stay,' said Mrs Earnshaw grimly . . .

The meeting was held on the second floor of the terminal building. While we waited, leaning against the grubby wall because there were no chairs, it became apparent that the Organization had commandeered the whole of the floor for the purpose of transacting business such as ours. Temporary signs gave the names of sub-colonies and a schedule of hearing times. Neatly dressed lawyers hurried to and fro carrying briefcases presumably loaded with clients' claims against the Organization. I saw a group of people emerge from a nearby room grinning, slapping each other on the back. They were from Inchtown South. They had pulled off a good deal.

The autocracy was finished. The omens were good.

Althea Gant looked tired. She sat in a small area which could hardly be dignified by the title of room: it was a part of the vast terminal concourse subdivided by temporary screens. These screens were well short of ceiling height and far from soundproof. From all around came the sounds of furious altercation, yelling voices and pounding fists, the constant reiteration of astronomical figures.

Miss Gant smiled at us ruefully as we sat down around the table. 'I don't suppose you people have heard of the terrestrial vulture. It's an unpleasant bird which only appears when death is approaching; it has an uncanny knack of sensing when another animal is in trouble. It moves in after the disaster, and picks the bones.'

Jane Swindon replied, 'You'd be surprised how much we know about Earth. Mr Moncrieff and Miss Lincoln were born there. There was another terrestrial creature called the dinosaur. I'm sure you'll have heard of it, Miss Gant. It grew too big and it couldn't adapt, so it died out.' Her voice grew harsh. 'Nature showed it no sympathy, Miss Gant, just as I have no sympathy for your fucking Organization.'

I could understand why the Colony Committee had appointed Jane as one of its representatives.

'Couldn't we just forget these tired old metaphors and talk in terms of cash?' suggested Mrs Earnshaw. 'I never get tired of that. Just tell us whether you propose to settle individually or jointly for the colony as a whole, and how much. Huh?'

Resignedly Althea Gant drew a sheet of paper towards her. 'The majority of Riverside inhabitants will be paid compensation for breach of contract based on two and one-half years' pay. Other specific cases will be dealt with separately. These people include Kli a' Po, the Swindons,' she glanced at Jane with wholehearted dislike, 'Kevin Moncrieff and one or two others.'

'What about Mort Barker?' I asked.

'Since he met an accidental death while employed by us, his heirs will be entitled to compensation. This will be based on full pay from date of death to normal retirement age.'

'And will that amount satisfy the Organization's conscience?'

'Before you ask stupid questions like that, Mr Moncrieff, you should define which persons you mean by the Organization. A corporate body cannot have a conscience. Only people can.'

The wrangling went on around me while I sat back trying to figure it out, trying to come to terms with my own emotions. The Organization was making restitution in the only way possible – by cash payment. What else could it do? It could hardly be tried for murder. Yet how could we – any of us human beings around this table – reconcile the ruthlessness, the crooked dealing, the attempted murder and actual murder, with this formalized, stereotyped discussion of cash compensation? I felt we ought to be outraged, we ought to be screaming in each other's faces, we ought to be finding scapegoats whose noses we ought to punch. Instead we were talking about bits of printed paper. We were talking about book figures in nebulous banks.

'Fuck you all,' I said suddenly.

They glanced at me, paused as though I'd said something of faint but not arresting interest, and then continued the discussion. Susanna stood, walked over to the window, and I joined her.

'OK, Moncrieff, you goddamned sentimentalist,' she said quietly, 'I know how you feel. We all feel the same, if we think about it. But we know there's nothing more to be done – other than to screw every goddamned cent out of these bastards that we can ... Otherwise, what can I say that will help? Except that I love you.'

Her eyes seemed to glow for a moment as she looked at me, then she turned and looked out of the window, looked at the hopeless, mindless line of amorphs shuffling past, shuffling endlessly across the arid concrete into the dark hold of a nearby shuttle. The leaders paused in dumb acquiescence between the legs of the huge machine. The elevator descended; twenty, maybe thirty amorphs entered. The elevator rose into the cloacal gloom twenty metres above the harsh brightness of the burning concrete. Simultaneously, an empty elevator descended, partly counterbalancing and saving power. It was terribly efficient. The amorphs shuffled forward again, were consumed.

A whole section of the line-up below us showed identical features, identical builds, clothing. They were men, dark-haired and very stocky. Their faces were pale and indeterminate. Something about their washed-out appearance suggested an underground mode of life. Then, as if by contrast, a small group of angel girls trooped past, bright-eyed and baby-faced, shop assistants and aquatic aeronauts...

'... and the Organization is willing to overlook the technical breach of contract committed by Mr Moncrieff, in the interests of goodwill.'

Susanna quickly rejoined the table. They were talking about me. I ought to be interested, but something about the mechanical procession of amorphs had numbed me. I saw different girls coming in the distance, emerging from a large shed, beautiful girls even at this distance somehow familiar. I was numbed, numbed.

Nearer, more familiar faces. Trudging past the window, the duplicate of Mrs Earnshaw. Mariette, small and plump. Sinclair Singleton, hermaphrodite. Others. Men and women I recognized from the colony. Paul Blake II and the beautiful girls behind, joining the line a hundred metres off, endlessly filing out of their shed...

I couldn't watch. I sat down again. I daren't watch...

'You're taking the amorphs from Riverside,' I said.

'Of course.' Althea Gant looked at me.

'The colony isn't going to like that.'

'Mr Moncrieff, we are not here to indulge in another of these ethical arguments. Ownership of the creatures is vested in the Organization and that's an end to the matter.'

There was something happening outside that window which I couldn't watch, dared not watch ... My whole body was trembling; Jane and Mrs Earnshaw were looking at me in surprise. If I sat still, I thought, if I sat still and didn't go near that window, then it wouldn't happen. But still I had to say it, still I had to torture myself...

'Listen,' I said. 'Is there any way you'd allow the amorphs to stay? I mean, if a person, say, forfeited his compensation?'

Miss Gant did not smile. She watched me, and her eyes were not cold. She said quietly, 'The amorphs are beyond your kind of price, Mr Moncrieff. I'm sorry.'

I said, 'I'd give you everything I have. I'll work for the Organization, sign a life contract, go anywhere in the Sector.'

'I'm sorry.'

'Listen. I'll ...' But I could think of nothing more. I was a mere human of the male sex, a lump of animated meat, and I couldn't match the price. I was trying to buy love, and Miss Gant and I knew it. That was why she wasn't selling, because I was wrong and she was right – and she knew it, and she was an OK woman.

I got up and stumbled over to the window, because I didn't want Jane Swindon and Bernadine Earnshaw to see my weakness.

Althea Gant said into the puzzled silence at the table, 'Uh. ... Miss Lincoln, I—'

'Don't tell her!' That was my voice, choked.

'Miss Lincoln, I'm afraid you'll have to come with us.'

And outside the window the beautiful amorphs shuffled along towards the space shuttle, an endless line of them. Susanna after Susanna after Susanna after Susanna ...

'Just what the hell are you talking about, Miss Gant?' asked Susanna steadily from her seat at the table. 'I stay with Kevin. Your goddamned Organization's not so big that you can tell me what to do.'

'Miss Lincoln, I'm trying to tell you you're an amorph. Please don't make it difficult for me.' Althea Gant was unhappy, too.

'You must be crazy. Do I look like an amorph, for God's sake?'

And outside the window they moved along, Susanna after Susanna after Susanna ... One of them happened to see me looking out of the window. She smiled up at me, friendly, nothing more. Then she saw my expression and looked away.

'Miss Lincoln, you wouldn't know.'

'My name is Susanna Lincoln. I was born in Exeter, on Earth. I went to Exeter University, where I got degrees in biology and physics. I got a job at the Falcombe Research Station under the direction of Dr William Stratton. We were engaged in temporal research and made certain discoveries concerning parallel worlds which I'm not at liberty to disclose. Following the death of Dr Stratton and the closing down of the Station, I emigrated to Arcadia. Is that good enough for you?'

'I'm afraid not. All you have done is to describe the real Susanna Lincoln. She is the Te of a man named Maine, a hotelier in the town of Falcombe you mentioned. Does the name Maine mean anything to you?'

I think now I was crying for Susanna, the Susanna in this room, the one sitting at the table and looking suddenly uncertain, and a little frightened as a person does who doubts their own sanity ... 'How could I have forgotten John?' she whispered.

'You were told to. You are what men call an ideal woman, Miss Lincoln,' said Miss Gant with no rancour. 'And your type is very useful to the Organization. We've used you all over the Sector, to keep men happy until the real women start moving in ... It's quite astonishing, the improvement in productivity. And occasionally we might use your kind in a key position; you represent insurance, you see. Any normal man would imagine himself in love with you, and could be manipulated ... Just as poor Mr Moncrieff was manipulated.' She looked up at me. 'Your involvement with the Organization hinged on the sinking of your first boat, the *Easy Lady*, which left you short of cash. Did you ever find out how and why that boat sank?'

No, I hadn't. But Susanna had been on hand to save me. She'd also been on hand to sabotage the pump in the first place at the launching ceremony ... But no doubt the Organization had neatly processed that memory from her mind before it even arose ... The very make-up of the amorph would render it peculiarly susceptible to post-hypnotic suggestion.

She was looking at me with her wide blue eyes, that alien whom I had loved. 'Listen to me, Moncrieff you bum,' she said with a brave return to her old manner, 'I didn't know anything about all this. I love you, huh? You know that. Remember it, will you?' Suddenly those eyes blinked, and a brightness appeared. 'I love you so goddamned much that I'm not going to ask if you still love me, and I don't want you to tell me.'

'Susanna ...'

'Shut up, you bastard!'

Her eyes flashed, then she was calm again, watching me gravely while she remembered things she didn't remember. While she became aware of great gaps in her knowledge of herself and her past which she'd never questioned before.

While she began to question those gaps, and more – the meaning of memory, the memory of freedom, the meaning of love...

Jane Swindon spoke, staring at Miss Gant with some hostility. 'I don't know what the hell you're trying to pull, but I don't believe any of it. I've known Susanna for months. She's no amorph. All this time she's been living with Kevin, if she'd been an amorph she'd have changed some. She'd gradually have come to look like his ideal – not the Te of some guy on Earth. And I tell you she hasn't changed. Not by one eyelash!'

Jane is a great person.

Althea Gant said, 'Look, you're forcing me to say this. The fact that the Susanna type did not change in Mr Moncrieff's presence is a measure of its effectiveness. He met her, and thought her so wonderful that she *created her own ideal*, you understand?'

And the Susanna type met my eyes dumbly, knowing memories that were not her own.

And outside, the pretty girls walked by.

'Did you really think a woman could be so perfect?' Althea Gant asked me quietly. 'We're not, you know. Our moods change with the time of day, the time of month. We can be illogical, unreasonable, and sulky. We can fart and vomit and compose moronic letters to newspapers. We can cut ourselves on a can-opener and stub our toes on a stanchion. We can be annoyingly enigmatic and stupidly transparent. In short, we have the same faults as me.'

'But Mr Moncrieff ... Did your Susanna have any faults?'

That angular ugly woman was sorry for me. She was trying to convince me *now*, so that the pain wouldn't be too drawn-out. She continued, 'Other people might have thought she drank too much, or that her language was too forthright, or too flip; or that she was too sexually aggressive. But what did *you* think?'

I shouted, 'Listen, I just thought she was great, that's all, huh? Do we have to define everything?' There was a huge crimson rage growing inside me and I thought I was going to burst, or else wake up and find myself back at the unit with Susanna cuddling beside me. I was aware that I was crying. I said, 'Some ... great types are going past the window right now.' I wasn't ashamed of the tears; I wasn't aware enough to be ashamed.

Althea Gant was beside me, staring down at the beautiful walkers, the standers-in-line. 'For God's sake,' she said helplessly. 'You should have been spared that.'

Then the ex-Susanna was taken away from us.

We stood at the window for a long time, four humans, watching the hot afternoon. Dust hung about the feet of the walkers in a low, long cloud. Sometimes one of them would look up at the window and see us.

One I remember in particular, a blonde alien girl, humanoid. She was very pretty but it was obvious that she'd been crying. When she looked up at the window and smiled, I could see streaks of wet dust on her face.

# epilogue

With the month of Teth the weather broke and the rains came, endless and saturating, turning the surface of the estuary into mist so that the trawlers looked like suspended ghosts, running off the hillsides so that the main street of Riverside became a new tributary. The roof of my non-standard unit leaked and I spent my nights listening to water tinkling into containers on the floor, waiting sleeplessly until they sounded full enough for me to get out of bed and empty them. It gave me something to do, during those aeons of darkness when Riverside slept.

Elsewhere the immigrants were arriving in droves by every incoming shuttle. A large proportion of the labour force was occupied in erecting the prefabricated dwelling units, fighting an endless battle with clinging mud and slippery plastic. Even in Riverside we'd had our share of newcomers: thirty in the last month. I had every hope of finding a purchaser for my boatyard: every week Jake was sending new prospects out from Premier City. It was only a matter of time.

Meanwhile Kli a' Po's farmhouse was completely reconstructed and enough cool weather crops planted to supply the colony for the next year. While this was going on, the fishermen had placed themselves at Mark Swindon's disposal and within a couple of weeks the fish pens had been rebuilt, and restocking commenced with the pick of the daily catch.

'Even Chill Kaa is helping,' Mark told me in some amazement, one day. 'And the fishermen know the pens will make the trawlers obsolete in a few years' time.'

There were new faces in the Club; before long Riverside would be back to its population peak of pre-Relay Effect days. John Talbot worked busily behind the bar, mixing drinks, chatting with the newcomers with an eye to future business.

One noon-hour Jane said, 'Do you have to go, Kev? It really looks as though things are going to be OK here, after all. You've got to hand it to the Organization – they know how to make publicity work.'

But the ghosts were among us suddenly, just for a moment in that crowded bar. I saw the large figure of Mortimore Barker, sitting in his favourite chair, emphasizing his points with a stabbing motion of his cigar, *When you've seen the Procyon waterfowl defending a nestful of young against the sawtooth swampcrawler twenty times her size, when you've watched her fight without yielding until the last nestling is evacuated by the male to a place of safety, then you can talk to me about love, man ...*

And Ralph Streng was there, grey-haired, broad-shouldered and intense, countering Barker point for point as the rest of us listened, enthralled, *The bird is a slave to its instincts, just like you or I. The concept of love, in its sentimental usage, is as meaningless as the concept of good and evil ...*

So different, so right and yet so wrong, those two men. And each in his own way – even though they would never admit it, the big sham and the cold fish – so *good* ... So human and so much a part of us all. And, most important of all, I missed them like hell. A purely selfish thing, that. As Streng put it once – *If you died, Kev, I would be sorry. I would regret the loss of a source of intellectual stimulation ...*

Somebody shouted with laughter and the ghosts fled, and the room was bright and noisy, and pretty dark-haired Jane Swindon was watching me, waiting for a reply.

'Listen,' I said carefully, because she was the one person who might possibly understand, 'I've lost too much in Riverside, you know what I mean? Everything I see, I have to subtract from. The sight of the trawlers, or the sound of the birds, or the feeling of climbing up the main street to the Club, everything I see or hear or think of is connected with something I have to make myself forget. So Riverside is a minus place, for me. I can't live like that: I'd go crazy.'

She said, 'If that was all it was, then I'd believe you. But there's something you're keeping from us, huh?' For a moment there was only the two of us; everyone else was talking to everyone else and there was room for just this one private conversation. Will Jackson was there, and Jed Spark and Perce Walters discussing the suicide of Ezra Blake. Mark Swindon talked Committee business with Mrs Earnshaw. Miss Cotter – back under the same roof as Mrs Earnshaw – sat listening to her employer respectfully. Nearby, Tom Minty drank noisily with his henchmen Jim Spark and Bill Yong. Jane and I were alone.

I said, 'There's nothing more. Nothing.'

'Nobody fools me, Kev,' said Jane. 'I wish you luck.'

A couple of days before I was due to ship out, I broke my

usual rule and went on a sentimental pilgrimage along the north ridge trail. It wasn't as bad as I'd expected. Maybe this was due to the weather: everything was dripping wet and the path heavy with mud, and somehow the place seemed different from the summer place where the alien and I had played and made love. So I was able to walk fast and to think, and to begin to get things in some sort of perspective.

I walked to the headland and looked at the sea, at the newly repaired fish pens dividing the shallows into neat rectangles, and the narrow ribbon of beach immediately below me, where the rusting remains of huge machines lay. The ocean was calm, the waves flattened by the drizzling rain which was finding its way through my clothes. The grass was short and slippery here, and the gaunt triangular skeleton of the hoist stood at the cliff's edge, to my right. Ghosts walked.

'Hi there! Kevin!' I turned round at the shout. The short figure of Enrico Batelli was hurrying towards me, oilskins flapping about his ankles. He squinted up into my face, rain flowing down his dark skin. 'I just happened to see you ... I thought maybe you'd like ...' His voice trailed away and he glanced down at the beach, ill at ease.

I had to chuckle. 'I wasn't going to throw myself off, Enrico. I have too much to do.'

'I heard you found a buyer.' He fell in step beside me as I turned and began to stroll back towards the colony.

'We sign the contract tonight. It's a good price, Enrico. With that, and the compensation from the Organization, I have enough for the FTL to Earth – and enough to come back, if I feel like it.'

He glanced at me curiously. 'Will you come back?'

'How should I know? Possibly. It depends on how things pan out.'

The trees closed in around us and the fine drizzle turned to sparse, heavy drips. Sticker plants extended their tentacles like wakers stretching, delicately picking at the ground, at the trunks of the nearby trees for those slimy creeping tidbits which the rain brings out. Worrals moved cautiously in the spiny branches overhead, waiting for the night.

'What the hell is that?' There was sudden alarm in the priest's voice.

I saw it too, a giant, menacing darkness in the undergrowth, the outline concealed by the mass of vegetation. 'Careful ...' I murmured. I stepped forward cautiously, dragged at a curtain of creeper, bringing a shower of raindrops on myself.

The rogue brontomek loomed over me.

Although its fading senses must have been aware of my presence and the sensor turrets twitched ever so slightly, it remained almost silent. Just a faint, tired hum acknowledged the existence of an organic life-form in its proximity; the lasers remained dead. The cab windows were shattered and the glass of the eye sensors missing, broken by countless collisions with trees during the monster's manic hunting. Several of the plates had sprung their seams and hung open like ragged wounds, while the whole surface of the machine was covered with a red patina of fine rust. One of the giant balloon tyres was missing, shreds of rubber still clinging to the wheel, causing the brontomek to assume a ponderous and inappropriate position of obeisance, like a kneeling elephant. It stared at the ground with its blind eyes, its heart barely beating, crippled beyond recovery, betrayed by its own mechanical weaknesses.

I had the fanciful notion that Batelli ought to say a few words.

'Thank God for that,' he said, which was as good as anything. 'Probably Walters will be able to cannibalize the thing. He found some useful stuff, back there on the beach.'

We resumed our walk. Batelli is a practical man, and the practical approach is very necessary in a priest on a young planet. The last thing any colonist wants to be taught is a pious fear of the Unknown – there are too many real perils about. 'A degree in psychology and a working knowledge of the inconsistencies of a dozen or so popular religions; that's all a planetary priest needs,' he once told me.

Now he said, 'I hope we see you again, Kev.'

I was going home to Earth. It would be good to see the people again: the busy cities, the quiet byways. There was so much to see; so much I'd never seen.

I'd never seen Falcombe, for instance, where a beautiful blonde girl had once worked at a Research Station. I would probably take a look at the place, talk to the people there; I had nothing to lose, nothing left to lose...

From Arcadia to Earth might seem a long way to go for the possibility of love.

Ralph Streng would never have understood me.

John Boyd

**The Rakehells of Heaven** 60p

Kevin O'Hara, a lusty Irishman with the gift of the blarney, and John Adams, an Alabama boy with an evangelical streak, should never have been sent on a voyage of space exploration together – but they were, and landed on the planet Harlech where an advanced culture is governed by autonomous universities.

Their efforts to 'humanize' the inhabitants suffer constant distraction from the females of the species who are not only the right shape but very, very, friendly . . .

Robert Sheckley

**Options** 60p

Tom Mishkin is forced to trek across Harmonia to obtain spare parts for his grounded spaceship.

To protect him from the bizarre and sometimes dangerous collection of creatures on this alien planet there is a Special Purpose Environmental Response robot. Unfortunately, beneath a cynical exterior, his robot buddy is definitely bewildered and something less than competent. Together they chart a zigzag course from the improbable to the phantasmagoric and beyond . . .